RISE *of* FIRE

RISE

of

FIRE

SOPHIE JORDAN

HARPER TEEN
An Imprint of HarperCollinsPublishers

Library of Congress Control Number: 2016949941
ISBN 978-0-06-237768-5

Typography by Brad Mead
17 18 19 20 21   PC/LSCH   10 9 8 7 6 5 4 3 2 1

First paperback edition, 2018

For every girl who finds hope in the pages of books.
Keep reading. Keep dreaming. Your turn will come.

ONE

Luna

THIS WAS DARKNESS.

Of course, I was sightless, so darkness was all I had ever known. It lived in me, *on* me, like scars written on my skin. But this darkness went deeper. Thicker. Denser. It suffocated me. Thick as tar, I was drowning inside it, flailing, searching for air to fill my starved lungs.

Diving underground after Fowler, I knew precisely what I was doing. Even if an earthen tomb would likely become my crypt, it was what I had to do. Fowler was gone. Dwellers had taken him. He was lost somewhere in this tar. Dead, maybe. Probably. I expelled my pain-laden breath. No. *Find him. Find Fowler.*

I dropped, falling into a thick pool of sludge. I swam through the mire and sucked in a sharp breath that felt like razors scraping the inside of my throat. My palms slapped the surface of emulsified earth, keeping me from sinking. I was already underground. Who knew what lay farther down? The very bowels of the earth, perhaps.

I lifted my fingers, letting them unfurl from their grip on ground that only seemed to break and crumble under my grasp.

For a moment, I wobbled on my knees, my balance thrown. Lifting my chest, I took another gulp of air and inched forward, patting wet earth. The ground started to dip, so I flipped to my bottom and slid down the slope.

Damp earth rushed past, sticking to every inch of me. Sludge clung to my hair and clumped in my lashes. I blinked, trying to clear it away. Rich, pungent loam filled my nostrils. I sucked in a breath and swallowed earth. Coughing, I spat out debris and sealed my lips shut, determined to not breathe too deeply down here.

I came to a stop, landing on actual ground. *Their* ground. I'd followed Fowler into their domain. For the first time I was the invader.

I sat still for a long moment, listening and taking slow sips of air as I attempted to still my racing heart in the dripping silence. I was certain dwellers could hear me. *Terrified* they could hear the wild beating in my chest, that organ that I'd thought dead. Fowler had killed it, crushed it with the awful truth, but the stupid thing knew how to keep beating, fighting no matter if it was dead. Fowler was Cullan's son. Cullan, the man who killed my parents and hunted me. The man who killed every girl in the land for the crime of *maybe* being me. That monster was Fowler's father. Fowler's past, his legacy, was wrapped up in that evil.

I shuddered and pushed out the thought for later. For now I couldn't think of that. I wouldn't. I could think only of saving Fowler and getting both of us out of here alive. Nothing else mattered right now.

I flexed my fingers and remembered that I still clutched my knife. I was comforted to feel it in my hand. Water fell overhead, echoing in tinny pings all around me. I shivered in the bone-numbing cold that permeated my wet clothes. I shifted uncomfortably, plucking at my tunic and vest. It was pointless. There was no relief, no way to feel warm or dry or safe.

I didn't feel at home like I usually did in the dark. There was nothing comforting. Nothing familiar. I wanted to crawl back out and escape through the quagmire. Except Fowler was here somewhere.

My breath came faster. My heart felt as though it might explode from my too-tight chest. *Fowler*, trapped in this world under our world. It didn't seem possible that strong, capable, unbreakable Fowler could be here—that this was his fate, that he had embraced it, sacrificing himself to dwellers to save me.

I shook my head against the terrifying possibility that I was too late. He was still alive. I would know if he wasn't. Something like that . . . I would know.

I deliberately shoved away the memory of the words he had said to me, that confession, that horrible truth that had always been between us like a serpent in the grass waiting to strike, waiting to inflict its poison with immense fangs.

I kept going. My legs felt wobbly. Bracing my hands along the moist wall of earth to my left, I continued to edge forward, half expecting to come face-to-face with a dark dweller. But no, I was always good at sensing them, at knowing where they were before they knew where I was.

Most dwellers were aboveground hunting, with the exception of the ones who had taken Fowler. Hopefully, they'd just dumped him and returned aboveground to hunt. There seemed no end to their hunger, after all.

I hastened forward, skimming my hand along the earthen wall, the odor of bracken and rot stifling. I shuffled one foot after the other, feeling my way rather than plunging headlong down another incline. With luck, the ground would stay level. I needed to keep my bearings.

A distant dweller's cry echoed faintly through the underground labyrinth of tunnels. I froze, angling my head and listening, holding my breath. No other cries came. Water dripped over the blanket of calm.

I started forward again, turning left when my hand met the open air of a tunnel. I focused intently, using my heightened senses and marking the distance my feet traveled, noting every turn I took so that I could find my way back to the spot through which I entered.

Another cry sounded, and this time it wasn't a dweller. It was wholly human. I followed the direction of the shout, my steps quickening as hope pulsed inside me. *Let it be Fowler.*

TWO

Fowler

I'VE ALWAYS LIVED in darkness. With dark dwellers and death, death and dark dwellers. The two were interchangeable but the same, and by some miracle I still lived.

I'd lost consciousness at some point, but I wasn't gone. Not yet. I remembered that rush of adrenaline as I flung myself from the tree into the arms of the waiting dwellers. I did it for Luna. I could accept that. I had no regret. As long as she lived, I was fine.

In this absolute absence of light, I waded through air like ink, lost.

My ears pricked, listening. Not far away someone wept. Panic bit me in the chest. Was it Luna? Had they taken her, too? She couldn't be down here as well. Fate wasn't that cruel. I tried to move my body, but my arms were wedged tight.

Maybe it was punishment for all my wrongs. I'd withheld who I was—what I was—from Luna long past the point when I should have told her. Fear held me back and now this was the price. Faulty logic, maybe, but it was all I could manage.

My head and shoulders were free, and I looked about wildly, tossing the hair back from my eyes and squinting into the darkness, peering in the direction of the person crying.

"Hello?" I called into the murk. The tears stopped abruptly as my greeting echoed over the chilled air. "Who's there? Luna?"

"Who are you?" a voice demanded. Not Luna.

Relief eased over me. "Fowler," I replied, and then almost laughed. What did my name matter? I was stuck in here with this hapless other soul and we were both about to die.

For a moment her ragged breaths were her only response. "I'm Mina. They took me . . . and my group. A few days ago, I think. I don't know. There were seven of us. I'm all that's left." Her voice cracked into wet sobs. "There are others in here, too. But I don't know them."

A few days? They'd kept her alive this long? And there were others. Maybe that meant I had more time. Time to give survival another chance.

Determined not to give up, I tried to move my arms again, hopeful that I could break loose. My breath puffed out as I exerted pressure. If I could get free, perhaps I could find a way out of here. There was a way in, so there had to be a way out.

There had to be.

THREE

Luna

I CHASED THAT echo of a cry long after it faded. Even when the air around me softened to mere drips of water, I didn't stop. I prowled down tunnels and passageways for so long that I worried it was only a matter of time before I came face-to-face with a dweller. I lost all sense of time in a world where every moment counted.

The space around me was empty. I moved, straining for any sound. My nostrils flared, the odor of dwellers rich around me: loam and copper. Metal in my mouth.

Even with the scent of them so strong everywhere, they weren't nearby. This was their territory. The stink of them embedded in the bones of this underground tomb.

The silence was finally broken again by another shout. Human.

I followed the sound, my lips moving in a silent mantra. *Let it be Fowler. Let it be Fowler.*

I couldn't be certain how long I was down here, but I sensed time was fading fast until midlight—that brief duration when the ink dark faded and a haze of feeble light surfaced and chased the dwellers back underground. In an odd twist, midlight was something I didn't want to occur. The idea of dwellers returning and prowling the same space I occupied made my steps quicken despite any reassurances.

Suddenly the ceiling above me started to shake and froth, mud dropping down and raining on my head. Was it a cave-in? I ran, trying to escape the earth falling on me, keeping my hand on the wall to my left. I ducked down the tunnel, chest heaving.

Pressed into the wall, I turned my face up and held out my hand. Nothing was falling anymore. The ceiling of earth was stable. Holding myself as still as possible, I listened.

A dweller's wet, sloughing breath filled my ears. Its dragging steps felt like a scrape of a blade across my flesh. The heavy weight of its body thudded and settled into the damp ground with each move. My heart beat so hard my chest ached. I heard the whisper of the sensors at the center of its face slither on the air, and smelled the drip of toxin.

The monster wasn't alone. A human struggled against the dweller's razor talons, sobbing and choking out garbled pleas.

Hopeless words. There was no reasoning with these creatures. Not pity to rouse. No help. No rescue.

They drew near the smaller tunnel where I hid, and I debated my next move. Hold still or run? Lungs locked, I held my breath, waiting for them to pass. *Hoping* they passed. If they turned down this tunnel it was all over. I was lost.

The dweller passed me, dragging the hapless human behind, and I swallowed against the dryness of my mouth. Fortunately, the dweller was so focused on its victim it didn't detect my scent. Or perhaps being coated head to foot in mud aided in disguising my smell.

I waited several long minutes before continuing. Part of me wanted to take cover and hide, but the longer I hid the closer we drew to midlight. And once midlight hit . . . I shivered. Dwellers would be coming home. I had to move. Fowler and I needed to be out of here before that happened.

I took several more bracing breaths, in and out, to calm my heart as I moved down the narrow corridor. I didn't hear that dweller or its poor victim anymore. Faint, very human moans trickled over the vaporous air. It was colder down here than above. My teeth clacked slightly as I continued, growing closer to the sounds of humans, my hand skimming the uneven wall beside me. The tunnel opened up into a great space where the air flowed swifter, the current similar to when I stood in an open field with the wind blowing, lifting the hair off my shoulders.

I hovered, standing at the threshold, shivering at the cusp of something . . . a great maw of space that contained several humans. They were trapped. Their moans met my ears, soft anguished cries lined with defeat. Their hands slapped and clawed at the ground, trying to pull themselves free. Some were injured. I smelled the cloying sweetness of their blood. I lifted my face, smelling, listening, assessing.

It was a nest, a vast stretch of earth with holes that imprisoned humans.

"Fowler?" I whisper-shouted over the pitiable sobs and pleas for help. Swallowing, I took on more volume. "Fowler! Are you in here?"

His response was almost immediate, alongside the cries of others, answering me, begging for their release. "Luna! What are you doing here?"

Elation burst inside me, sweeping over me and making me almost limp. "Fowler!" I started to step forward, but his sharp warning stopped me.

"Careful, Luna. You'll fall in. Drop to your knees and crawl."

Lowering to my knees, I started forward, patting the ground ahead of me. It didn't take me long to figure out why I should crawl. The ground broke off into a pattern of holes. I crawled between them. Sticky residue was everywhere. I practically had to peel my palms off the narrow stretches of ground between holes.

Other people pleaded with me, calling for my help, but I kept an even line to where Fowler was lodged. His voice was a steady wind of encouragement that I followed until I reached him. My hand landed on his shoulder.

"Fowler . . . are you hurt?" I skimmed the curve of his shoulder, quickly understanding that he was wedged deep in the hole, his arms trapped. This must be why none of them were moving.

"Luna, you have to go." Panic sharpened his voice. "You don't have long. Get out of here before they come back—"

"I'm not leaving you. I'm here. Now help me get you out." My hands roamed, trying to find some leverage to pull him out.

"I'm stuck tight and this sticky mess everywhere isn't helping. It's like one giant spider's web."

"Then I'll cut you out," I declared.

"What do you—" His words died abruptly as I used my knife and started hacking at the edge of the hole trapping him. I worked hard, panting as I cut and clawed the crumbling ground away from him with my fingers.

"Luna, there's no time."

I shook my head, pelting mud-soaked strands against my cheeks. I'd come this far. I wasn't leaving without him.

He released a grunt of frustration and then started struggling, apparently grasping the fact that I wasn't giving up and he might as well try to break loose.

My arms burned as I hacked at the ground. He jerked inside the hole, wiggling his upper body as I widened the opening a fraction at a time.

"It's not . . ." Whatever he was about to say was lost as one of his arms suddenly broke free. He flung his body to the side and squeezed the other one out. I grabbed his shirt and helped haul him out, although now that both his arms were free he managed most of it on his own.

The others came alert and called out, their voices ringing around us, begging for help.

Fowler grabbed my hand and tugged me to crawl after him, ignoring them.

"Fowler," I began, listening to the sound of a woman near him, crying and begging for us to save her. "We need to help—"

"There's no time, Luna." His fingers tightened on my hand as if he feared I would slip free.

I turned my head, facing the direction of her sobbing pleas.

"Please, please help me, too. Don't leave me here. Don't leave me here to die!"

I pulled against Fowler's hand.

"Luna!" he growled, turning his body to snatch me by the shoulders. "We have to go! They're lost. Most of them are covered in toxin, and it's nearly midlight!"

For once in my life, midlight signaled the end of safety. Not the dawn of it. The irony wasn't lost on me.

I shook my head, but then everything started shaking. The very ground we crawled over vibrated. The underworld cavern trembled and shuddered, great clumps of earth falling from the ceiling.

"Dwellers," he growled over the buzz of their return, as though I didn't know. As though the rot of them wasn't choking. "They're coming."

This time I didn't resist as he pulled me after him.

A woman screamed, her cry of despair bouncing inside my head as we crawled over the nest and ran. My chest constricted, aching at the cries of the others we left behind, certain they would haunt me forever.

We ducked into the tunnel that I took to get to the nest. The earth still trembled as we ran down the tunnel, wet chunks of dirt showering all around us. I felt the telltale draft and knew we had come to the crossroads. Fowler started to pull right, but I stopped him, tugging him hard to the left. "This way!"

This time I led the way, clasping hard to his hand, relying on my memory.

"Not much farther," I tossed over my shoulder, backtracking the way I had come. "We're almost there." I could smell the brackish water running softly down the chute that spat me out no so very long ago.

The rumbling intensified. More mud fell, showering us in thick clumps. Except it wasn't just mud this time. *Dwellers.* Entire bodies emerged like infants pushing their way into the world. *Their* world. We were the interlopers in it. Never did I feel that more keenly.

"There are too many of them," I murmured past numb lips, a calm settling over me as I tilted my face to the deluge of sludge and dwellers.

"No! This way." Fowler jerked me into another tunnel, his strong fingers clenched hard around mine. He didn't even care if we were going in the wrong direction. The goal was escape. Desperation drove him and his fear. The emotions filled my nose like burning feathers on the air.

His grip bit into me, each finger a burning imprint. He wasn't going to surrender. It wouldn't be like before. He wasn't going to dive in headfirst. There would be no embracing of death.

But we couldn't escape them. They met us in every direction, the stench of them thick, their moist breaths ragged as they began filling the space around us. Fowler uttered a stinging curse as more dwellers dropped from above, landing with fat plops all around us. Clawed fingers scored the ground as they shoved to their feet.

He swung around, yanking me with him. I felt dizzy for a moment as he pulled me one way, then another, moving us forward in a wild zigzag pattern.

I grabbed his shoulder, but he kept going, dodging their ice-cold bodies. "Fowler! Stop!" I dug harder into his arm. "Stop!"

He finally froze, pulling me into a pocket in the wall of a tunnel, shielding me with his body, his breath falling hard against the side of my face. I faced him, savoring the sensation of his eyes on me. His breath continued to fall in savage pants. It was hopeless.

"Fowler," I pleaded, fighting to tune out the sounds of dwellers closing in—the rasp of their sensors, the shuffle of heavy feet. We didn't have long before they would be on us, ripping flesh and sinew from our bones. I could almost imagine the weight of them on me, crushing, killing. "I don't want to spend my last moments running."

"Luna," he choked out, his hand flexing around mine.

"Why did you have to come . . ."

"Shh." I cupped his face with both hands. "You're not the only one who gets to play knight in shining armor, you know." My thumbs brushed the planes of his cheeks, letting go of my anger. In this moment, what was the point? "I want in on some of the fun, too." This was easier than being angry, easier than accusing him of betrayal.

He dropped his head until our foreheads rested together. "You're supposed to live."

I swallowed back the impulse to tell him the truth. Me living was never going to happen. It was only a matter of time. He'd told me as much when Sivo first insisted that I leave the tower with him. This world, full of darkness and monsters and tyranny, wasn't for the living. Fowler had tried to tell me that so many times.

Since the moment I discovered that innocent girls were dying in Cullan's quest to destroy me, my fate was sealed. My only regret was that I wasn't able to stop him. That he would continue killing girls because of me.

"No more running," I whispered, trying to block out the sounds of dwellers, focusing all my senses on the boy in front of me. The heavy steps and rotting, loamy aroma of dwellers closing in. The horrible gurgling breaths. All of it vanished. "That's not how I want my last moments to be."

"Very well." His head nodded in the clasp of my fingers. "No more running." His breath fanned my lips and I lifted up on my tiptoes.

His mouth closed on mine, stealing my breath. Blood rushed to my head, precisely what I wanted—a rush of white noise in my ears to block out the army of dwellers coming at us.

His arm wrapped around my waist and hauled me closer. Everything else melted away. Fowler's chest mashed into mine, and I even forgot the miserable sensation of my wet clothes sticking to me like a second skin.

I felt his heart pounding into my ribs. His fingers delved through my mud-tangled hair as he kissed me, lips devouring me in precisely the way I wanted, in the way I needed, in a way that made me forget his lies and my shattered heart and the monsters bearing down on us.

FOUR

Fowler

I KISSED HER harder than I ever had before. It was no gentle meeting of lips over hushed endearments. Nothing slow or leisurely. I claimed her mouth, determined that it be everything. Everything a last kiss should be.

The kiss burned and left its mark, burrowing past flesh and tissue to the very marrow of us—to all that would be left. It imprinted on our souls. When the dwellers tore us apart this kiss would still remain.

I slanted my lips over hers, going deeper, my hands gripping her, ignoring the pain that throbbed in my one arm . . . ignoring the dwellers moving in, so close. I kept my eyes closed, losing myself in her taste and texture. One of her hands curved around my head, molding to the shape of my scalp, and I felt her pulse in the press of her palm on me. Luna's life merged into mine.

My mind reeled, thinking of the first time I saw her, shooting an arrow at a dweller, saving my life—a bold girl who moved as though she belonged to the woods. As though she belonged to this world, as natural as the darkness itself. I'd resisted her, fought the attraction, but now I knew. She was not something I could resist. It was what she asked for, even if not in so many words. No more running.

I inhaled cold air through my nose and dove deep into the taste of her, pushing my fingers into her mud-caked hair.

A sudden scream blasted over the air, long and eerie as nails scraping glass. It jarred us apart. The sound resembled a horn or trumpet, except no instrument had ever created this. It was animal-like and loud enough to make ears bleed, blaring long and deep, tinged with impatience.

With a cry, Luna staggered, colliding into the earthen wall. I held on to her arm as she flung her hands over her ears. The dwellers stopped cold. The nest of sensors in the center of their blocky faces writhed, the only movement made. Dozens of them hovered on every side of us, locked in some kind of frozen spell. One was so close, it only needed to lift an arm and stretch its taloned fingers to reach me. This close, I could make out the dark stain of blood on the tips of those thick talons, bits of human flesh and gore stuck there like meat on a bone.

As abruptly as it started, the screeching stopped. The

dwellers still didn't move. I held my breath, assuming they would lurch back into action. I eyed the one nearest me cautiously. Its mouth gaped, sensors dripping with glistening toxin, but it still made no advance.

I tightened my grip on Luna. "Come," I whispered.

Her hands dropped from her ears as I pulled her back to my side. She exhaled, and I felt that breath shudder through me.

"Fowler?" she asked, her voice shaky. "What's happening? Why aren't they moving?"

I knew her well enough to know that even without vision, Luna behaved as though she could see. There were very few instances where one was alerted to the fact that she was blind.

I eyed the army of dwellers all around us and opened my mouth to reply, but that savage scream started again with renewed force.

I winced, and Luna covered her ears again. I could just barely make out her eyes in the near darkness, jammed tightly shut as she covered her ears, as if that would somehow help ward off the sound. I shook my head, but the action only seemed to bring more stabbing pain to my ears.

The dwellers turned almost as one body, still ignoring us. Several passed us, their cold, pasty bodies brushing against us with slow drags. It was almost unbearable, being this close to them. Feeling them, smelling their stink. My throat tightened as one passed, a chunk of its hairless skull missing, someone's hatchet still embedded there.

They moved in the same direction, walking away from Luna

at the briskest pace I had ever seen them move. I didn't know they could even move at that speed. Most of the time they doddered, and this was the salvation of many lives.

"They're leaving." Bewildered, I held her close as dwellers passed, parting like a tide around us. We stood holding each other, two pebbles undisturbed in their path. It was like they didn't even see us anymore. We were invisible . . . unimportant.

Whatever that scream was, wherever it came from, it was manipulating them. I watched for a paralyzed moment as they shuffled along, fading away and leaving us alone in the narrow tunnel. The deafening scream continued, punctuated with brief pauses, and I wondered if it was their language, or a code dwellers alone understood. I had long thought they communicated with each other through their shrill cries . . . and this scream was the mother of all that I had ever heard in the years that I journeyed the Outside.

It was only supposition. I didn't know what was happening, and I didn't know how long it would last. It couldn't last long.

Luna stretched up on tiptoes to speak in my ear. "They're following the scream." She pressed a hand against the earthen wall, her slim fingers splayed wide as if requiring the balance. "And it's more than that. There are vibrations, too. I can feel them in the earth. In the air." She lifted her chin as if she was detecting those sound waves now. Her next words confirmed what I suspected. The chill of my skin wasn't only from the cold. A sick dread took hold of me—a suspicion that there was something down here bigger, more powerful, than any single dweller. Something strong enough to control an army of dwellers. Whatever that something was, we needed to remove ourselves from it.

"There's something else down here. It's controlling them," Luna finished.

I shook my head as though it didn't matter. I slid my hand down her arm to seize her hand. By some miracle we had our chance, and we needed to take it before the window of opportunity disappeared. "Let's go."

I led us. She pulled on my arm at one point when I tried to take a right turn. "This way," she instructed, guiding me.

Of course, she would know the way out. I followed her. Luna never forgot a path taken. I hardly remembered being dragged down here. It was all a blur of sound and pain.

She stopped at a slippery slope and started to climb upward, stabbing her knife in the slick wall and using it for leverage. I came up behind her and gave her a boost. It was slow progress. For every two feet she advanced, she slid back down one. I grunted, fighting the pull of weariness, shoving her up, struggling to keep her moving. I was so damnably weak.

She wiggled higher, taking the momentum of me pushing to claw up the incline until I couldn't see her head and shoulders anymore.

I started after her, ignoring the ache in my muscles and the burn in my arm. Freedom was close. I heard her suck in a deep breath and surge up through the quagmire above our heads. Her legs disappeared, followed by her feet, until she slipped totally out of sight, vanishing into the marsh above.

I followed, dragging a deep breath inside my lungs, filling them to capacity before I plunged into the icy muck. I kicked and used my arms, assisting gravity in bringing me to the surface, where the water was a few degrees warmer at least.

I broke clear with a gasp, tossing my head and filling my aching lungs, pulling sweet air inside me.

Lifting my face, I let the paltry rays of midlight wash over my face.

"Fowler! This way!" Luna was there, hauling herself out of the bog. She turned back over her shoulder to call for me.

"Here," I said, scarcely recognizing the hoarseness of my voice.

I swam through the dense bog, forcing my leaden limbs to move. My strength was dwindling. I hefted myself up, pulling my legs free. For a moment, I collapsed on the sodden ground, resting, facedown and panting with labored breaths.

We made it. We were alive.

"Fowler." She breathed my name somewhere above my head. "We can't stay here."

I pushed up onto my trembling legs, knowing she was right and trying not to collapse on the spot. Not after all she did to rescue me. I had to keep going. "Of course."

The hour would end and darkness would descend again. With it dwellers would return. We couldn't count on that *thing* that had called them down there to hold them at bay from us forever. "We'll find shelter." She nodded as though this would be a simple matter. "This way."

We tromped through the marsh side by side, avoiding where the water was the deepest. I fixed my gaze on Luna, focusing on her and not the excruciating discomfort pounding through my body.

She was a mess. Her shorn, muddied hair jutted about her head like black straw. The milk of her skin was nowhere to be seen. Not an inch of her was spared mud and that greenish sap from the dwellers' nest.

She was the most beautiful thing I ever set eyes on.

"You saved me," I uttered, a fair amount of awe creeping into my voice. I doubted anyone ever went belowground and returned to tell of it.

"A fair exchange. You saved me first by jumping from the tree and letting them take you so that they forgot about me." Her strides struck harder and she almost overtook me. I increased my pace to stay abreast with her. "Fool thing to do! What were you thinking?"

"I was thinking of *you*. There was no sense in both of us dying. Which is exactly what would have happened if I didn't jump from that tree when I did."

The ground grew more solid beneath our feet. Rocky and uneven. I scanned the hazy landscape, spotting rises and out-croppings ahead. Maybe we could find cover there.

"So you thought to make a grand sacrifice?" she snapped. "No one asked you to do *that*! I didn't ask it of you! I don't want anyone to die for me. Not even *you*."

"Oh, but it's a familiar concept, is it not?" I shot back, letting her feel my full temper. Gone was the moment of that kiss when we pushed aside every anger and betrayal. We were alive and safe for now, and our differences resurfaced with nowhere to hide. "Senselessly sacrificing yourself for others is something you're only too willing to do?"

Her body stiffened. "It's not senseless," she whispered.

"Let's consider that. Returning to Relhok and throwing yourself at the feet of Cullan so that he might lift his kill order on girls? How is that any different from me sacrificing myself for you?"

She paused for a moment and turned her face in my direction, her expression startled before she masked it and continued walking, her boots biting into the ground with her ire. "It's not the same. Not the same at all."

"It is," I insisted over ragged breaths, struggling to keep up. I swallowed, fighting for stamina, cursing this maddening weakness that sucked and pulled at me.

"Very well then," she snapped. "If it's the same, then you understand about necessary sacrifices. You *should* understand why I need to go to Relhok City. Why I have to stop Cullan." She halted, and I tried not to sigh my relief. Her pace was killing me.

I flexed my fingers, willing sensation back into my hand . . . sensation other than searing agony. She faced me as though she could see me, her liquid dark eyes flitting over me unseeingly. It was eerie the way I always felt exposed around her. Maybe now more than ever. I had nothing left to hide. No secrets to keep from her. This was just me standing before her.

"Cullan," she repeated. "You know. Your *father*."

The accusation was clear. Apparently we would have this conversation now. I inhaled a pained breath. "Luna, let's not—"

"Why not? It's the truth. He's a tyrant. Brutal. Evil."

All truths I would rather not waste precious time discussing. "He's no father to me—"

"Except he is your *father*. A convenient bit of truth you kept to yourself." She nodded as though willing that bitter fact to sink in and take root.

I stared at her for a long moment, futile words welling up inside me that would mean nothing to her. The only thing she felt was betrayal. *My* betrayal. It was too raw. Nothing I said would change that. At least not yet. It would take time. Time I didn't have. Wincing, I shifted my arm. I couldn't move my fingers anymore.

"You left me, Luna. You ran from me so that you could go after Cullan," I reminded her in a hoarse whisper, determined to make her remember, make her care again. Only then could I sway her from the path she had chosen for herself. "Do you have any idea what that did to me? Waking up and finding you gone?"

"Don't do that. He's your father. Don't call him Cullan like he's not."

"Who my father is doesn't erase what we have."

"*Had*," she cut in, her voice quiet. "Had, Fowler. We don't have that anymore. It's finished. There are more important things. Matters of the heart are immaterial. You taught me that.

Remember? Everyone dies. No one lasts in this world, and it's pointless growing attached to anyone."

"Luna, I didn't—"

She swung around and kept moving, her pace swift. I fell in next to her, holding my burning arm close to my side.

I nodded to the outcropping not far to the right of us. "Rocks ahead. Let's rest."

"We should keep going."

"I need to rest." I hated that I had to say the words. In all our time together, I usually forged our path. I never complained of tiredness or weakness. It stung my pride that I had to do it now.

She sent me a peculiar look, clearly thinking the same thing, too. "Very well."

We made our way to the rocks. I clambered up the incline ahead of her, grunting cold gusts of breath. At the top, I noticed a crevice between two rocks. I reached for her hand, briefly grabbing hold of her fingers with my good hand before she pulled away. The rejection stung. She wouldn't even let me have that much of her.

Her chin shot up and she shook mud-stiffened hair back from her pale face. "I can manage."

Shrugging like it didn't bother me, as though I didn't feel her distance from me like a physical ache, I squeezed through the opening into the chilled space, relieved that it widened to a larger area. The area was wide enough for us both to stand with arms outstretched. I collapsed onto the cold stone, the chill at my back a welcome contrast to the fire in my arm.

She lowered herself down on the ground, keeping her distance and folding her hands on her bent knees. The closeness we'd had underground—*that* kiss—felt like a lifetime ago. Not forgotten, but buried deep with the dwellers and bones of the dead. I settled on my back and let my head drop back on the solid ground with a dull thud.

Now that we had escaped, my body let every pain, big and small, assert itself. I closed my eyes, not even caring that I slept on rigid stone. I ached—and not just my arm. My head throbbed, flushing with heat. My arm burned so much that I began to wonder if it wouldn't feel better simply severed from my torso. I chuckled lightly at the morbid thought. There had been days when I thought death might be better, easier than this existence. Then I had met Luna and she convinced me that life could be more. That together we could have *more*. Now she had decided she had been wrong.

Luna's voice burrowed past the growing fog of pain. "You can get me inside the capital, Fowler. You know the city. You have to know people there. Maybe you still have friends who—"

My laughter slipped out again, unbidden, and rusty as a forgotten plow blade in one of the fallow fields all across this land.

"Why do you continue to laugh at a time like this?" she demanded.

"It's just that the only reason you want me around is to help you on your suicide mission—a mission that would bring me back to the place I swore never to return."

"You can't run away from this."

I sobered, levity disappearing as I shook my head. "All I do is run. It's the only thing I know."

She nodded, understanding.

I added flatly, "Even if I could, I wouldn't. You need to give up on this insane quest."

"What do you mean *even if* you could? You're saying you can't. Be honest for a change. Tell me the truth. What you're really saying is you *won't*."

I wished it were only that.

I took a slow breath, wondering when I should tell her that I might not be able to make it twenty yards, much less trek across the country to Relhok City.

She continued with a sneer, "He's your father. They would fling open the gates for you. Throw you a grand party."

Something twisted inside my chest at the way she said that. She thought less of me because of my blood. She thought less of me and she always would. "Don't call him my father." Even if he gave me life, he was no father to me. Nor was he any kind of husband to my mother. The man knew nothing of paternal bonds. Nothing of love or loyalty.

Moistening my dry lips, I tugged at my shirt, peeling it over my head and off my burning flesh with a wince. "Fact is, I'm not leaving this cave." I balled up my shirt and wiped at my arm with the fabric. A hiss of pain escaped between my teeth as I attempted to wipe it clean.

She stilled, her arms wrapped around her knees. "What do you mean?"

"I'm asking you not to go." I settled my gaze on her face, not above manipulating her with my grim reality. I always knew it was a matter of time before I died. It wasn't as though I expected to live to a ripe old age. In this world, that wasn't a possibility. "My dying wish, Luna. Will you deny me that?"

She uncurled her arms from around her knees and inched over to my side, her expression giving away her concern. "What are you talking about? You're not dying. We made it out—"

I held up my arm. "Can you smell that? My arm?"

She froze, her nostrils flaring as though she was in fact smelling me—inhaling the bittersweet aroma of poison.

"It's dweller toxin, Luna." I glanced down to the glimmer of it on my skin. "It's all over me. The worst of it on my arm." I grimaced. "I didn't get out unscathed. Like I said, you shouldn't have come for me."

She lifted her hand to touch my arm, but I pulled it out of her range. "Don't touch it. You don't want to get it on you."

"Fowler," she whispered, bringing her hand up to cover her mouth, her stricken expression forcing me to confront the truth of things.

I laughed roughly, but the sound twisted into a hacking cough. I had always prided myself on being so very skilled at surviving. Even when I didn't particularly want to live, I always somehow managed to survive. Not anymore, though. Now, when I might want to live, when I might have found someone I wanted to live with—someone to live *for*—this happened.

She shook her head. "I fail to see any humor in this."

"No, you wouldn't. You, who wants to save the world. You still risked your neck for me even when you ran out on me, even when you want nothing more to do with me." I brushed my good hand against her cheek. "You're too decent for this world, Luna." Too good for me.

"Fowler." There was such pity in that single sound of my name that I felt relief. At least it wasn't hatred. Me dying stopped her from despising me. I snorted. That made me pathetic, but there it was. I had a flash of that kiss underground. Too bad I hadn't died then, swiftly amid the swirling windswept taste of her. No, instead my death would be a lingering agony. "I—I don't want you to die."

I sighed, lowering my arm back to my side. "I'm already lost, Luna."

FIVE

Luna

I SPENT THE next day trying to make Fowler as comfortable as possible. I went out and left him to fetch water several times. He slept more and more. Half the time he wasn't even aware of my comings and goings. I rinsed his arm with water until I couldn't smell the toxin on the surface of his skin anymore. It wasn't really gone, though. The poison had buried deep, settling past his flesh and coursing through his blood. I lifted his head and guided him to drink, hoping that helped in some way. Whenever I had been ill, Perla always pushed for me to drink. I missed Perla now more than ever, certain that she would know how to help him. I, on the other hand, was less than useful.

I washed off Fowler's face, chest, and arms. Then I turned my attention on myself, washing up as best as I could, too. My situation was hopeless. I gave up on my matted hair. I'd managed to get most of the mud off my skin, but my hair was a lost cause. Not that I worried much about my appearance. I had bigger concerns.

Fever trapped Fowler in its grip. There was no more conversation. At least nothing intelligent. He muttered, thrashing on the cave floor, incoherent words tripping from his lips. More than once he cried out for Bethan. The name made me flinch. Obviously she was someone important to him. Someone he had never seen fit to tell me about. It was another reminder that there was a great deal I didn't know about him.

Sitting beside him, watching him die, my mind roamed down paths better left alone. He'd been there when his father killed my parents and seized the throne. He was just a child then, a boy, but he'd been there. He'd reaped the benefits, living in the palace, taking my place, enjoying what should have been my life as the king's heir to the throne.

I knew nothing about *that* and yet I thought I loved him. I believed that maybe he loved me, too. *Enough to die for me.* I shook off the thought. He'd never shared anything real about himself with me. I didn't really know him at all. And now I never would.

I picked up his hand, clutching it in both of mine as I hovered over him, feeling alone even though he was still here with me. It was a shell of him, whimpering and shaking with fever.

"You're strong, Fowler. You can beat this." I squeezed his hand, attempting to convey what strength I could to him.

I racked my brain for everything Sivo or Perla had ever said about dweller toxin, thinking there had to be something more I could do. They'd said it was lethal, but they didn't know everything. What had they done except hide away from the world and all its dweller problems? There had to be a way to survive it. He only had it on his arm and he was young and vital.

A scratching outside the cave brought me lurching to my feet. I clutched my knife, flexing my hand around the hilt, bracing myself to use it. Dweller or man, I would defend us.

A sudden low growl accompanied the snuffling outside the cave. A dweller wouldn't make that noise. Besides, they never roamed over anything except penetrable earth. Sivo said it was because they didn't want to be caught far from underground access should they have to flee to home quickly.

Even so, this growl was familiar. Not dweller familiar, but familiar.

My grip on the knife relaxed a slight fraction. Still wary, I whispered, "Digger? Is that you?"

The tree wolf's nails clacked over the rock floor at an easy pace as he stepped inside the cave. He greeted me with a whimper.

"Digger," I breathed, my shoulders slumping as the tension melted from me. My arm fell to my side, the knife loosening within my fingers.

The wolf snuffled at me, slipping his muzzle under the palm of my free hand. I stroked the velvety texture of his nose. "You found me, Digger." Dropping to my knees in front of him, I looped my arms around his neck, my chest lifting and falling in quick succession—like a tightening and loosening of a knot. Suddenly I didn't feel quite so alone anymore. "That's a good boy."

I buried my face in his coarse mane of hair. The beast whimpered again, but didn't pull away from me. My fingers delved deeper into the thick fur. Right now, he was all I had, my only friend in the world.

He abided my embrace for a few moments, the swish of his long, looping tail over the rocky ground a comforting sound. Until he decided he had enough. Never one to stick around for long, he licked my face and departed. I listened to the light clack of his nails, not worrying if I would see him again. He'd be back. He'd gone through the trouble of finding me. I was confident he would return.

I curled up beside Fowler to wait, forcing sips of water down his throat and feeling his scalding-hot brow, holding out hope that his fever might yet break. That he might be immune to the dweller's toxin. It could happen. Perhaps. In this world, anything was possible. The last seventeen years had taught me that.

Digger returned a few hours later, perhaps more, perhaps less. It was hard to know. Usually I was a good judge of passing time, but I felt like I was in a haze where time ceased to exist.

The pungent scent of his fur and clatter of his nails announced his arrival—along with the hare clamped between his teeth. He dropped the dead animal at my feet and then sank to his haunches, tail swishing, waiting for his praise, expecting it as his due.

"Good boy, Digger," I crooned, petting his head before turning and dressing the animal. Even though Sivo had usually performed the task, I knew what to do: from skinning the animal to preparing a fire and setting the hare over the flame to cook. I busied myself, glad for the task. It beat watching Fowler with my heart in my throat, jerking at every ragged breath, terrified it would be his last.

As I prepared the hare, Digger shifted his weight and inched closer to where Fowler rested. He sniffed at him cautiously. I paused over the hare, tensing, making sure Digger's intentions were friendly and he wasn't going to take a bite out of Fowler. He continued sniffing, nails scratching rock as he edged closer and closer, and then there was a slight snuffing and blowing against Fowler's hair.

I half-smiled, suspecting he was trying to rouse him. Digger gave up with a huff and then settled down close to Fowler. It made my chest ache a little—that this wild beast could find tenderness inside him not only for me but for Fowler, too. It made the world seem just a little bit better. Not entirely dark and hopeless. A little less bleak.

I focused on cooking the hare over the fire, mindful not to burn myself. I couldn't afford the injury. I had Fowler to tend. It was up to me to pull him out of this. And I would. I had to.

Cooking was a risk, I knew, and not because I might burn myself. The aroma could attract dwellers willing to risk the rocks, but I needed the food. I needed to keep my strength up.

They would not risk the rocks. We were safe from them for now. I let the mantra roll through me, needing to believe it. It was my sole thought as the hare finished cooking over the small fire. I sat beside Fowler, coaxing more water down his throat, talking to him, letting him hear my voice.

Digger reclined nearby, his great furred back a warm pillow alongside my body. It almost felt safe, warm and comfortable. If only Fowler weren't fighting for his life.

Digger's hackles flared up an instant before the low rumble of his growl filled our small sanctuary. My apprehension was misplaced. I didn't need to fear dwellers finding us. I patted his back, feeling every hair there standing on end. "What is it, boy?"

Digger hopped to his feet and trotted out of the cave to investigate. I bit my lip, resisting the impulse to call him back, even if I did feel alone and vulnerable. Indeed, I had no wish to make a sound at all, to make myself a more obvious target.

Instead, I reached for my knife again, all of me as tense as a slat of wood. My hand flexed around the knife's edge, palm growing slippery with sweat.

My free hand reached for Fowler, clasping the hard curve of his shoulder. Even like this he still felt vital and strong. Maybe that was simply the fever. The heat of his skin imbued with warmth in the chill of the cave. Warmth that intimated health and comfort and well-being.

I patted him for reassurance—for me, I supposed. He was out of his head with fever, unaware of me.

I felt every sound. The flap of a bat's wings in the far distance outside the cave. Breaths panting in exertion. The sound of multiple footsteps reached my ears long before I heard voices to alert me that men were approaching. I knew their gait, so very different from the dragging steps of dwellers.

I released my grip on Fowler and lurched to my feet, my blade brandished before me in hands that were slippery with sweat but surprisingly steady.

I counted three as they appeared, one by one, squeezing through the mouth of the cave.

They invaded our space, filling it with their smell: sweat and an underlying odor of horseflesh. That meant they weren't traveling on foot. Somewhere outside the cave, horses waited for them. On the rocks, no doubt. They wouldn't have left them in the open, vulnerable to dwellers. My mind raced, thinking about the ground Fowler and I could cover if I we had those horses.

And then reality crashed down on me. How could I get Fowler atop a mount? How could we travel at all? He wasn't even awake.

"You were right, Jabon. There is someone up in here. Two somebodies, it looks like."

Another voice, presumably Jabon's, answered gruffly, "Always trust my nose, Kurk. Never leads me astray, especially where food is concerned, and I told you I smelled roasting meat."

The words made me want to kick myself. Cooking the hare had brought them here. I'd led them here. I'd brought them to Fowler.

I did this.

There was a slight chink as one of the men moved, and I instantly recognized the sound of chain mail. Sivo had kept his chain mail in a trunk. As a child I had donned the much-too-large tunic of mail before, playing dress-up, pretending to be a grand knight like Sivo. Like my father. Of course, Perla would fuss at me whenever she caught me, reminding me that I was a girl . . . the one true queen of Relhok. According to her, queens did not don chain mail. My chest ached and burned. I missed them. Especially now as I faced these men and whatever degradation awaited me at their hands.

"Come, lad, put down your blade." It was the rough, guttural voice again.

I shook my head, lifting my knife higher. "Get back!" Thus far, experience had not led me to count on any soldiers in chain mail being remotely like Sivo or my father. I wasn't so naïve to expect that.

"We don't aim to hurt you," another voice volunteered, still male, but decidedly lighter and younger than the voices of the other two men. "We're a convoy returning home from Relhok."

They came from Relhok? Just this admission gave me a small measure of hope. If they came from there, then I could get there.

He continued, "I've lived all my life in these parts, and I have to say you haven't the manner or speech of a Lagonian."

Lagonian? As in the country of Lagonia? I knew enough from studying geography with Sivo to know that Lagonia bordered Relhok. Had we drifted so far east that we crossed into the neighboring country?

For a moment, my chest lightened. The kill order on girls was a Relhok edict. It was not a Lagonian law. If we were in Lagonia, I was safe from that threat at least.

The moment the thought entered my mind, I shoved it out. I was never safe. Not even here. Especially not among these three strangers. *Soldiers.* Even worse. Soldiers were a rough, brutal sort. I knew they had to be to survive, but I still wanted no part of them. Astonishingly, I would rather be back in my tower with my loved ones. I'd taken them for granted.

"We mean you no harm," the soft-spoken one continued. "How about you share a bit of your meal with us and we'll provide you escort into Ainswind."

We must be fairly close to the city if he was offering escort into the capital.

"What makes you think I need an escort to Ainswind?" I snapped, doing my best to keep my voice deep. I still couldn't reveal my gender. Even if these were Lagonians, we weren't far enough from Relhok for me to announce that I was female.

They doubtless knew of the decree. By their own admission, they'd just journeyed from Relhok City. My head would fetch a nice price for them no matter their country of origin.

"Oh, you don't want to go to Ainswind, then. The nearest bit of civilization . . . safety . . . is there. Why wouldn't you want that? People are dying, truly dying, to get in its walls." He paused, and tense silence stretched between all of us. After a few moments, his smooth voice continued, "I'm only suggesting a trade. Our escort for a bit of that delicious hare. It's just the two of you, yes?

And your friend looks in bad shape. We can help you. My name is Breslen. What's yours?"

It was tempting to believe Breslen. Fowler needed care, and I might not have it in me to give it to him. I might not be enough.

"We're stronger in numbers," he coaxed, his easy tone suggesting I already knew that. It was reasonable. Logical. Weeks ago I would have agreed with that logic even though Fowler had never believed that. He thought the bigger the number, the greater the target you were.

Only what choice did I have? There were three of them, a nearly dead Fowler, and only one of me.

I lowered my knife, deciding that aggression would get me nowhere. I would have to figure my way through this. I motioned to the ground like it was some fine table before us. "Have a seat. There's not much, but I'll share it."

"Good lad." The three soldiers sat near my fire and fell upon the hare. I waited, not demanding anything for myself. I doubted I could eat anyway. My stomach was suddenly tied up in knots. I was too tense, essentially alone and defenseless in the company of three strange men.

I fixed a neutral expression on my face. So much to hide, so much to guard against. Keeping all my secrets was exhausting. I was a female. Blind. The one true heir to the Relhok throne. And now I had Fowler's secrets to keep, too. My temples pounded.

"Relax, boy. Here. Take this." At Breslen's offer, I held out my hand, smelling the bit of steaming meat being stretched out to me. Even though I wasn't in the mood for food, I accepted it and forced myself to chew, clinging to my armor under the crawl of their gazes.

Never far from my memory was the last strange man we met. He tried to kill me for my head. These men could try to do that to me. Or worse. There were other things to fear.

I picked at the greasy meat, forcing down another bite. My lack of appetite didn't escape their notice. "Eat. We're not so inconsiderate that we would eat all your food," Breslen encouraged. "Go on, boy."

With a tentative nod, I forced another bite down my throat.

"Take some more."

Grudgingly, I accepted, almost wishing the soldier wasn't so generous. The meat was hot enough to singe my fingers, but I didn't drop it. I brought the roasted hare to my teeth and nibbled, my stomach still too knotted to consume much more than that.

"What's wrong with your friend there?" one of the deeper-voiced men asked. Kurk, I thought. He was bigger, too, constantly shifting his large girth in the small space, brushing against the rock wall. "Don't tell me it's your cooking?" He guffawed at his own joke.

"No," I said softly, still holding my voice at a deep pitch.

"Dweller get him?" Breslen asked. For one so young, he was perceptive. I'd already gathered he was the leader of the three. Not the brawn, but the brains.

I nodded.

"Shame," Kurk said around a mouthful of food. "Nothing to do for it. Great deal of suffering ahead for him. Kindest thing to do would be to stick a knife between his ribs and put him out of his misery. I'd be willing to oblige you if you haven't the stomach for it."

I sucked in a sharp breath, understanding what he was saying, but no less horrified. Even if he was right, if it was the merciful thing to do, I couldn't do it. I could never do that. And right then I knew. No matter who he was or what he had done, I still deeply cared about Fowler. I still wanted him. Even if his father was evil and responsible for everything bad in my life. Even if I had no room in my existence for such tender feelings because I had a tyrant to kill and my country to save. It was weakness in me, to be certain, and I would not let it get the best of me. I would crush it beneath the pulse of obligation buzzing through me.

"Don't touch him," I growled.

"It's what I'd want," Jabon chimed in. "Sure it's not what he wants?"

"Fowler's a fighter," I insisted, lowering my hands that held the stringy meat, debating picking my knife back up. Would I need to defend Fowler?

"Fight don't matter." Kurk snorted, his big body scraping over the ground again as he shifted.

"Fowler?" At the soft query, a ripple of unease traveled down my spine. It wasn't such an uncommon name, but I regretted having said it aloud. It had just slipped out, but how could I know that it would strike a chord with this soldier . . . emissary. Whatever he was. Breslen was no friend to me. I supposed I should have known that the less said the better. "Is that his name, then?"

I fixed my expression into something that hopefully didn't

reveal panic. He couldn't know Fowler. The names of kings and princes were notoriously popular.

"Is he from Relhok City, by chance?" He lifted up from where he sat, sliding his slight frame closer to where Fowler shivered through his fever.

"No," I said. "We've never even been there."

"Interesting. Your accent says otherwise."

Of course I would sound like I was from there. I was raised and surrounded by two people who were born and bred there.

He did not respond to my lie, but I felt his stare.

"You lie," he finally pronounced, that gentle voice flaying me like the cruelest whip.

I flinched.

"He's been to Relhok City before." He spoke quickly, clearly thrilled by his discovery. "In fact, that's where he is from."

The other two soldiers adjusted their weight, clothes rustling as they leaned forward as though they required a look at Fowler, too.

I tried for an air of bewilderment, shaking my head. Truthfully, bewilderment wasn't far off. How could he know Fowler? "What do you mean?" Even if he'd ever glimpsed Fowler from afar, it had been years. In the time since, Fowler had been living a hard life on the Outside. He couldn't resemble the well-fed, undoubtedly pampered aristocrat from years ago. No, this hard-edged Fowler couldn't look the same at all.

"I know him. This is the prince of Relhok, the king of Relhok's son and only heir."

Jabon to my left made a whistling sound with his teeth while

Kurk demanded, "What? I thought he was away on some diplomatic trip to Cydon."

I absorbed that. Obviously this was the story Cullan had spread to explain his son's absence. Never mind how unlikely it was that Cullan would permit his one son to go anywhere outside the safety of Relhok City's walls. Whatever story Cullan put forth was taken as truth. No one opposed the bastard.

"Lies, apparently," Breslen answered smoothly. "King Cullan wants no one to know that his one heir is missing. Interesting. What is he doing so far from home?"

I moistened my lips, my heart thumping so hard I was certain every single one of them heard it. Breslen leaned forward over Fowler. I held my breath, listening, braced and ready to spring should he touch Fowler.

"What are you doing here with him?" Kurk directed the question to me, and his tone was decidedly less friendly than earlier. Suspicion hugged every word.

I shook my head. "I don't know anything about him being . . . royalty. You must be mistaken. He's just someone I met out here . . ." I waved a hand, gesturing to the world that I couldn't see but felt like a throbbing heartbeat in my chest.

That's what I thought about Fowler in the beginning, at least. He was just someone exceptionally good with a bow. Someone who knew how to survive in darkness . . . as though this world belonged to him and he to it. That's what I had thought. That's what I wished were true now more than ever.

A slight rustling of fabric alerted me to the fact that Breslen was now touching Fowler. I jerked forward, the tiny hairs on my arms prickling. "Don't touch him!"

"Easy, boy. Just checking his injuries. Assuming you want us to save him."

I froze. "Save him? You can do that?"

"It's not *impossible*."

The tension ebbed from my shoulders. I hadn't realized how close I had come to giving up, on ceasing to think Fowler had any hope, until I heard the desperation in my voice.

"It's possible. If he is King Cullan's son, I am certain King Tebald would go to great lengths to see that he lived. *If . . .*"

He let the word hang there, a clear bribe for the truth. I felt their stares then, fixed on me, waiting for an answer—waiting for me to confirm that he was in fact Cullan's son. I swallowed against the thick lump in my throat. It was tempting. And yet I knew Fowler would have me deny it. Even if it meant his death. He wanted no connection with his father. He'd forged his way, risking death every day without claiming Cullan as his father. It had wrecked him to admit the truth to me. I couldn't admit it to them.

In the stretch of silence, as though sensing my indecision, Breslen volunteered in his encouraging voice, "Perhaps you did not know the true identity of our companion. But you do now. Your friend here is the prince of Relhok."

I blew out a breath, clinging to denial by a thread. "This is madness—"

"Indeed. It is most unusual to find a prince stuck in a cave, dying. Most unexpected." He chuckled lightly. "I've been to Rel-hok City two other times as King Tebald's emissary. I've seen your companion there before. Of course, he was dressed far more grandly at the time. And I seem to recall there were many rumors surrounding him."

"Rumors?" I murmured because I couldn't help myself. I knew so little about him, especially the Fowler who had lived in Relhok City—in *my* place, living the life that should have been mine.

"Yes; he was in love with a girl that his father didn't approve of. Peasant girl. It was quite the castle gossip. His father was very displeased with him."

Fowler was in love with another girl? What was the name he'd called for in his sleep? Bethan? Again, another layer revealed proving how much of a stranger he really was to me.

"Don't worry," Breslen continued. "Relhok and Lagonia are allies."

One of the other soldiers snorted and muttered, "Today, anyway."

Breslen continued as though he hadn't spoken. "They would welcome Prince Fowler with open arms and take care of him . . . cure him, even."

My head lifted higher, hope thrumming inside my blood. I gulped a breath and fought to control my racing heart. This could happen. I could get Fowler the help he needed, and once he was in good hands and on the mend, I could continue on my way.

I could still finish this. I had to. An aching heart did not matter. The creeping fear that threatened to consume me around these men didn't matter either. I had to resist that and fight it as I did everything else. I couldn't let it conquer me.

"They would treat him?" I pressed.

"Indeed; the king's own physician would see to his wounds."

"But he's been poisoned. It's not too late? The toxin has—"

"If we get him to Ainswind quickly enough, he can be treated."

I lifted my chin, letting this sink in, letting hope fuel me and turn me in a new direction. "Very well. Then let's get moving."

SIX

Fowler

My world swayed and pitched. I felt like I was still on the boat in the lake outside of Ortley with black waters rolling under me. Even though something gnawed at the back of my mind, telling me that wasn't quite right, it was the only thing I could cling to.

I wanted to be in that boat, headed to shore, out of immediate danger and returning to Luna. We'd take our kelp and go.

Gripping what I told myself was the side of the boat, I thought of Luna. I thought of the Isle of Allu, a place where dwellers didn't exist, where she didn't have to pretend to be a boy; where I didn't have to be so relentless, where I could be something other than this version of myself.

For a while there, with Luna, I believed I could have that, a sanctuary amid this world. She convinced me of that—not with her words but in her unflagging optimism that life could be something more than pain and blood and a straight line to inevitable death.

A nervous energy buzzed through me. Something wasn't right. I frowned and angled my head, listening to the wind over water.

"Fowler?"

I cracked open my eyes and looked in the direction of the voice. It was familiar and not. A little like Luna's voice but different, as though she were speaking to me through a layer of cloth.

Everything was darkness, but that wasn't different from any other day. I lifted my hand and dragged it down my face, trying to wipe away the clinging fog, as though that motion would be enough to make everything clear.

"His eyes are open," a voice said. This one was not familiar. It was deeper, and rough as sharp pebbles against my skin.

"Give him some water. See if he'll take any."

I blinked and realized they were talking about me.

Suddenly a flask was at my mouth. Water splashed my lips and I drank greedily. In that moment all I cared about was the water, wet relief sliding down my throat.

"Not too much. You'll be sick."

The flask vanished and I mumbled a protest, groping for it but seizing only air. The motion sent hot agony sizzling through my arm, a reminder of just how bad things really were. I might not be dead, but the toxin pumping through me would eventually finish me off. But while I was still alive I could protect Luna. With my dying breath, I could try. I couldn't shut that impulse in me down. It was even more than impulse. I owed her a debt. For my father's transgressions, for everything he stole from her. I owed her more than I could ever give back. Inhaling, I fought to swallow down the mind-numbing pain and focus on Luna, and making certain she was all right.

I blinked some more and peered into the darkness, searching for her, waiting for my vision to acclimate to the thick, vapory gloom.

There were shapes moving around me. All atop horses. The faint sucking sound of hooves on soggy ground confirmed this. I was atop a horse, my body rolling with its movements, and a thick wall at my back.

I struggled to sit straight, fighting down a wave of nausea and pushing away from the wall with a surge of determination. That's when the wall came alive behind me. A hand clamped down on my shoulder. I jerked, realizing it was a man. A very big man.

I flung the hand off me and tried to twist around, ready to attack my captor. The colossal hand on my shoulder squeezed tighter, showing me just how impossible that feat was. I shrank under the pressure, as weak as a broken bird.

"Fowler, don't fight. They're helping us." Again I thought the voice belonged to Luna, but it was different. I opened my mouth to speak, but a croak escaped. My mouth was as dry as a barren creek. I worked my throat, attempting to swallow as my gaze sharpened, identifying the gray outline of a figure etched against the darker night. A face stared at me, dark eyes glimmering like coal. Luna.

She sat atop a mount, but she wasn't alone. A man sat behind her, no bigger than she was. She blocked most of him from view, but I marked his eyes peering over her shoulder at me. They were impossible to ignore.

My thoughts churned like tufts of feathers floating through air, looking for a place to land. The savage urge to reach her seized me, but I held back, remembering I couldn't even help myself, much less her.

I sat rigidly, not relaxing against the giant behind me.

The horse plodded along under us, and I felt the strain of his muscles in every rolling stride. Our combined weight had to be a burden. We would have to stop soon to rest the horses or they would collapse. This thought gave me hope. Perhaps then Luna and I could get away. Or Luna at least.

"Fowler, these men are taking us to help."

She made it sound so *possible* that they were helping us, that I could be anything other than dead at the end of this.

I opened my mouth and then closed it, uncertain what to say, what Luna had told them. I had no idea what they knew or didn't know . . . whether they even realized she was a girl. For her sake, I hoped not.

She said they were trying to help us. Could that even be true?

The man-boy sitting behind Luna spoke. "Glad to see you're awake. We've been traveling as hard as we can to get you to Ainswind quickly, and you haven't hardly stirred through it all."

"How long?" I managed to get the question out of my still-parched throat.

"How long have we been traveling together?" he asked, his tone all politeness. "We discovered you and your companion here three days ago. We're almost to Ainswind now. Once there, we will get those wounds the attention needed."

If we were almost to Ainswind, then we were in Lagonia. I peered through the dark at their soiled tunics stretched over chain mail, my vision becoming clearer. The Lagonian hawk was emblazoned across the front of the fabric. They were soldiers. A foul taste rose up in my mouth. Going to Ainswind was almost as bad as returning to Relhok City.

I took a bracing breath, shoving the pain aside so I could think clearly. Someone might recognize me there. Lagonia and Relhok shared a border. There had been an on-again, off-again accord between the countries—at least before the eclipse happened. Relhok and Lagonia had been in a cautious truce through most of my life. My father worked hard to maintain that truce. Lagonia's durability was the chief reason my father fought so hard to establish the alliance. Their fortifications were stronger than Relhok City's. Their numbers, too. *Stronger* could be applied to them in general, and that fact filled my father with endless frustration and forced him to act with diplomacy when it was his instinct to conquer.

Ever since I could walk, I'd been told that I would marry the princess of Lagonia and bring relief and stability to Relhok. Behind closed doors, my father never minced words on the matter. He told me we would find a way to get rid of the king and crown prince of Lagonia after I married the princess in order to rule both countries. It was the vision of a madman, I knew that now, but as a boy it was just one of many things my father said. I wished he were all bluster, but I knew differently. He did horrible things. Killing Luna's parents had just been the start for him.

I didn't know how things had transpired between Relhok and Lagonia in the years since I left. Apparently friendly enough, if convoys journeyed there.

King Tebald's emissaries had been to Relhok more than once while I was part of my father's royal household.

If my identity was exposed, I wasn't certain what my reception would be. There was also the fact that my father would likely hear of my presence in Lagonia. He'd issued an edict for the slaughter of all girls. It would be nothing for him to send an army after me.

My thoughts spun with too many questions to ask—especially with these soldiers as an audience. I decided to stick with the most important one.

"Why are you helping us?" There was no such thing as altruism in this world, in this life. Certainly not from these soldiers.

Perhaps the question was a waste of breath. No one was completely honest, after all. Even Luna had kept her secrets, holding them behind those deep, soulful eyes for so long. Like a fool, she took me in. I fell into the fathomless eyes, and kept falling . . . into *her*, without even knowing who she really was. And once I did know, it changed nothing. Not even when she ran from me did my feelings for her change. After that night together, after I had bared myself to my most raw and vulnerable for her, she still left me. She drugged me and slipped away as though I were a bad dream she could outrun.

I lied to Luna, too. The contrary thought slipped inside my head. I wasn't the most forthcoming person either, but I would never hurt her.

These men . . . they were capable of anything. Luna had a bounty on her. They could decide to take her head at any moment.

"We're close now. Ainswind is just half a day's ride." No one answered my question.

I stayed my tongue, wincing and holding my dying arm close to my chest. *Half a day.* Bleakness rose inside me. How was I getting us out of this in that span of time?

The smaller man continued talking from behind Luna, his voice deceptively amiable. "It was good luck to find you and the boy here." My shoulders practically slumped in relief. They didn't know she was a girl. That was one less worry. For now.

The Lagonian soldier was still talking, and I concentrated on his voice. "Imagine our surprise to find you with him. In your condition, no less." At these words, the hairs on the back of my neck prickled. He made it sound like he was surprised to see me *specifically*. "We'll see you mended. No fear, Your

Highness. You're in good hands."

His words hit me with a jolt. Cold dripped down my back and settled into my spine. He'd see me mended, but my arrival in Lagonia would be no secret. My father would know. He'd come for me eventually. I was his heir. As far as he was concerned, that meant I was his property.

The man leaned around Luna, his gaze clashing with mine across the distance separating us, pinning me with the hard truth.

He knew.

Grinning, he nodded to a spot ahead. "Let's rest the horses here." He dug in his heels and hastened ahead of us. We fell into pace behind him and Luna. I stared after him, trying to remember where I had seen him before. He knew me, so I must have seen him somewhere, but I couldn't place his shadowy face.

It all clicked into place. I understood why he was even bothering to bring me back to Ainswind. I was a commodity—the prince of Relhok to be hand delivered to King Tebald. My hope for escape died a swift death. He wasn't going to let me slip away. Not considering who I was. But perhaps Luna could. Luna was just a boy to him.

We stopped near a grove of trees. I dismounted with little grace, my arm hugged to my chest. Even with it immobilized, every movement sent pain ricocheting through me.

Luna was at my side, moving hastily. Her lack of sight was another thing they didn't know about her. That was for the best, too. Better that they not see her as impaired in any way.

"I've got you," she murmured near my ear, and I grimaced as

we hobbled toward the tree, needing her help more than I should. It wasn't supposed to be that way. I was supposed to protect her. That's what I'd promised to Sivo when we left the tower.

"You shouldn't be doing this," I whispered, anger frothing, mingling with the pain bubbling in me.

"Doing what?" she asked, turning her head slightly, listening to the three men behind us. Always careful, always vigilant.

"Helping me," I growled. "You need to look after yourself."

"Like you did when you saved my life, oh, at least a dozen times? I actually think we're pretty good at saving each other."

I didn't acknowledge that she might have a point. That would only encourage her. I kept a careful gaze on the three soldiers as they stood near the horses. "You have to get out of here, Luna. Before they find out you're not a boy. I don't trust them. They're only taking me to Ainswind because they expect some reward for handing over Cullan's son. They're out for themselves. You'd be a prize they couldn't pass up either. We're not so far from Relhok. They still could take your head and turn it in for a bounty."

She sighed as she wrapped an arm around my waist and helped lower me to the ground. "You worry too much." Once on the ground, she crouched near me and pressed a palm to my forehead. "You're still warm. Too warm."

I snatched hold of her wrist. "I'm not going to make it—"

"Don't say that. They said they have medicine that can cure you."

"They'll say anything. As long as they get me to Ainswind, dead or alive, they'll be rewarded in some manner."

Luna frowned and directed a look back at the soldiers as if she could see them. It was always eerie the way she did that. To these men it made her look normal, fully sighted, but I knew Luna was anything but normal. Even over the pain buzzing along every nerve, pain that ran so deep and intense it made my teeth ache, my gut tightened thinking about her and just how *not* normal she was. She was special. An anomaly. She shouldn't even be alive, but she was. She lived, and I wanted to pull her inside me, absorb her and keep her until I knew her as well as the shape and protrusion of my own bones. Until the taste of her was as clear to me as my own.

But none of that would happen. It couldn't.

"I'm not leaving you here," she vowed.

Still holding her wrist, I pulled her close until her face was almost nose-to-nose with mine. She winced at the pressure of my hand on her arm, but I didn't relax my grip. I had to make her understand. "Don't let them take you into the city, Luna."

"You need to rest, Fowler." She peeled my fingers off her arm. "Don't think about it. I can handle this."

I knotted one fist and beat it dully against the ground. "What's it going to take for you to do what I say just this once?"

She opened her mouth, but whatever she was going to say died abruptly. Rising to her feet, she whirled around suddenly.

I gripped the end of her tunic and gave a tug. "What is—"

She cut a hand through the air, silencing me. "Hear that?" she said, her voice so low it was practically inaudible.

I held still, listening, trying to decipher what it was she heard, but my ears weren't as good as hers. No one's were. Well, except perhaps for dwellers themselves. She shared that with them.

Several moments passed, but there was no telltale shriek that signaled the approach of a dweller. Exhaling, she crouched back down at my side. She'd cleaned her face. The freckles stood out starkly against her milk-pale features as she closed a hand around my good arm. "Horses are coming this way. Half a dozen at least."

I squeezed her wrist with hard fingers and studied her with an urgency I hope she felt. "This is your chance. Go. Slip away."

She shook her head at me, her voice a fierce hiss. "You wouldn't leave me. I'm not leaving *you.*"

"Is that what this is? Some stubbornness contest? Well, enough of it, Luna. You win. When you get an opportunity, you go. Don't look back. You run."

She made a sound of frustration. "No . . . "

The distant sound of hooves stopped all conversation then. Blades sang out on the air as the soldiers with us took position, drawing their weapons and standing in front of us. I tugged on her arm, signaling that this was the moment she should go. They weren't even looking at either one of us, too focused on the impending arrivals. She could slip away. They probably wouldn't bother to give chase. After all, I was the prize.

I struggled to rise, huffing out a pained breath, pushing the flat of my good hand down on the ground. My head spun with a surge of dizziness, but I managed not to topple over. Luna was there, of course, ignoring my command, wrapping an arm around my waist for support. Half the time I didn't think she needed me. That she did now, when I couldn't be all that I should be, all I had to be, for us to survive . . . it killed a part of me.

"You should stay resting," she reprimanded.

I shook my head once, ignoring her as she ignored me. I wasn't going to be on my back, defenseless against whatever was headed our way.

Sweat beaded my brow and my limbs trembled but I stayed on my feet. The horses materialized from the darkness, at first smudges of gray shapes against the moonlit night.

They moved with practiced stealth. As with all trained horses, they had been taught covertness. They even kept their heads relatively still so that there was no jingle from their harnesses. As they drew close, their hooves beat a muffled cadence on the soil. The shapes of the men atop the animals grew more distinct. They were armed to the teeth and with superior weaponry, too.

Luna's hand slid down my arm, stopping at my wrist. Her slim fingers circled my thicker bones, clinging to me as though she needed me right then and not the other way around. It made my chest tighten and swell a little. Even as sick as I was, as helpless, it made me feel useful.

From the very beginning, from the moment Sivo had foisted her on me, I knew I would probably fail her. No one lived long on the Outside. No one lived long with me especially. History had taught me that. I knew this. I'd accepted it.

It didn't, however, stop my will to fight.

SEVEN

Luna

THEY NUMBERED CLOSER to ten. I didn't hear them until they were almost upon us, which was a testament to how *good*, how quiet, these riders were at maneuvering around in the Outside. They had adapted to this world. As one did. Adapt or die.

They wore the same chain mail as the other men accompanying us. I could hear the faint grind of metal beneath their tunics as they shifted their weight atop their mounts. A well-rested energy hummed about them. Their bodies were mostly clean. A hint of mint and sandalwood soap clung to them. They didn't smell ripe of the Outside as we did. As everyone else I had ever encountered did. There was none of the loam and bitter metal that always seemed to find its way onto my tongue. They lived nearby. Someplace warm and dry and dweller free. Someplace safe.

My breath came a little faster as they stopped before our group. Fowler gave my arm a tug and turned to me, whispering, "Slip behind me."

Anger slicked through me. He still sought to protect me when *he* was the one mortally wounded? "Stop it," I hissed at him. The least he could do was trust me. After everything, he could give me that.

For three days I had traveled with these soldiers, caring for Fowler, not giving away the fact that I was a girl. Did that not count for something? Could he not have more faith in me?

I'd managed well enough while he slept, blissfully unaware of our situation. They would get Fowler to safety—get him the care he needed. It was his only chance. Once he was healed, I could slip away and continue on to Relhok as I needed to do. That hadn't changed, but I had to see that Fowler survived. I didn't allow myself to consider that I was putting Fowler ahead of the rest of the world . . . ahead of all the girls who fell even now, prey to Cullan's kill order. I didn't permit myself to question the rightnesss of that. There was no choice.

I could not allow Fowler to die. Later, I would let him go, but I wouldn't let him die.

The soldiers who had found us relaxed. Tension ebbed from them as they lowered their weapons and greeted the new arrivals with warm familiarity. Evidently they were fellow Lagonians.

"Your Highness, out on a hunt?" Breslen asked, his tone and manner that of total deference.

My heart struck a hard beat and held there for a moment before receding again into a normal rhythm. *Your Highness?* As in the king of Lagonia? He dared to leave the safety of the palace to travel the Outside?

There was a slight shift in the air and then dull vibrations on the ground as the three men escorting us dismounted and lowered to one knee.

I listened raptly, fascinated at the prospect of meeting the man who ruled Lagonia. *He'd known my parents.* Sivo and Perla were the only people I knew who had known my parents.

"Breslen, good to see you returned safely. We were beginning to worry." The leather of his saddle creaked as he shifted his weight. "Although there were two more of you that originally set out, were there not?"

I frowned slightly at the sound of his voice. He did not sound like a man of advanced years. Deep as his voice was, he sounded young, his voice smooth polished stone. Even without Breslen addressing him so formally I would know he was important. His words flowed with authority.

"Sad to report they were lost, Your Highness."

"Well, perhaps next time I shall go with you and lend you my sword arm."

Another voice from atop a horse spoke, this one older, guttural and raspy. "As much as they would benefit from your sword, I do not think your father would permit that, Prince Chasan. He dislikes the risk you take on these hunting forays as it is. He'll not let you cross into Relhok."

So he was not the king. He could not have known my parents. My chest deflated a bit then, even as my thoughts raced with the realization that he was a prince, heir to a kingdom. Like me. Or, depending how one viewed it, like Fowler. No one recognized me as a royal. The world thought I was dead.

The prince chuckled. "Don't underestimate my skills of persuasion." There was something underlying his voice, a silky quality that indicated that this prince in fact knew how to talk. Confidence radiated from him. Arrogance, too. He was accustomed to getting what he wanted—an anomaly in a world where nothing went right for anyone.

He addressed Breslen again. "It appears, however, you've gained two additions to your group. Who is that behind you?"

Fowler's hand slipped from my arm as all attention swung to us.

"We happened upon them returning home, Your Highness. A surprise for your father."

"Why should my father be surprised over these two haggard-looking individuals? The bigger one there looks ready to collapse."

"He's the surprise, Your Highness."

"And how is that?"

"He's King Cullan's son. Prince Fowler."

Fowler had held silent during the exchange, but at this declaration he stiffened beside me. I suspected it had been a long time since he'd considered himself a prince—or Cullan's son. Perhaps even longer since anyone addressed him as such.

Prince Chasan swung off his mount swiftly. He strode to where we stood near the tree, his tread muffled by soft-soled boots. He stopped before us. I listened to his breath several inches higher than my head and knew he was tall. "So this is the prince of Relhok. He doesn't look well," the prince announced. "Is he diseased?"

"*He* is right here," Fowler growled. "I can speak for myself."

"Is that so?" Amusement curled the prince's silky voice. "Are you unwell, then, Prince Fowler? As thrilled as my father will be to make your acquaintance, I don't think it wise to take someone sick near him. My father is healthy and I would like to keep him that way."

I bristled at his arrogant tone and opened my mouth to inform him that he need not fear contamination.

"Just a little dweller toxin in the arm," Fowler replied in a caustic-thin voice that did nothing to disguise the pain he felt. I felt it radiating off him. Standing on two feet, enduring this conversation with any semblance of dignity, was costing him.

"Oh. Toxin? That's all? I thought it might be something serious." The prince's attendants laughed deeply at his sarcastic remarks, and I had a flash of him at court, surrounded by groveling courtiers. He was accustomed to being the center of attention, his every word applauded. My upper lip twitched. Already I did not like him.

"They told us the king's physician can help him. Cure him," I bit out, tired of the conversation. We weren't far from the palace, from help, and here we stood talking.

The prince of Lagonia turned his full attention on me. I felt the prowl of his gaze over me. His scrutiny lasted several beats, intent and heavy. I resisted shrinking away.

"And who are you?"

I couldn't find my voice at the simple question. I hadn't picked a fake name. In the last three days, it hadn't been necessary. No one asked me for my name. They didn't seem to care about my existence. Only Fowler's.

Tension radiated from Fowler beside me and I knew he was willing me to say something, and quickly—convince everyone that I was just a boy and no one worth consideration.

"They're friends," Breslen answered for me. "He was traveling with the prince when we found them."

"Indeed?" Prince Chasan murmured, his voice closer now because he had moved closer to me and I had not even heard him. What was wrong with me?

My chin went up. He was so close. I felt his breath on my face, fanning over my cheek and nose and lips. I caught more of the mint I had smelled earlier. "Are you absolutely certain, Breslen, that you've found the prince of Relhok? Because I have my doubts."

Fowler's breath hitched a little beside me. I don't know if it was the question or because Prince Chasan lifted his hand right then and tugged my cap from my head, exposing my mud-caked hair to the chilled air.

"Your Highness, I am certain," Breslen insisted as I suffered the prince's examination. My skin burned everywhere his gaze brushed—which was all over. "I remember him well from the two other times I visited Relhok City. He put on quite the memorable archery display at court. He's an exceptional archer. I'm sure once he's healed he can put on a demonstration for us. Also, I never forget a face. He's a little older, his face more gaunt, but it's him."

The prince stepped back, apparently done examining me. My shoulders slumped slightly in relief to be finished with his scrutiny. He gave a grunt that didn't sound entirely convinced. "I can hardly see his face beneath the scruff. He needs a good razor. I'm sure he did not look like this at King Cullan's court. Can you not be mistaken?"

His arrogant tone pricked at me. I knew he was born to privilege and all the honors of his rank, and it stood to reason he should sound so haughty. It shouldn't bother me. And yet it did.

Being born to privilege didn't mean you had to be full of such arrogance. Fowler didn't sound or act that way.

I couldn't stop myself. I spoke up. "He is who he claims. We're not lying." Hot defiance draped my words.

Fowler reached for my arm again, squeezing for me to hold my tongue. He should know me better by now.

"Is that so, little one?" Prince Chasan took a step in my direction, and I instantly had second thoughts about calling his attention back to me.

Fowler slid a step closer to me, as though he would shield

me—he who could hardly stand on his own two feet.

"I'm not mistaken, Your Highness," Breslen offered resolutely.

"Interesting." Mint breath was on my face again. It wasn't an unpleasant smell, and I resented that. Unpleasant people shouldn't smell nice. "I cannot decide whether I trust your judgment, Breslen. Especially since you are so glaringly wrong about the boy here."

I jerked at this reference to me. I was standing right in front of him. I felt his stare on my face, and yet he spoke about me as if I were some inferior species.

"What do you mean, Your Highness?" Breslen asked, indignation thrumming in his tones, robbing him of his usual reverence despite his formal address.

The prince did not seem to note it. Or he simply let it slide. "This *boy* is not a boy at all. He's a girl. Trust me. I'm an authority on the subject of girls." Dry humor spiked his voice, which did nothing to lessen my burst of panic. He knew. He took one look at me and knew.

Breslen sputtered as Prince Chasan continued, "You failed to notice this most obvious truth, but I'm to believe you're perceptive enough to remember and recognize the prince of Relhok?"

My mouth worked to say something. *How?* How did he know? What had I done to give myself away to him so quickly and not the others? For three days I had traveled among them, my true gender undetected.

"You're wrong," Fowler offered beside me, clinging to the lie, unwilling to give up. He forced out a cracking laugh as if it were an absurd suggestion and only worthy of mirth. I swallowed miserably, knowing it was a lost cause even if Fowler wasn't willing to admit that yet.

"Indeed. Am I?" Prince Chasan asked in a mild manner, his elegant tones as slick as glass—as if he were remarking upon the taste of his soup and not something significant. Not something that could spell death for me. "Because it would be an easy enough matter to prove." There was a beat of silence as this sank in. My stomach dipped and then heaved back up. "Shall I?" he asked, testing us.

He snapped his fingers, and suddenly two soldiers grabbed me by the arms and hauled me away from Fowler's side. I struggled, but they were bigger and stronger.

They held me in front of Prince Chasan, arms stretched wide at my sides like some sacrifice. And that's how I felt. Exposed and open for whatever awful thing he wanted to do.

Fingers slid down the skin of my throat, warm to the touch, but that didn't stop my shudder. I yanked my head to the side, trying to escape the brush of the prince's fingers. The hard hands holding me only tightened their grip, bruising me through my garments. The pads of his fingers were surprisingly callused, rasping my dirty skin as they roamed, stopping to rest at my hammering pulse. An egg-sized lump lodged itself in my throat.

Shivering, I tried to wiggle away from the contact, but I was pinned to the spot, held up for inspection—for anything and everything the prince wanted to do to me. It was a hard bite of reality. I could do nothing save wait for him to make his next move. My utter sense of helplessness was perhaps the worst thing I had endured so far.

His liquid voice was close, sliding on the air and sinking through me like falling rocks. "It's hard to tell beneath all the mud and filth, but I would hazard to say she's a fetching thing."

I forced my chin up, not cowering, swallowing back a whimper as his fingers dipped lower, stopping at the center of my throat, in that tiny hollow between my collarbones. "The softest skin," he mused. "How could you think her a boy, Breslen?"

There was a violent surge of movement to my left. "Take your hands off—" Fowler's voice stopped abruptly, almost saying it. Almost confirming I was the girl.

My heart hiccuped painfully as I turned my face in Fowler's direction. I felt his gaze and tried to communicate with him, tried to convey that maybe we should just confess the truth and be done with it. Anything to get Chasan's hands and attention off me.

"Her?" Prince Chasan finished for him, sounding so smug and satisfied that I wanted to claw his face. "You'd like me to get my hands off *her*?"

Fowler didn't answer. He sucked in an angry breath, but said nothing.

"Fowler," I croaked.

"Still won't admit it, then?" The prince tsked and paused, giving me and Fowler time to volunteer the truth that was fast becoming unavoidable.

I waited, dread pooling in my stomach, my voice lost deep

inside me as I listened to the rasp of Fowler's breath, wondering at his next move. Prince Chasan sighed as though greatly aggrieved. "Very well."

His fingers curled into the throat of my shirt and yanked down hard. The sound of fabric ripping was violent and obscene on the loam-soaked air.

Crying out, I surged and writhed, unable to break free. I just hung there between the soldiers, my tunic ripped down the center, my torso bare except for the binding covering my chest. My naked stomach quivered as cool air washed over me.

For a moment, there was only silence in the hum of darkness.

Everyone's attention focused solely on me. Their gazes felt like hot coals raking over me, blistering my flesh. Bile surged in the back of my throat.

The air shifted, crackling with a dangerous energy that hadn't been there before. My nostrils flared, smelling it, the foul intent of their thoughts coiling around me.

Fowler broke the stillness, lunging forward. He swung an arm, smashing his fist into one soldier's face with a crack of knuckles on bone. He'd been violent before, when desperate, but not like this. Before he was always controlled and precise, but this was wild and savage and brutal. Fowler launched at the other soldier holding me, and he went down like a heavy slab of stone, unmoving. I was suddenly free. "Run!" he shouted.

I lunged only one step before the prince caught me up in his arms. I struggled against the lock of his embrace, assailed with his scent—mint and leather and wind and that hot pulse of adrenaline that coated the back of my throat. "Oh, no, you don't," he breathed near my ear.

There was a flurry of movement. Boots shuffled over gasps and cries. Bones crunched. Fowler grunted and I knew they were striking him.

"Stop! Let him go. He's sick and your men are hurting him!" I struggled, the flaps of my torn tunic flapping open, but I didn't care in that moment. I could have been stark naked and I would only care about Fowler—helping him, reaching him. Saving him.

"Now that all depends. Are we going to be honest with each other from now on? Are we going to admit who we are? These are dangerous times, and I can't surround myself with deceivers. I can't bring anyone into the palace who isn't who they claim to be." His hand drifted back over me, his fingers brushing my bare belly and making my skin revolt with goose bumps.

"Rot in hell," Fowler snarled.

Prince Chasan tsked. His fingers curled at the edges of the binding wrapping my chest, getting a good grip on the fabric. I shuddered at the scrape of his blunt-tipped nails in the valley between my mashed breasts. The steel tip of a knife pricked my skin. I ceased to breathe, not daring to lift my chest even a scant inch for fear that the blade would pierce me.

"What do we have here?" he asked. The binding dipped with the slightest pressure beneath the prince's knife. "Now why would a boy be wearing something like this? Are you trying to hide something?"

He tugged on the tight fabric concealing my breasts, pressing the knife deeper against the edge of the fabric. I gave a small yelp as some of the threads popped loose. The binding was on the verge of giving way.

"Stop! Let her go!" Fowler spat, lunging toward us.

"There you go! Was honesty so very difficult? She's a girl . . . and you're the prince of Relhok. Isn't it better now without any lies between us?" Prince Chasan's fingers slipped from my chest binding, leaving it intact. He still kept one hand lightly on my shoulder, though, not completely letting me go.

Fowler staggered to his feet. I felt his presence in front of us. Heat and fury radiated off him. "Touch her, and I will kill you."

I trembled at the hard bite of resolve in his voice. I didn't doubt him, and that didn't bode well. We were in Lagonia. The entire country—or at least what was left of it—would come after us if he so much as ruffled one hair on the prince's head.

Swords hissed on air and I knew they were drawing on Fowler. His threat would not go unanswered. They couldn't ignore it. They didn't care if Fowler was the prince of Relhok or not. They were in Lagonia and these were Lagonians.

"Easy," Prince Chasan chided, but I wasn't certain if he was talking to Fowler or his men. His men, I supposed. I heard them lower their swords, and some of the tension ebbed away.

I sidled away from the prince. This time he didn't stop me. My heart hammered a wild beat in my chest as I took my place at Fowler's side. I inhaled, smelling the sourness of his feverish skin. He wasn't doing well. He'd used up whatever strength he had. I didn't know how he was still standing and talking and fighting, but I didn't think he could for much longer.

"I understand," the prince said. "She's yours. And you have to protect what's yours. I would do the same."

I didn't bother correcting him and telling him that I didn't belong to anyone. I shivered anew, sensing his scrutiny on me. I tugged the flaps of my shredded shirt back together as best I could, grasping what modesty available, however flimsy.

"Smart of you to disguise her," Prince Chasan continued. "It couldn't have been easy for you traveling through Relhok. Not with the bounty on young females. A shame, that. Not sure what your father could be thinking to come up with such a decree. Such a travesty . . . the murder of so many girls." He clucked his tongue.

Fowler suddenly buckled beside me. I made a grab for him, slipping an arm around his waist. "Are we going to stand here all day, then?" I snapped.

Fowler choked out my name near my ear. "Luna . . . "

I ignored the warning in his voice. His weight sank deeper against me, and I had to wrap both arms around him to keep him from falling. He was still much heavier than I was, and I staggered under the bulk of his body.

"I would like to get him to the physician that was promised to us." Exerted pants punctuated my words. "Unless that has changed and you want to stand idly by as the prince of Relhok dies?"

I arched an eyebrow and pulled back my shoulders, awaiting their verdict and trying to feel as though I wasn't begging. As though I weren't completely at their mercy.

"Breslen promised. And a promise is a promise." The prince snapped his fingers and soldiers moved forward, quickly relieving Fowler's weight from my arms.

"Your Highness?" that older, scratchy-rough voice asked. "What of our hunt? Shall we continue on and let the others take them back to the city?"

"No, we shall escort them ourselves. We can catch dwellers another time."

Catch dwellers? Before I had time to inquire what he meant by that, the prince himself was pulling me along toward one of the horses. "Come along. Luna, was it? You can ride with me."

I looked over my shoulder as though I could see Fowler. "What about—"

"He'll be fine," he assured me.

"Fowler?" I called out as I was hauled up in the saddle in front of the prince.

"He's lost consciousness."

The explanation left me feeling hollow inside. I was truly alone with this arrogant prince who cut my tunic away as if it were a small matter and not anything that might shame or terrify me.

He turned his mount around and we traveled for several minutes in silence. The terrain grew craggy and it was a rough ride. I tried to sit as high in the saddle as possible but the jarring motion forced me back against him.

A swarm of bats flew overhead, their loud flapping wings and cacophony of chirps deafening, making me jerk a little in the prince's arms. I'd heard plenty of bats before but never such a large flock and never so close to our heads. I couldn't help ducking slightly.

"We have lots of bats around here. They thrive in this area with all the mountain caves. They never bother with us, though. You'll get accustomed to them."

I bit my lip to stop from saying that no, I wouldn't be getting accustomed to them because I wouldn't be staying.

"How did you come to meet Fowler?" he asked, his voice close to my ear.

I shrugged, gasping when the hard band of his arms circled my waist and pulled me back against him.

"Come now. Don't pout simply because I uncovered your secret."

"I'm not pouting," I retorted, almost tempted to fling at him that he wasn't as perceptive as he claimed. He hadn't figured out that I was blind yet.

"Then don't be reticent. It's a few hours to reach the palace. Must we journey in silence? That would be needlessly dull. Regale me with your adventures with the prince of Relhok."

"I'm not here for your entertainment."

"Interesting. Most people are, you know."

I leaned away from his mouth. "I'm certain that's not true."

"It is. Most people exist for my amusement."

I snorted. "You're serious. Is that a requirement of princehood? Spoiled arrogance? I'm glad Fowler is nothing like you."

I wondered if I would be like this, too, had my parents lived. If the eclipse hadn't happened.

"Indeed he's not." His voice turned to flint at my insult. Apparently I'd hit a nerve. "For starters, he's lucky if he will live out the day. We might be bringing him to the physician too late. You should consider that, girl . . . consider where that will leave you once your precious prince is dead."

I knew exactly where that would leave me. It would leave me at the mercy of him.

He understood that well enough, too. His voice felt like a cold winter wind near my cheek. "It would not hurt you to make a friend of me."

Apparently no longer interested in talking to me, Prince Chasan dug in his heels, and the horse broke into a run under us. I buried my hands in the coarse mane, and held on.

It was all I could do.

EIGHT

Fowler

I FADED IN and out. I knew it was happening, but that didn't make fighting the thick press of unconsciousness any easier. The pain pushed me into it with a hard, two-handed shove. I tumbled in, the pull of numbing darkness too strong. It continually dragged me back under into nightmares with dwellers chasing me—and worse, chasing Luna, capturing her, grabbing her up in their clawed hands and tearing her apart. Her screams rang in my ears and I wasn't sure what was real or a nightmare.

I did know that every time I emerged into consciousness, my arm burned with a deep, unholy fire. All movement jarred me and sent agony shooting to every nerve in my body.

At one point, I opened my eyes and it was midlight. I blinked at the milky air as I swayed in the saddle, the soldier behind me the only thing keeping me from falling. A great castle of rock rose up before us, the pale-milk stone etched against the feeble light like something from a dream. A ghost of yesterday when this world was once prosperous and made up of towns and villages and castles that looked out over countryside of fertile fields.

The stench greeted me with all the force of a fist to the face. The reek of urine and cooking meat, unwashed bodies and live-stock, mingled into one great maelstrom of stink. In short, it smelled of life.

Our party stood before the gate, waiting as a great draw-bridge lowered with a groan. Archers wearing tunics emblazoned with the Lagonian hawks stood along the top of the parapets, smudged shapes staring down through slits in their helmets, their arrows at the ready. The drawbridge struck the ground with a reverberating thud that I felt to my very bones. If possible, the vibration made my head ache harder.

I'd never been to Ainswind before but I knew I was staring at it now, passing through the shadow of the barbican, the horses' hooves clattering over the bridge that led through the gatehouse and opened into a vast courtyard bustling with people and soldiers. A slapdash assortment of buildings dotted the wide space, some squat and single storied, but most were several levels high. Stalls with vendors hawking wares and pens of animals lined narrow lanes. It was almost normal. A normal that I scarcely remembered.

And there at the far end of the courtyard a castle jutted out of the craggy limestone mountainside, home to Tebald and his offspring.

I'd heard that the city was built right out of the side of a mountain, impenetrable to dwellers, but thought such tales exaggerations. It was impossible to identify where the mountain ended and the castle began. It looked like one enormous white-skinned fortress as big as the sky, stretching so high into the air that my neck had to drop back to take it all in.

My father had cursed Lagonia often enough, jealous and bemoaning that it was better equipped to survive the eclipse than Relhok City. Unfair, he insisted, that they should withstand the dwellers better than the rest of the world.

"Fowler." I turned at the sound of my name and found Luna, mud-encrusted, her hair sticking out all round her head in stiff clumps, sitting before the prince, her hands anxiously worrying the horse's mane of hair. For a moment she blurred and I was staring at three of her. Blinking several times, I brought her back into focus. She looked so small, slender as a reed in front of the prince's larger frame. All these people crowded into one space. The intense smells and sounds. For a girl who spent the majority of her life isolated in the tower, this had to be sensory overload.

Chasan was attired in a royal-blue tunic without a speck of dirt or mud on it. I doubted he'd ever been dirty. He'd probably never felt the pains of hunger in his belly either.

I knew that because that had been my life. Others had gone without food, but not me. I knew what it was like to exist levels above everyone else so desperately fighting for survival. I knew what it felt like to have your life valued more than others, your stomach full each day, every precaution taken to ensure your safety and comfort and to hell with everyone else. As far as my father was concerned, everyone else was dweller bait.

Like Bethan.

The only difference between Prince Chasan and me was that I turned my back on that life and left it to find something else. Anything else. He was what I used to be.

Chasan stared at me, his expression blank, as my horse pranced over the cobbled rock littered with dung. His eyes, however, were bright and alive, an ice blue more ice than blue. He glanced at the back of Luna's head before looking at me again, a faint smirk curling his lips. He knew. She was my weakness.

She stared in my general direction, looking a little lost. My chest clenched; I wondered how much longer she could keep from them that she was blind.

"I'm fine, Luna," I managed to get out, the sound of my voice a dry crack. The effort to speak made my head pound harder, but I did it for her—so that she would feel some reassurance.

We rode deeper into the crowded courtyard. Soldiers and peasants stopped to stare. The distinction between the two groups was greatly visible even without the uniforms. The soldiers were cleaner, leaner, obviously well-fed, while the citizens of Ainswind looked like they could use a good meal or two—along with a bath. A stiff wind might break them.

The soldiers used staffs to push back the peasants and make room for the prince and the rest of us to pass. We rode down narrow lanes between buildings and pens of pigs and goats, hooves clacking over the rocky ground. Eyes watched us from ground level as well as every window and perch above.

I started to slide off the saddle, too weak to hang on, but the soldier behind me caught my arm and held me up. I hated such frailty in me, but there was nothing I could do. Sweat beaded my lip. It was hard to fathom a cure for this slow death. I had seen too many die from toxin before.

I had many regrets; the final and greatest, however, would be leaving Luna here among these strangers. If Chasan was like the me I used to be, then he couldn't be good or trustworthy. In that same vein, if King Tebald was anything like my father, then she needed to forget about me and get far, far from here.

My head dropped back and I stared up the great, towering lengths of the buildings on either side of us. Heads and arms hung out the countless open windows and balconies, watching us speculatively as we advanced toward the castle. Hopefully, this place and these people would not destroy her. Hopefully, she could find one friend, one ally, in this sea of strangers.

We finally stopped before a long stretch of steps that led to a pair of massive doors. The ornate carved wood parted to reveal several figures. One robed man at the center drew my gaze. He descended the stone-polished steps at a leisurely pace, gold-trimmed robes of blue flashing at his ankles. Several other figures surrounded him, similarly garbed, but no one needed to tell me the man at the center was King Tebald. Even without the crown on his gray head, he held himself with an air of superiority, his chin lifted.

He floated down to the base of the steps and stopped. His retinue hung back several steps, careful not to step past him. He held his arms wide, his broad sleeves floating out at his sides like wings. "My son, I see you've returned with different quarry than what you set out to catch."

"Indeed, Father. We happened upon Breslen and what was left of his party."

Breslen dismounted and made an elaborate bow. King Tebald held out his hand and his man accepted it, pressing it to his bent brow.

"Breslen, I trust you have happy tidings to share with me from Relhok."

"Indeed, Sire. Discussions went as we expected. The king did not produce his son. However, I now realize why."

The king arched a thick eyebrow. "Pray, enlighten me."

Breslen cast me a quick glance, anxious energy buzzing about him. "He did not have him, Sire."

The king digested this, puffing out his great barrel chest, his lips working as though he tasted something foul. "He's dead. Just as I expected. All these years of silence, of Cullan's evasions—"

"Not dead, Sire," Breslen dared to interrupt. "Simply gone."

"Gone?"

"Yes, and fortune shone on us. I have found him, Your Highness."

Those great bushy eyebrows lifted. "You've found him?"

"Yes, and I've brought him to you." Breslen turned sideways

and gestured to me with a wide sweep of his arm.

Tebald's gaze followed. He scowled. "Him? The boy? There doesn't look like there's much to him." His lip curled faintly as he surveyed me. "He barely looks alive."

Hard hands helped me down from my saddle unceremoniously. My knees gave out and I buckled to earth, proof of the king's low estimation. I didn't stay prone for long before each of my arms was grabbed and I was dragged before the king. They released me and I dropped, head bowed. I struggled to lift the weight of my head and meet the king's gaze.

He stared down at me, still with that faintly curling lip. "This is the crown prince of Relhok?" He flicked beringed fingers in the air over me.

"Sire, I've visited Relhok City several times, as you know. I've dined with him. Spoken with him. I watched him demonstrate his great prowess with a bow and arrow." Breslen stabbed a finger in my direction. "This boy *is* the prince of Relhok."

His declaration carried far, and gasps and titters broke out from the crowd assembling around the castle. I understood their disbelief. From what I observed, Lagonian peasants looked better off than I was, and yet I was supposed to be royalty.

King Tebald stared at me unflinchingly. I inhaled labored breaths, trying to keep myself upright and not disgrace myself by collapsing again. My head and shoulders slumped, the weight unbearable, but I didn't look away from his eyes. It was one lesson my father had taught me that I held close—always hold a man's gaze.

"Is this true?" he finally asked me. "You're the prince of Relhok?" There was a beat of silence, and then he added my name. "Fowler?" Impatience hummed off him. He was tidy and well-groomed, his gray hair and beard close-cropped. "Well? Answer me."

My breath came in violent spurts. I moistened my dry and cracked lips, reaching for my voice, but the words were buried just out of my reach. My head spun. Faces whirled in a kaleidoscope. I couldn't hold on any longer. I fell, toppling over and rolling to my back.

My last sight was the gabled peaks of Tebald's castle etched against the chalk sky.

NINE

Luna

"FOWLER!" I CRIED out, recognizing the sound of him collapsing. Without waiting for assistance, I dismounted, sliding quickly to the ground and rushing to where he had crumpled into a pile.

My hands landed on him, gingerly assessing, trying to determine if he still lived. His chest lifted with the barest rise of air. My shoulders sagged with relief and my head dropped as I took a moment to find my composure. This was all on me.

I lifted my head and swung my sightless gaze around at all the people I sensed watching. "Help," I said in a surprisingly commanding voice. No one moved. "Help him!" I shouted, louder and with more force.

"Who is this?" a voice rang out with total authority.

"Your Highness, this is the prince's companion. She was attending him most diligently when I found them."

The king shifted his weight from his perch several steps above me. I heard him sniff as though catching my scent. He coughed slightly and cleared his throat, evidently finding it unpleasant. I would suspect as much. After days of traveling, sleeping on Digger's musky pelt, and diving underground to wade through the dwellers' tangled labyrinth, I probably smelled like a latrine. Not that the courtyard of this city smelled much better.

"Is this true? Come closer, girl."

I shook my head and continued to touch Fowler, needing to assure myself he was still with me. I brushed my palms over his burning-hot face and barely moving chest.

There was a slight snapping of fingers and I was hauled to my feet. Rough hands dragged me up the few steps. A relentless grip at the back of my neck forced me down on my knees. My forehead struck a stone-polished step with an unforgiving whack. Gray spots flashed across the darkness of my mind. Pain radiated throughout me.

"Bow before the king and answer when spoken to," a harsh voice rasped in my ear, a voice that didn't belong to any man in our group. After three days, I knew everyone's voice distinctly. Also, Breslen and the others had never been so harsh with me. Even the prince himself had not been this savage. This hand at my neck, this voice in my ear . . . he enjoyed brutality.

"You were his companion?" the king pressed.

His man's cruel fingers fisted in my hacked hair and yanked my head back on my neck, presumably to grant me a view of the king. I swallowed a whimper, committed to putting on a brave front—and determined to remember his voice, his faintly musty smell. I would not forget this man.

Steps sounded beside me, and then I recognized Prince Chasan's voice. "Easy there, Harmon. It's not necessary to cave her head in on the palace steps."

My head throbbed. I inhaled through my nostrils and tried to quell the nausea, attempting to focus in front of me where I knew the king stood. "Y-Yes," I stammered over the ringing in my ears.

Harmon's voice growled in my ear again. "You *will* address the king properly." He gave another yank on my hair, the roots dangerously close to being ripped from my head.

I swallowed a whimper. "Yes, Your Highness."

"Is it true, then?" the king asked, unaffected by my suffering at the brute's hands. Was ruthless indifference a feature among all kings? Was my father that way? From everything Sivo had told me, he had not been like that. Perhaps if he had been, he would have seen Cullan's treachery coming. Perhaps then he would still be alive. "Your companion? He is the prince of Rel-hok?" Even though he asked the question, I sensed he didn't care one way or another about my response.

Harmon's grip tightened in my hair, prompting an answer. I gasped. "Why ask me? I'm no one to you."

Harmon's fingers twisted, but thankfully he didn't yank again.

The king answered evenly, "True, but I'm curious for your answer. What do you know of your companion? How long have you been together? Liars don't last very long around here. I have no tolerance for them."

"He only introduced himself as Fowler to me." Not a lie.

I knew Fowler didn't want these people to know who he really was, but it seemed useless to continue pretending. He had tried to deny it earlier, but then I thought of him, lying on the ground in a broken heap as I went back and forth with the king of Lagonia. Suddenly it didn't matter to me that Fowler wanted to protect his identity. I wanted him to live. With that burning thought, I admitted, "It was only recently that he revealed his true identity to me."

Silence met my words. Even the onlookers held their tongues. I felt the king's stare on my face.

Suddenly he laughed. "You're correct, Breslen. You brought me something far greater than news from Relhok. You brought me the crown prince himself." He clapped his hands. His joviality seemed to be the signal for everyone else. They all broke out in cheers and applause.

I don't know what I said or did that convinced him I spoke the truth, but he believed me. "Guards," he called. "Quickly. Carry him inside and call for my physician. I want him well attended. He must live."

My shoulders sagged as movement broke out all around me. Fowler was going to be taken care of. He would heal.

"What about her?" Prince Chasan asked near me, revealing

he hadn't forgotten about me in all the revelry.

"A friend of the prince of Relhok must be our honored guest, too. Never let it be said that the king of Lagonia was a poor host. See to that she is given a room, fed, and bathed thoroughly. She offends my nose."

Harmon relaxed his grip on my hair with a grunt, practically flinging me from him. My hands slapped palm-down on a step as he moved away from me.

Prince Chasan helped me to my feet. "There now. Keep telling the truth and no one will hurt you."

I dragged a shaking hand down my face, wondering if that could possibly be true.

"Chasan? What are you doing?"

I stiffened at the nearness of the king's voice, closer than before. I inhaled, catching the improbable aroma of roasted hog. I'd tasted wild pig only once. Years ago Sivo had caught one. I was very little, but I still remembered the rich aroma of the meat and the roasted acorns and wild berries that Perla had stuffed inside it.

"Just talking to the girl, Father."

"Whatever for? Let one of the servants attend to her. You and I have much to discuss with Breslen. I want you there."

"I'm seeing to her comfort, Father. I was thinking she might enjoy staying in the rose suite."

"The rose suite? For her?"

I lifted my chin at his bewildered tone, my ego getting the best of me. Perla's voice filled my ears, reminding me of who my parents were, my grandparents, the long line of kings and queens who came before me. Their blood ran in my veins. I could not stop myself from flinging his words back at him. "I am your honored guest, am I not, Your Highness?"

Suddenly my chin was seized in a brutal pinch of bony fingers. My face was turned hard left and right. I felt Tebald's gaze, his hot breath on my cheek as he examined me.

"Have I seen you before, girl?"

My heart stuttered at the question and the implication. I looked familiar. "N-No, Your Highness. We've never met. I've never even been to Lagonia before."

He still clung my chin, looking me over. I held my composure and tried not to think about how I must look—shorn hair stiff with mud from the bowels of the earth. I clutched the shredded edges of my tunic with a single hand, hugging my modesty close.

There were so many people watching, devouring me with their judging eyes. I heard their low murmurs, and the shifting of countless slippered feet. Here they wore kid slippers that never stepped from the sanctuary of this city. They had no need of sturdy boots like I wore.

"You're familiar," the king finally concluded. "It will be interesting to see you without this layer of filth." He released my chin. "The rose suite it is."

He left me, ascending the steps.

"The rose suite is beautiful, Luna. It's in a corner tower. Excellent view," Chasan remarked, his tone conversational and cordial, as though I were an invited guest and not some manner of peasant in their eyes. "Enjoy it."

I nodded, my legs trembling as a servant arrived to lead me up the steps and into the palace.

TEN

Luna

EVEN WHEN I lived in comfort with Sivo and Perla, I had never known luxury like what waited for me in the rose suite.

Three women attended me, chattering amicably as they dunked me in a copper tub full of warm, scented water—this after they exclaimed in horror over my shorn hair and ruined garments.

They gossiped. Names of people I didn't know bounced off me. It was just as well. It was hard to think as they lathered my aching muscles with sweet-smelling soap. One scrubbed at my nails, determined to rid them of their grime. My head drooped under their ministrations.

Any modesty I had in those early moments fled. They scrubbed every inch of my skin until it felt raw and new. Following that, they guided me out of the tub and wrapped me in a fluffy, stone-warmed towel. They led me over a plush rug to a thick cushioned bench positioned before a dressing table, where they proceeded to lather me with lotions that made my skin sigh in appreciation. I perked up at the mention of Chasan's name.

"Did you hear about Prince Chasan and Susa?"

"The girl who works in the laundry?"

A knowing *hmm* responded to that. "That's what you get for aiming above your station," the servant woman added. "She always did think too highly of herself."

The servant who was rubbing a silky mixture in my hair clucked her tongue. "What was she thinking? He would make her his queen? Ha! The fool."

The three of them made sounds of agreement over this. I listened, fascinated despite myself.

"That Susa never did possess a peck of common sense. Everyone knows that Prince Chasan enjoys a pretty face. Only the very stupid think they can matter to him beyond the moment."

"Well, Susa's just like her mother. Fair of face, empty of head." More laughter followed, but I was beginning to get a sense of who the prince of Lagonia was. I had heard the arrogance in his voice, but now I knew the full extent. He was handsome and powerful, preying on the girls of his kingdom.

Once I was clean and feeling like a new person, they dressed me in a gown that laced up at the front.

"We need to fatten you up," one of the women said, offering me a tray of iced biscuits. I knew the pastries were before me instantly. I smelled the sticky-sweet icing as my fingertips sank into the goodness. I moaned as I bit into one, the warm biscuit giving way under my teeth the same moment the creamy icing hit my tongue. It was bliss.

"Careful not to get it on your gown," one of the servants chided.

I nodded and reached for another one, practically shoveling it into my mouth.

"Gor, never did see such a little thing eat with such a fury."

A heavy door creaked open. I didn't stop inhaling the biscuit, assuming it was another servant; a female from the sound of her slight tread.

I plucked a third biscuit and proceeded to devour it as thoroughly as I did the first two.

A slight giggle penetrated my love affair with the delicious pastries.

"Careful there. You might eat your fingers." This new arrival didn't sound like the other servant women. Despite her giggling, her voice was youthful and she fairly bounced as she walked, the fine satin of her gown swishing as she advanced into the room.

I chewed fiercely, trying to swallow the last bit of biscuit. Holding fingers to my lips, I attempted an apology.

"Oh, I'm just teasing. Keep eating. You look as though you need it."

I gulped down the last of my mouthful. "It's very good," I said as an attempt at an excuse.

"Cook is a wonder. He could make a stick of wood the most scrumptious thing to cross your lips. Not that I've ever eaten wood."

I smiled at her exuberance and shook my head. "Who are you?"

"Oh, I'm sorry. I'm prattling on." She cleared her throat. "I'm Maris, princess of Lagonia."

King Tebald's daughter? How many children did he have? Would another one appear?

At the awkward stretch of silence, I realized she was waiting for my introduction. "Oh. Hello. I'm Luna."

"I know. I've heard all about you. You were traveling with Prince Fowler. How exciting! Tell me of your travels together."

I blinked at the strangeness of that. Only someone who had little to no exposure to the Outside would say such a thing.

"You've heard *all* about me?" I echoed.

"Yes."

I nodded, wondering what *all* she could have heard about me since there was essentially nothing any of them knew about me. Who had she been talking to? Chasan? What had he told her?

"You must tell me everything." She plopped down on the bench next to me, crushing my skirts beneath her.

I tugged them out from under her. "About what?"

"Fowler, of course."

"Fowler?" I repeated dumbly as one of the women behind

me began snipping at my hair, evening out the ragged and jagged ends.

"Yes, silly. Is he as handsome as rumored?" She giggled as though we were lifelong friends. An unusual sensation. I'd never had a friend—especially of the female variety. "Father won't permit me to visit him yet, but I will, never fear. Later this evening I intend to see him, in fact."

"I-I'm sure," I answered, still feeling slightly bewildered by her interest in Fowler. I didn't feel sure of anything about this girl . . . except that she reminded me a great deal of her arrogant brother.

She leaned forward, bringing her voice closer and crushing my skirts again. "I need to know something, *anything* about him. I've waited all my life to meet him."

"Fowler?"

"Yes," she retorted, and this time she sounded exasperated. "We've only been betrothed since my birth."

My stomach bottomed out at her words. It was a casual utterance for her, but it cut me like a blade. I pressed a hand against my diving stomach.

She must have read some of my reaction. "Are you . . . what's wrong? Did I say something? You look pale."

I shook my head and ducked, averting my face as a lump rose up in my throat. "No. I'm fine."

The surge of emotion I felt wasn't right. Even if I hadn't been running from Fowler and racing headlong into a fate that did not include him, he had turned his back on this shining world—on this girl. He had turned his back on his father and whatever betrothal had been arranged for him. Except he was here now. *Because of me.* I squashed the niggle of guilt. I might be the reason he was here, but he could have died out there.

"Well, come now, then. Don't be so reticent. Tell me about Fowler."

I cleared my throat. She pressed closer on the bench, the soft linen of her gown brushing my arm.

I shouldn't feel this awful swell of heat in my face. It shouldn't hurt to realize this girl sitting beside me was *his* fate—even if he had walked away from it. She was the fate he was running from . . . and I was beginning to realize that it was impossible to run from your fate.

My whole life I had been hiding from Cullan, avoiding the death intended for me. I should have died that day alongside my parents. Sivo and Perla had stolen me from that fate, but now I would embrace it for the survival of others, for the good of the kingdom that I had been born to rule.

The princess sitting next to me was still talking, but I didn't hear her—not the actual words coming out of her. I understood her perfectly. She wanted Fowler. Without even knowing him, without even meeting him or seeing him, she wanted him. And she would have him.

She was still talking beside me, her words falling into place. "How did you come to be together? Was he journeying here to finally meet me?" As if a journey across two countries in this day and age was a simple matter? As if the eclipse had never happened and the world wasn't doused in dark brutality. "Has he spoken of me at all?"

I snorted. No. He had conveniently left out any mention of a betrothed.

"I only recently learned that he was a prince." That much was the truth at least. "I don't believe he wanted it common knowledge that he was the prince of Relhok."

"Why ever not?" She tsked. "It's his right. His due."

The girl was naïve. Did she think a royal prince should announce his identity? Especially on the Outside, where enemies could hunt him for ransom? I was still not convinced that these Lagonians knowing the truth of his identity was a good thing.

The woman working on my hair began pinning and twisting the mass atop my head. The bottom strands were too short to be pinned, so they fell loose to curl against the nape of my neck.

"You'll have to ask him." I shrugged as if what he was to me was of little consequence. "When he wakes, I'm sure you will have much to discuss."

Princess Maris sighed happily. "Indeed. I cannot wait for that moment." She leaned forward and began rifling through one of the serving women's baskets. "Here, put the pearl drops in her hair."

"Yes, princess." The woman began stabbing the little pearls randomly throughout my hair, sometimes poking my scalp.

"Ah, I knew it. Lovely against your dark hair," Maris murmured. "Don't you think?"

I nodded.

"Come, Luna. You did not even look at the mirror."

Discomfort at being put on the spot made my skin itch. I deflected the question with one of my own, airily waving my hand. "Why are we going to such trouble with my appearance?"

"We dress for dinner."

"I'm to dine with you?"

"Yes, Papa insists. Er, or maybe it was Chasan." She shrugged beside me, the motion sending a waft of floral scent circling the air. I knew about fragrances. Perla had told me she used to be a skilled perfumer. She'd made signature scents for my mother and every lady at court. *No use for such extravagances these days. The last thing we want is some sweet fragrance leading dwellers to our door.*

Sound logic, but nothing that seemed to affect them locked away safely inside this mountain castle. It was as though they lived here untouched by the eclipse.

Maris stood. "You look ready. Come along. We can go in together. I hope you did not ruin your appetite with all those iced biscuits. Although Cook will be glad to hear that you approve of them."

"I can still eat," I assured her, rising to my feet, smoothing sweating palms over my skirts. I'd worn dresses plenty of times in the tower, but it felt odd to be in skirts again—as though years had passed since the last time and not a mere month.

Princess Maris looped her arm through mine. "You look lovely. You shall have to beat the swains off with a stick."

I smiled, but it felt more like a grimace as I marveled at what a strange world I had entered. I didn't want the attention of a bevy of swains, but maybe it would offer some distraction during my brief time here—because I wouldn't be staying.

Dinner was no small affair. I heard the din long before we entered the cavernous hall. My steps slowed. "How many people are eating with us?"

"It's full court this evening," Maris replied, urging me to resume walking. "Papa is in a celebratory mood." I could only infer that this was because of Fowler. "Several nobles and their families reside here in the palace. They've been here as long as I can remember, keeping safe in the city rather than venturing out to whatever is left of their estates. When Papa feels like it, he invites them all to sup with us in the great hall. The company provides a diversion."

Ainswind was an alien world buried within the darkness I knew. As we strolled down the wide corridor, my slippers whispering over a lush runner, the warmth from lit sconces bathed my face, drenching me in light. This place hummed and glowed with no fear of monsters.

None of this is real. None of this is real.

The words rushed through me, a reminder that I should not be lulled into safety. No place was wholly safe. Even this fortified castle.

I couldn't stay. I had my mission. I wouldn't forget it. I couldn't. Every day I remained here, every moment that passed, more girls died. Cullan needed to be stopped. The first chance I got, I would put this place far behind me. Once I assured myself that all was being done for Fowler that could be, I would leave this bewildering place. If they tried to stop me, then I would find a way out on my own. It wouldn't be the first time I'd executed an escape.

The voices grew louder as we approached, and I had to fight every instinct to not turn and flee. I felt more vulnerable than usual in this strange new place. Sounds, smells, people . . . it was long ingrained in me to avoid those things that attracted dwellers.

The Outside, for as much as it carried death in its fold, felt more like home to me. Here I was exposed, no weakness concealed. I flattened a hand over my racing heart, where so much skin lay bared. After pretending to be a boy, the exposed skin felt odd, too.

"Now, I can't sit with you . . . as much as I would like to." She patted my hand as we entered the bustling hall. The space was large, the air churning around me and lifting high into vaulted ceilings. "There is a seating protocol, but I shall place you beside someone charming. Trust me."

"Thank you. That's very kind."

"That's me," she trilled. "Oh la! Look at all the eyes on you. I told you that you looked fetching. We don't get too many new faces. I can count on both hands the number of guests we've had over the years. You shall be all the rage."

"I'm sure I won't," I murmured—or rather, I hoped.

I doubted King Tebald permitted anyone inside the palace who wasn't perceived as important, and that most certainly wasn't me. I was only here because of my association with Fowler. My newness aside, I was sure little care would be given me. Everyone would be in a dither over Fowler's arrival—even if he wasn't present for the meal. He was the prince of Relhok, after all, and betrothed to Princess Maris.

Elegant slippers and fine boots shuffled over the hard stone surface of the floor. There were too many bodies to count and that made me jumpy, as though my skin were stretched too tight over my bones. I inhaled the delicious aroma of food I couldn't even begin to identify. My stomach rumbled. At the far end of the great hall, an enormous fire burned and crackled. Several hounds lounged in front of it, their panting breaths and pungent, baking fur eddying around me, flaring my nostrils.

I pushed a hand against my bodice self-consciously and stuck close to Princess Maris, unwilling to be left alone in this room full of strangers. They already saw too much of me in all this glaring light, in this dress with its low-cut bodice. I would not have them see anything more about me.

Following close behind Maris, I sucked in a breath, trying to pick out all the sounds over the band of musicians playing in the corner. No easy task.

A bell pealed loudly over the jumble of noise.

"That's the signal. It's time to take our seats. You're over here."

I cleared my throat. "Which seat?"

I was grateful to feel her hand close around mine. She had the softest hands, like a child's. "You can sit next to Gandal. He's the royal physician's son. He has very fine eyes." Her tone lowered suggestively.

I perked up a little at this. Not because of his fine eyes—the part about him being the physician's son. Perhaps he would have news of Fowler? It wouldn't hurt to inquire. The sooner Fowler's well-being was established, the sooner I could abandon this place that made me feel dizzy and so out of sorts. "Thank you."

I was ushered onto a bench. Princess Maris made the introductions and then slipped away, moving to the head table that was elevated upon a dais—where the important people dined. The distance between that table and me told me how low I ranked on the social hierarchy.

I tracked Maris's progress, marking the soft tread of her footsteps ringing hollowly up the wood steps and across the raised platform. Once she settled into a chair, I turned my attention to those around me, listening carefully over the music to all the voices, marking each individual and trying to follow the anecdotes swirling on the air like a tangle of threads in the cavernous echoing space.

One woman complained because she hadn't been able to find her hand mirror and suspected her maid, that "lazy, shiftless girl," had taken it. The gentleman across from her assured her that a mirror wasn't necessary, as she looked ravishing. The lady laughed coyly and I knotted my hands in my lap, wondering at this place and these shallow people who acted as if there were no hungry monsters at the gates.

It was a large table, seating at least fifty, maybe more. I

wasn't certain of the exact number, and that was something that troubled me. I was blind but had never felt impaired, never lost or floundering. Until now. Multiple conversations rolled on all around me. I focused on keeping track of them, even when it made my head hurt.

Outside there was a rhythm, a cadence in the soft chirps of insects, the yips of giant bats, the ebb and flow of wind through dying trees. And Them, the dwellers, sending out their eerie calls. They could be relied upon, too. In here there was only the unknown, the machinations of people my gut told me not to trust.

After the initial introduction with Gandal, we exchanged a few pleasantries before he ignored me in favor of the lady to his right. The princess was wrong. I wasn't nearly as appealing as she proclaimed. My conversational skills were perhaps even worse than I'd thought. Or it was simply that I was unimportant—a nobody even for the son of a physician.

I folded my clammy hands together in my lap. The aroma of well-seasoned meat was more pronounced than ever, and my mouth watered. I had never smelled so much food. Surely we would eat soon.

"I almost did not recognize you."

I started at the warm voice sliding near my ear. A voice that I instantly recognized. I should have heard him coming. My pulse sputtered in alarm at my throat. This place was ruining me, eliminating my edge. Before I knew it, if I wasn't careful, I would be as weak as all of them.

"It's astounding what a little soap can do, Prince Chasan," I rejoined, rubbing at the goose bumps that puckered the skin of my arm.

He chuckled. "Indeed. Do I not smell better, too?"

I opened my mouth and shut it, stopping myself from pointing out that he had not smelled foul to begin with. "I can't claim to have a strong sense of smell, Your Highness," I lied.

"No?" His body sank down on the bench to my left and I started a little, concerned that he meant to stay beside me. I didn't want his attention. I wanted him gone.

I wanted to be gone.

I felt Gandal at my right lean forward, his clothes rustling on his seat as he anxiously peered around me at the prince. "Greetings, Your Highness; good evening to you," Gandal said.

The prince ignored him and continued assessing me. I didn't have to see to know. I felt his stare like a breathing, living thing working its way over my face and down my body. I resisted the urge to lift a hand to shield my face.

"You have the most extraordinary eyes, Luna." I tensed at the compliment.

"Th-Thank you," I stammered, motioning toward the dais. "Are you not expected to sit there?" Perla and Sivo had regaled me with enough of my parents' life before the eclipse for me to know rudimentary household protocol.

"I am quite content here." The prince leaned back, his weight creaking the wooden bench as he settled his palms along the edge.

Heat burned my cheeks. I could feel the unsubtle glances from others.

I let his words sink in, turning them over, wondering if there was a double meaning there. I couldn't decide. My anxiety only grew as he continued to stare at me. I lowered my head, hoping that he would take the action as shyness. I didn't want to face him. Not this close. Not in this brightly lit room. I might give myself away.

"Can you not look me in the face?" he queried. "Have I said something to offend you?"

"No." I shook my head. "This place is . . . different. I can't relax. Any moment I feel as though dwellers will storm the hall. I know your defenses are impregnable—"

"Nothing is impregnable."

"Not very comforting as I sit here without a weapon and wearing a dress that would hamper my movements should I need to run."

"You can always use your cutlery."

The idea of defending myself with spoon and fork almost made me smile.

"Ah, I see I've amused you," he added.

His words killed my almost smile. "Not at all."

A deep thumping struck the floor several times, a signal that reverberated through the room. The musicians ceased to play. A hush fell over the crowd. No one stirred. Even the smelly hounds near the great hearth stopped swishing their tails.

Looking up, I leaned slightly to the left, asking the prince,

"What is that?"

"They're heralding my father's arrival."

King Tebald entered the room. I heard the whisper of robes over the floor as he cut a path toward the dais, a small retinue following him.

Suddenly he stopped before us. "Chasan, what are you doing sitting here?"

The prince rose to his feet. "I thought I would sit here tonight, Father, and visit with our new guest."

At this, low murmurs broke out through the room. My cheeks heated; I knew this was a breach in etiquette.

"Guest?" Tebald said blankly, as though he had no memory of visitors, much less me.

"Yes, Father. You recall the prince of Relhok's companion." There was no response, and even Chasan sounded uncertain as he added, "Luna."

"You're the girl from today." There was a touch of wonder in his voice.

"Yes, Your Highness." I self-consciously brushed a hand over my hair near my ear. Clearly I had undergone a transformation.

"Stand," he commanded.

The bench was pulled out so quickly I nearly fell. I'd almost forgotten the existence of the king's guards. Sadists. Apparently they were never far.

The prince caught my arm, steadying me while turning me to face his father, but he said nothing. I'd almost prefer to hear his arrogant tone right then. In that moment, I realized the prince did not frighten me nearly as much as his father did.

The king stepped forward. No one else moved or spoke, making it simple to mark him in the now deathly silent hall. He held total dominion, and that unnerved me. He could do whatever he wanted and everyone else would just sit back and watch no matter how they felt about it.

"Turn around."

I hesitated a beat too long because the guard stepped forward again, grasping my arm and tugging me in a small circle. The king was so close. I could hear the puff of his breath.

"Father?" Chasan voiced.

"It cannot be," the king muttered so quietly I knew he was talking more to himself than anyone else. Wariness crept over me. My pulse hiccuped at my neck, fighting to break free from my skin.

Chasan spoke beside me. "What? What is it, Father?"

"You are the very image of her," Tebald whispered. His fingers grazed my cheek and I flinched.

"Who, Father?"

My heart dropped to my feet. Before he said anything I was already beginning to suspect that he knew. Perla's many words came back to me. She had told me stories of my parents, and I had always hung on every word.

Your mother had many suitors. Nobles from all over the land wanted to marry her. Princes and kings . . . but she chose your father.

A woman like that, my mother, would be memorable.

"Avelot."

At the hushed sound of my mother's name, I lifted my chin high.

"The late queen of Relhok?" Chasan finally asked, his voice rife with bewilderment.

"Yes. This girl is identical to her. The mirror image. That face. Those eyes. Everything about her. The curve of her lips."

My hand drifted, touching my mouth. Perla had made similar remarks, and I always thought her merely embellishing, or trying to forge a connection in my mind for the mother I would never know.

"Father, the king and queen died at the start of the eclipse. As did so many."

Those words woke and shook me from a lifelong slumber. *No.* My parents did *not* die at the hands of dwellers. I could have understood that. Not the betrayal. Not their slaughter at the behest of someone they trusted. Anger that I thought beyond me after all these years burned like a fever through me.

"If this is not her, then it's her child. The one she was carrying at the time of the eclipse. She would be of a like age," the king intoned. "The child must have survived, and this is she."

I dragged in a shuddery breath, astonished at how accurately he had deduced the truth.

"That's not possible," the prince said.

"It is possible. I know what I see before me." King Tebald's gaze roamed over me, and I felt his absolute certainty. He knew. I could deny it. I could let his son continue to tell him he was wrong. But he knew.

"The queen did not survive the dweller uprising on Relhok City. She never gave birth." Prince Chasan spoke in a coaxing tone, as though his father were feeble-minded. He wasn't even addressing me and yet his words hit a nerve. My last frayed nerve.

I couldn't hold silent. Not with fresh outrage pumping through me. And did it really matter? There was no hiding the truth anymore. The king knew.

"No," I growled, straining forward as that last nerve snapped free. "Dwellers did not kill my mother. Or my father. My parents were killed at the hand of the royal chancellor, the false king who now sits on the throne of Relhok."

A long pause followed my outburst before voices erupted all around me. My bravado fled in the volley of sound. The din was overwhelming and made me cringe and shrink into myself.

The prince grabbed my elbow, his grip once again hard, as it had been on the Outside. He swung me to face him. "Luna, what the hell are you—"

A steady clapping thundered through the room, close and deep and resounding. "I knew it! Splendid. Brilliant!" Tebald cheered. The buzz of voices ebbed at the king's applause. "The true heir to the kingdom of Relhok stands before us."

Cold washed through me. My secret was out. Suddenly the light around me felt brighter, hotter on my skin. Sounds were more jarring, painful to my ears, the smells more overwhelming.

I should have convinced him he was mistaken and there was no connection between the late queen and me. It didn't matter how convinced he was; I should have tried to deny the truth.

"Luna?" It was Chasan's voice, hard and questioning, full of menace.

I gave myself a swift mental shake. It would have only been a delay to the inevitable. The moment I arrived in Ainswind, it was simply a matter of time before I was exposed.

There was no going back now.

ELEVEN

Luna

I WAS LED to the dais at the far end of the room and seated to the right of the king as his honored guest—a fact that he declared loudly and effusively to all in the great hall. The initial excitement faded away, but I was far from forgotten. The prince was at my other side and Maris was close, to her father's left. I sat stiffly, hands clutched in my lap in an attempt to still their shaking.

Fortunately, I was given something to do when the food arrived. I ate with gusto, falling on the food like I had never eaten before. Apparently the biscuits had not been enough to tide me over. I stopped short of moaning, overcome at the taste and sheer abundance of it all.

It also didn't hurt that eating saved me from conversation. Chatter flowed around me, and I did my best to answer the king between bites of food and sips of a drink that made my head feel warm and fuzzy. As with the food I tasted, the drink was like nothing I had ever experienced, and I imbibed freely, licking the exotic juice from my lips, not wanting one drop lost.

At one point a warm hand covered my own as I reached for my goblet again. "Have a care, *princess*. Those bigger and stronger than you have lost their heads over too much of this stuff."

I did not miss the emphasis the prince placed on the word *princess*. As though it were something loathsome and dirty on his tongue. Why should he resent the truth of my identity? It was almost as though he preferred me before, when I was just a peasant to him.

And that's when I sensed it. I felt their stares. Not all of them were delighted with my rise from the dead. Their resentment and dislike were palpable.

I tugged free, eager to be rid of the sensation of the prince's hand smothering mine. Lifting my goblet back to my lips, I took a greedy gulp and sighed, making the sound deliberately loud. "You don't know me, Your Highness." *Nor do you have any inkling of the strength that lies in me . . . what I'm capable of . . .*

"No, *princess*. I don't."

"Indeed," an older voice that reminded me of crackling leaves inserted. The sound of it made me stop chewing and pay closer attention to the man seated on the other side of Chasan. "He does not. Nor do any of us know you. Sire," he called out, the chair creaking as he leaned forward, "how can you be certain this girl is the heir to Relhok? For all we know, a fraud sits at your table."

I forgot my unease with Chasan and all those other hard-eyed gazes, asking the prince, "Who is that?"

"Bishop Frand," the prince answered, sounding smug.

"Even if the girl had not admitted it, I would know," King Tebald insisted in lofty tones as he stuffed something into his mouth. He chewed for a moment, lips smacking before adding, "I spent many hours in the company of Lady Avelot. Her portrait hangs in my gallery. Take a look for yourself."

My head snapped in the king's direction. "You have a portrait of my mother?"

"Yes; I shall be happy to show it to you, my dear. Would you like that?"

I nodded dumbly, because what else could I say? Of course a daughter would want to see a portrait of the mother she never knew. If only I could see. But I couldn't. I would never see my mother. Never hear her voice. Never know her. But this man did, and it struck me as wholly unfair. It made me stuff food into my mouth faster, as though that would somehow fill the hollowness inside of me.

"Yes, perhaps we should all inspect this portrait and make a comparison," the bishop agreed, his voice snide in a way that made my shoulders tighten.

"Bishop Frand, I can't imagine why you need to weigh in on the matter at all." The king's voice lashed like a whip, a firm reminder that he alone was king here and the one to decide anything, most notably whether I was the heir to Relhok. Admittedly, it comforted me. For now, he was on my side. If we were at odds, it would be a different matter, but I didn't need to think about that right now. Not yet. Hopefully, I would be gone from here before I ever had to worry about that.

"I am certain you may wish to reflect on this more, Your Majesty. You're never one for hasty decisions." The bishop adopted a conciliatory tone, but his voice was no less grating. "The king of Relhok will not recognize this girl's claim to the throne. It throws his and his son's claim into jeopardy. And where will that leave your daughter, who is betrothed to King Cullan's son?"

With those words I knew the peril in which I'd just landed. Anyone here who did not want Cullan's claim to the throne contested would not tolerate me. Suddenly, standing Outside surrounded by dwellers felt safer than this.

"Should we really discuss such affairs right now?" the prince asked, his smooth voice sounding bored . . . and yet a tension emanated from him that belied the tone of his voice.

The king slammed his goblet down on the table with a heavy clang. "I care not what might offend Cullan. He's kept his son from me for two years, stringing me along, never revealing that he in fact was gone. Prince Fowler and Maris should have already wed. I am quite finished playing puppet to Cullan's whims."

Still the bishop talked. "If you insist that she's the late king's daughter, consider what this means for our alliance, for our kingdom." He did not know when to stop. Even I knew Tebald's temper was high and he didn't need to be pushed further.

"Bishop Frand," the king cut in. "I was not aware that you were appointed to the role of advisor. Nor are you so insightful that you can call yourself an oracle. No, we have not been fortunate enough to have an oracle in over twenty years. An oracle would be someone useful. We are left instead with you and your unbearably long sermons."

A taut silence fell over the hall. The king's displeasure became thick, palpable as the steam that rose from the platters of freshly roasted meat that servers had just deposited on the tables.

"Perhaps you need to take leave of us this evening and drop to your knees in prayer, Frand. After deep and thoughtful reflection, your insights might become something more valuable, something that I may require in the future." The dismissal was clear.

A heavy, awkward pause followed before the bishop pushed back his chair. The legs scraped over the stone floor, discordant and jarring in the silence. I felt his gaze scour me before his tread signaled his departure, his heavy receding steps indicating a man of great girth. In a world where people were starving and eating bats that led them to madness, he was corpulent.

After he left, the hall gradually revived with conversation and the sounds of eating.

Chasan leaned into my side again. "Already making friends."

I hesitated in tearing a piece of flaky bread that was seasoned with herbs and a flavorful oil that I had never tasted before. "That's not my purpose here."

"Oh. You have a purpose, *princess?* Enlighten me."

His derision warned me that Frand wasn't my only enemy. For whatever reason, this boy did not like me either. "Not that it's your concern, but once Fowler is well, I'll be on my way." He chuckled at that. I stiffened. "Am I the butt of a joke?"

"I'm merely amused."

"Why is that?"

"You just revealed yourself to be the late King Relhok's daughter . . . the true heir to Relhok. Cullan, the current ruler of Relhok, is my father's greatest enemy or ally depending on the day." He paused, and his arm stretched along the back of my chair, brushing my shoulders in a way that made me lean forward to escape him. "You aren't going anywhere, princess. Possibly ever."

The food in my stomach suddenly felt like rocks as I turned his words over in my head. It seemed pretty clear then that the only way I was leaving this place was through a calculated escape. First order of business: ferret out information on all entrances and exits into the castle.

"Scribe!" the king called, his voice carrying over the conversation of everyone in the great hall and drawing my attention from Chasan. "Send for the scribe!"

Moments passed, and whisper-soft footsteps scurried over the polished floor. "Here, Your Majesty."

"Are you ready? Take a missive." King Tebald didn't wait for an answer before continuing, "It is with great joy that I share the news of the princess of Relhok's survival and good health . . ."

The scratching of quill on parchment filled the air. "She is safe and well and resides with us where, fear not, she will continue to prosper under our most diligent care and affections . . ."

"Father, are you certain that you should alert him that we have her?" the prince asked, an edge to his voice.

Have her. As though I were a possession.

The significance of this sank in, and hope flared to life in me. Cullan would know I lived. He'd have no reason to continue killing girls in his hunt for me. "Yes," I blurted. "Do it. Let him know." *Please, please, let him know.*

Chasan leaned closer again, his liquid voice turning acidic. "You're not fully apprehending the situation. If Cullan killed your parents to control Relhok, he will not wish you well. He believes you dead now. Are you certain you wish to alert him to the contrary?"

"He already knows," I responded, my tone urgent, excited at stopping the slaughter of so many innocents with a mere letter from Tebald. "He's looking for me. That's what motivated his kill order. If he knows I live, he'll lift the kill order. There will be no need for it."

"He may very well be looking for you, but he doesn't know where you are."

"Let him know," I boldly tossed down.

At my emphatic words, the king chuckled lightly, alerting me that he had been listening from where he sat addressing the scribe. "You do remind me of your mother. She was a fine, spirited lass, too. Kind and full of mettle." I smiled. I couldn't stop myself. I no longer had this—no longer had Perla and Sivo whispering of past things.

I listened with a light heart as the scribe finished taking down the king's message.

"Idiot girl," Chasan muttered beside me.

I bristled, liking him even less with every passing moment.

"That takes care of that," Tebald announced. "Cullan will know you live now and that you are here. You and Prince Fowler."

"How long will it take for him to receive the missive?" I asked, anxiousness making me sit up straighter.

"Not long. We'll send a courier bird out with it at once."

I ducked my head, so overcome with relief that tears burned my eyes. The senseless killing would stop. I wasn't foolish enough to think Tebald's motives altruistic, but the fact remained that he was helping me save lives. For that I was grateful.

I sucked in a breath, relief warming a path through me. "Thank you," I murmured. It was everything I wanted, after all . . . for Cullan to know I lived so that he would end his bloodthirsty hunt to find me. That had been the goal. Now if he wanted me dead, he could come after me directly. And maybe he would. I swallowed against the bitter lump in my throat, thinking of Chasan's warning.

I gave myself a hard mental shake. It didn't matter. The importance of my life waned when held up against scores of others. All those girls, faceless innocents, would not die because of me. The only monsters they had to fight were the ones we all had to fight.

Besides, I would be long gone from here before Cullan's men showed up. I was uncertain where to go next. Could I continue on to Allu? Continue the journey I had set out on with Fowler? It seemed so long ago since we'd left my tower.

I didn't need to go to Relhok anymore. Not unless I was ready to lay claim to my throne . . . if that's what I wanted to do. Did I *want* my throne? Did I need it to be mine? I had to sort out what was right—not just for me but for the people of Relhok. I winced. I knew that Cullan at the helm of the kingdom wasn't what was right or best for anyone. Even Fowler, his son, knew that.

"You're quite welcome." Tebald looked at me. I could feel his stare, cold as an icicle. I'd have to get over that. Perhaps it was just the way of kings—to stare so hard that their gazes felt like blades scraping the flesh back from your bones.

We continued to eat, the conversation flowing more naturally, except from Chasan. He sat beside me, detached. "And how is it you come to be with Prince Fowler? That's quite the coincidence. To say nothing of unusual," he murmured after some moments. "Considering that you claim his father murdered your parents, he is the last person I would suspect you to ally with."

I bristled at the word *claim*. "You doubt the manner in which my parents died?"

"A great many died in those early days of the eclipse." He shifted in his chair beside me and I sensed his shrug. "I'm not saying you're lying. Only that you could be mistaken."

The king spoke through a mouthful of food. "You don't

know Cullan as I do, son. Of course it's true. He was always overly ambitious." He snorted and slurped at his goblet. "Indeed, I know Cullan and I knew her parents. Traveled to Relhok often as a young man. I didn't spend my youth sequestered inside this city. I rode the expanse of my kingdom and beyond, learning my allies as well as my foes. You've done nothing of the kind. It's limited your understanding."

I did not mistake the veiled insult. It was a cutting insinuation that Tebald was better than his son.

Chasan did not miss it either. "I was not given a choice," he quickly replied. "I'm not allowed a stone's throw from this castle without fully armed guards. Otherwise I might know Lagonia and its neighbors better."

Tebald grunted. "You'd be dead. And I cannot afford to lose my only son. You're too valuable."

Valuable. Not loved or cared for. He was a commodity. The sleeve of Chasan's tunic rustled slightly as he lifted his arm. "We can't have that, can we, Father?"

"No, we can't. Your responsibility is to live and further our line."

"I will remain ever dutiful and not step out of your prescribed boundaries." Despite the very correct words, derision threaded through his voice. The king did not miss it either.

"Scorn my rules all you like, but you'll stay alive. You and your sister. Our legacy will not die out. Isn't that right, Princess Luna?"

My head snapped up; I was unaccustomed to being addressed

by my title. I wasn't certain how to reply. And what did I have to do with any of it? "I'm certain you shall all continue to thrive here. Your fortifications are remarkable."

"Indeed. And now that you're here, we're assured of that. Tell me, Luna, do you value duty?"

I felt as though the question was a test. The thought of my parents flashed through my mind. I knew from Sivo that my father believed in serving the people and that his responsibility as king was for that very purpose. Then I thought of myself, and what it was that I should do with my life. Especially now that the kill order would be lifted. Surely I was meant to do more than survive. There had to be more than day-to-day survival. What was my purpose?

Sivo and Perla predicted that I had a great fate. I didn't quite know what that fate was, but here I was sitting at the king of Lagonia's table—and he had just sent a missive out declaring me alive to Cullan.

I was starting to believe they might be right.

"Yes," I answered. "I believe in duty." I just needed to figure out what it was.

TWELVE

Fowler

I WOKE WITH a groan.

Agony clawed through me in unrelenting waves, twisting everything inside me to a fine edge of pain. I attempted to prop myself up on my elbows, but failed, collapsing back down with a shudder.

I sucked in another breath, my chest rising high as my eyes flew wide. A swirl of color greeted me, but I processed nothing. I blinked, attempting to focus.

The ceiling stretched high above me. Great beams criss-crossed the rafters. I didn't know this place. *Where was Luna?* After everything, I had lost her. An oath escaped me and I struggled to rise again, only to fall back down on the bed with another curse.

A coarse chuckle rewarded my efforts. "Got a foul mouth on you . . . quite unseemly for a prince," a voice said.

A face popped into my line of vision. A face I didn't know. It all came back to me. Lagonian soldiers found us and brought us to Ainswind. We were guests of the king. *They knew who I was.* That was bad for me and bad for Luna. It was difficult to say who was in more danger. I had to get us out of here.

I struggled to rise again. My efforts to get out of bed cost me. I only felt worse. Moaning, I turned my head away, my stomach rebelling. Leaning over the bed, I heaved, emptying the contents of my stomach over the side of the bed. Amazing how I could heave up anything at all when I couldn't even remember the last time I had eaten.

A cool cloth was pressed to my forehead. The hand holding it eased me back down on the bed and I was staring at the face of the wizened old man again.

He leaned over me. "There now, lad." He wiped the wet cloth over my face and I whimpered. There was no relief. The coolness only contrasted with the hot flush of my skin and heightened my misery.

I grunted, glad when he stopped.

But then he poured on fresh torment.

He took my arm, which I had curled protectively on my chest, and stretched it out at my side. As if that wasn't uncomfortable enough, he slapped on some foul-smelling ointment. I lifted my head with a hiss as he lathered the concoction up and down from shoulder to wrist.

The face grinned widely, revealing a smile barren of teeth, save for one rotting canine—a brown teardrop in the gaping maw of his mouth. "Stings, I know."

"Are you trying to kill me?" I demanded, dropping my head back on a pillow as the maniacally smiling old man slapped more of that wet concoction on my arm. The fire in my arm raged to new levels.

"If I wanted to kill you, I wouldn't be bothering with this stuff. Now cease your squirming. This will heal you."

"So I'm not going to die?"

He shrugged one bone-thin shoulder. For all his rotting teeth, he was well groomed, wearing a fine velvet tunic with embroidery at the cuffs. They hadn't sent some peasant to look after me.

His words only confirmed this. "You most assuredly will die. Only not today. You're fortunate. The king wants you alive or I wouldn't be here. I'd be feasting in the hall with everyone else."

Feasting in the hall with everyone else.

With Luna? Was she there with everyone else? With Prince Chasan? I didn't like the way that arrogant peacock looked at her. He knew there was something different about her. He'd figure it out soon. He was no fool. It hadn't taken me very long to conclude she was blind. My face burned hotter at the memory of how I had first discovered that about her—the intimate moment when she had walked in on me naked. It just drove home how vulnerable she was here in this den of snakes. The last thing I wanted was for them to mark her as weak.

All thoughts scattered as the burn in my arm grew excruciating. My mouth opened wide on a silent cry. I arched off the bed, my hand flying to the afflicted skin, ready to wipe the awful ointment off.

The physician held my hand away. "I'm drawing out the venom."

He called over his shoulder for someone. I hadn't even realized anyone else was in the room, but two servants were suddenly there, restraining me to the bed with ropes.

"'Tis for your own good," the physician puffed.

"Luna," I moaned as though she could appear to give me relief, solace.

"Ah, your friend is in good hands."

Through my fog of pain I detected something in his voice. Something I did not like. Panic flared inside me. I surged harder. The servants exclaimed and threw their weight even more on top of me.

I strained against their hold, against the pain, until I couldn't strain anymore. Until I couldn't fight.

Closing my eyes, I let go and fell into darkness.

THIRTEEN

Luna

I COULDN'T SLEEP.

This late, the world inside the castle was silent as a crypt as I paced the confines of my bedchamber, learning its layout, committing it to memory.

I thought of Fowler, wondering where he was and how he fared inside these thick stone walls. When I asked after him, I was simply told he was being well tended and not to worry. As though he was no longer my concern. As though nothing should ever be my concern again.

After dinner I had been escorted to my chamber and dressed in a billowy nightgown. A maid sat me down at a cushioned bench and brushed my hair until it crackled around my head. "This will grow out long again before you know it," she assured me, as though that assurance were necessary.

Then I was tucked into bed.

Maris made a little more sense to me now. If this was her life, if this was how she had been treated all these years, I could understand how marriage to a stranger would be a welcome prospect. Because it was something, *anything*, to break up the absolute tedium of her days.

I stepped out onto the balcony, marking its width, gripping the stone railing. Wind lifted my hair back from my ears. I was definitely high above the ground. The current hit me strong, as though there had been nothing in its way until it collided with me. No trees, no cliffs or rocky terrain. I inhaled deeply, marveling at the absence of loam on the air. There was no whiff of dwellers. One could almost imagine they didn't exist out there. Here inside Ainswind, I felt insulated. It was a dangerous sensation. Nowhere was safe.

Leaving the balcony, I stopped before the heavy oak door of my chamber and pressed my ear to its length. I heard nothing on the other side. Closing my hand on the latch, I slowly opened the door and stepped out into the wide corridor.

A rasp of breath and rustle of fabric alerted me to the fact that I wasn't alone, after all. I spun around to face the individual.

"Can I assist you, Your Highness?" a guard asked.

I flinched. It still startled me, hearing that designation applied to me so naturally. Would I ever grow accustomed to it?

I lifted my chin, grasping for an air of imperviousness, imagining that was the regal thing to do. The guard was actually shorter than I was. The sound of his voice fell below where most men spoke. I angled my gaze downward as I answered him. "I would like to see my friend, Prince Fowler—"

"I'm sorry, Your Highness, you're not allowed to see him."

I frowned. "What do you mean?"

Maris had seen him by now. I was certain of it. She said she would see him this very night, and I doubted she had been turned away. Later, I would likely hear all about it from her—including how handsome Prince Fowler was . . . how he was beyond all her imaginings. An ugly sensation took hold of me. It was unreasonable, but I was jealous that she could see him while I could not. I needed to let that go. The only thing that mattered was that he was receiving the help he needed. Once I had that assurance, I could escape from this place.

I settled my hands on my hips and addressed another question at the stoic guard. "Were you assigned to guard my door?" That would toss a hurdle in my plans for escape.

"Just for the night, in case you should need anything, Your Highness."

"Am I free to wander the castle?"

"With an escort, of course."

I inhaled thinly. "I don't need a watchdog."

Silence met the statement. Sighing, I shook my head. "Very well. Escort me to Prince Fowler. I'm certain with an escort it's acceptable—"

"No one is allowed in to see him without express approval of the king." Although he spoke in a deferential manner, there was an edge of iron to his voice. He would not be swayed.

"You mean *I* do not have the king's approval to see him?" The guard shifted uneasily on his feet, but neither confirmed nor denied me. "Very well."

I spun around and jerked the door to my bedchamber open again. Without another word, I plunged back inside the chamber and resumed my pacing, my thoughts churning as I tried to think of ways I could see Fowler. I couldn't go until I did.

Several minutes passed as I came to accept one glaring fact.

I was a prisoner.

I fell asleep eventually. My exhaustion must have been deeper than I'd realized. When I woke, there was a lightness to the air. It was midlight.

Instinctively, I relaxed, the tension that greeted me the moment my eyes opened ebbing away. I stretched my arms above my head, pleasantly pulling my aching muscles and marveling at the sensation of a bed beneath me again.

"Your Highness, you're awake," a feminine voice said.

I sat up on my elbows, smoothing a hand over my mussed hair.

"Come," the woman said, a different servant from the one who'd attended me last night. "I'll help you dress and escort you to the dining hall. You missed breakfast, but it's almost lunch. You must be famished."

I *was* famished. The prospect of food had me hopping from the bed. I stood still for her, malleable if not anxious as she dressed me in a gown and pinned my hair back on my head. "There you are now," she said, patting one last tendril into place. I followed her to the door, where a different guard waited. He escorted me down a corridor and winding stairs into a dining area that was smaller than the great hall. The smell of food tantalized my nose and hunger pains clawed me.

I hovered at the threshold, my senses prickling as I marked the sounds, the various voices, the clink of silverware, and the tread of servants circling a great round table.

"Ah, she has woken at last!" King Tebald exclaimed.

My face warmed at the sudden attention swinging toward me. I inched forward carefully, hoping that I merely looked shy and tentative.

"Come, there is a seat for you beside Maris. We reserved it for you just in case you roused in time for lunch."

At the king's declaration, I nodded in thanks, my ears perking at the sound of a chair being pulled out, its legs scraping the floor. I tracked this, stepping carefully in case there were any steps or obtrusions. Reaching the chair, I gathered my skirts and sank into the seat, lifting myself slightly as I was scooted in with the aid of a servant.

"You're looking well," a voice breathed at the back of my neck, and I realized it was no servant holding out my chair, but Prince Chasan himself, with his liquid-silk voice. "Blue is a fine color on you."

I nodded again, the only form of thanks I could muster. A niggle of sympathy for him wormed through the back of my heart as I recalled how his father had treated him last night. It threatened my resolve to not like him. He sank down in the chair beside me. I realized I was wedged between brother and sister— both of whom I didn't precisely want to be around, but here I was, trapped.

I had just managed to pick up my spoon and take a sip from a hearty broth before Maris whispered excitedly, "I saw the prince. He is as handsome as rumored."

I swallowed my soup. "How does he fare?"

"Oh, still feverish, but the physician vows he'll make a full recovery. I intend to visit him again after lunch. I want to be the first face he sees when he wakes." This last bit was a breathy sigh from her lips.

My chest pinched tight. "I am relieved he's on the mend." And I was. That was the only thing that mattered—not my petty emotions. Fowler would live.

Now I could escape this place.

"Princess Luna." The king's voice boomed across the table, claiming my attention. "Cullan has replied to our message this very morning."

I startled a bit at this pronouncement. He wasted little time. Something loosened and unfurled inside me. King Tebald had accomplished what would have taken me weeks, perhaps longer to accomplish. Perhaps I never would have done it.

I nodded once, decisive, consoled. It was done, then. Cullan knew I was alive. He knew that even though he had killed my parents, he had not destroyed everything about them.

"Already?" a voice I recognized as Frand asked.

The king chuckled. "I imagine he did not want to prolong his response. My message probably put him in a state."

"*Indeed*, Your Majesty," the bishop agreed. The word hung, bloated with meaning. He wanted to say more, wanted to convey his disapproval, but knew better after the last time the king had sent him from the room with his tail tucked between his legs.

I cleared my throat. "Your Majesty, might I ask how he responded?"

"As expected. He claims you are an imposter and demands your head." Chasan tensed beside me and I turned slightly toward him, curious at his manner. A hushed silence descended on the table, awaiting the king's next statement. "He also demands the return of his son."

I swallowed and moistened my lips. "He wants Fowler back?"

"Naturally. You, the true heir to Relhok and the"—he paused as if searching for the proper word—"*disputed* heir."

Disputed? Fowler's position was now disputed? Because of me? It shouldn't have been a surprise, but I hadn't thought about it.

"Now he can no longer lie to me and put me off when I press for him to produce his son to wed my daughter. If in fact that is what I still wish to happen."

If. Maris released a tiny gasp beside me. I exhaled. He might not wish for his daughter to marry Maris anymore? Because he had me. What did that mean for Fowler? Specifically, what did that mean for his safety here? His position?

I shook my head. No. I couldn't worry about him any longer. I was escaping. And once I was gone, Fowler would become a commodity yet again. Perhaps me disappearing was more important than ever.

"What will you do, Father?" Chasan asked.

"Nothing," the king said simply, slurping at the soup from his bowl.

"Nothing, Your Majesty?" the bishop asked carefully. "You will not reply to him?"

"Oh, eventually. I shall make him wait as he has made me wait all these years. I shall enjoy that. It's my turn now to let him writhe on the line that I hold."

"*Eventually*," Chasan said, echoing him, "what will you then reply?"

It was vexing, waiting on this man's word. He held all the power while we waited on his whims. My knuckles ached from clenching my spoon.

"I think that when I next contact him, it shall be to invite him to the wedding," the king said cheerfully, pausing to gulp from his drink. "Two weddings, perhaps. It's unlikely that he will come, but who knows? Travel is fraught with danger but not impossible."

"Two?" I echoed, a sense of foreboding sweeping through me.

"Yes. It shall be a notable year in the history of Lagonia. Two weddings. Two celebrations after years of so much . . .

unpleasantness. Something bright in all this darkness. A ray of hope for all."

"Who is getting married?" Chasan asked, and there was something in his voice, something that echoed the bewilderment that swept through me.

"I suppose the marriage of Maris to Prince Fowler is long overdue." Tebald sighed, clearly not thrilled about the idea, but at least he hadn't totally dismissed Fowler. As much as the idea of him married to Maris flustered me, I was relieved to know that he wasn't in danger.

"Even if it's no longer a necessity, it might be a wise precaution. Just to help solidify our ties to Relhok so that our claim will never be threatened under any eventuality."

Even though I knew this was happening—ever since Maris opened her mouth to me about waiting her entire life for Fowler I knew it could happen—it hurt.

"And the other wedding?" Chasan asked. "You mentioned two?"

"Yes." The bishop spat out the words. "What, pray, second wedding could you mean?"

My lips felt numb. There was only my heart, thumping madly, aching and twisting like a fist inside my chest. Everything else felt deadened.

"Is it not obvious? Luna's wedding to our house is a necessity. Surely you understand that, my son. And you, too, Luna. Your marriage to my son legitimately ties our kingdom with Relhok. With both these marriages, in any circumstance, it cannot be disputed that Relhok will become a part of Lagonia someday."

I couldn't stay here. I couldn't marry Chasan. I couldn't stand by and watch as Fowler married Maris.

My head spun as if I had just twirled in a speeding circle. I set my spoon down, my hunger forgotten as Maris hopped happily in her seat beside me, clapping her hands. Chasan didn't move or make a sound. If not for the steadiness of his breathing, I would not have known he was still there.

It made perfect sense for Tebald to play it this way. It was safe. It was smart. For both kingdoms. Even I could see that.

Accepting what was safe and smart, however, was not so simple.

FOURTEEN

Fowler

I WOKE ABRUPTLY with a gasp. I had been dreaming that I was still underground, running, searching, calling for Luna lost somewhere within the dwellers' web.

I blinked, my gaze swerving around the strange chamber with its vaulted ceiling, remembering at once where I was. I'd woken one time since the physician slapped the foul-smelling, skin-burning salve on me. A girl had been there, holding my hand, wiping my feverish brow. She'd declared herself the king's daughter, Maris. She also called me things, endearments that left no doubt she considered herself my betrothed. I'd opened my mouth and tried to explain that we couldn't be betrothed, but speech was lost to me then.

"Glad to see you are healing well." My gaze jerked to the man sitting in a chair beside my bed, and I knew he was the reason for my sudden state of wakefulness. He passed the smelling salt he held to the physician hovering beside him. Folding his hands neatly in his lap, the king smiled tightly. "You've slept long enough, my young friend. It is time we talk."

My chest lifted with panting breaths, as though I had in fact been running through tunnels and not merely dreaming about it. I pushed up on the bed, wincing. I felt as weak as a child, but I wasn't going to have a conversation with a man as ruthless as my own father while lying on my back.

Tebald eyed my bandaged arm with lifted brows, as though he could see through the wrapping to my arm itself. "You should belong to the dwellers, but thanks to me, you are still here." I nodded slowly, even as I thought: *Thanks to Luna I'm still here.* "Barclay here says you should be able to leave your sickbed and walk soon."

"I can walk now." At least I would have liked to attempt it. No more sickbed. No more weakness. No more lying defenseless while Maris stroked me like her new pet.

There was that slow smile of his again. It didn't reach his eyes. It didn't even crease his ashen cheeks. He brushed a finger along the line of his well-groomed beard. "Maris tells me you're stubborn. Even sick, you fight and resist the help you need. I see that now."

I tensed. So he knew his daughter had been visiting me.

What else had she said about me to her father? I watched him, careful to keep my expression blank. Maybe he even encouraged her to come to me. There was that ridiculous betrothal between us, after all—made when I was barely walking and Maris was still in a cradle. Maybe he thought to honor it. Or rather, he thought to make me honor it.

Tebald continued, "Rest easy. No rush on walking yet. You could relapse, and we want you well. We need you well."

I didn't mistake his emphasis on need. It was the reason I lived at all—the only reason I had been brought back to the castle and treated by the king's own physician. The king and Lagonia needed me. Maris claimed to need me as well. I recalled that from when she sat at my bedside. But that was more tied up into want than need. She was a child and I was the bright and shiny toy for her. Nothing more than that.

"Thank you," I replied because he stared at me so expectantly, compelling me to speak.

He inclined his head slightly. "Ah. Gratitude is a good thing. It means people understand . . . they know their place in the order of things."

He leaned back in his chair, lacing his fingers together. "This kingdom has lasted seventeen years. Others have fallen. And others are just skeletons of what they once were." His gaze narrowed on me. "Relhok hangs on by a thread. True, your father wields an iron fist, and his human sacrifices serve as timely feedings that keep the dwellers in check for now, but how long can that continue before his people revolt? Or the dwellers grow hungry for more?"

He wasn't saying anything I hadn't thought of before, or even anything I hadn't said to my father, trying to persuade him to change his ways.

Tebald continued, "But here Lagonia stands. We're surviving in these walls. My legacy will continue. If only one royal house is still standing when the eclipse lifts, it will be mine. Be assured of that." He nodded resolutely, a fanatical light gleaming in his eyes. I supposed there had to be a bit of the fanatical in anyone determined to survive the eclipse. "The question, Fowler, is whether you will be part of this house . . . if your legacy will live on."

The threat was subtle. Join him or perish. And there was only one way to join him that he would accept. We stared at each other for a long while.

"You don't want me to marry your daughter," I said quietly, thinking not only of me in that moment but of her, too. I could never love her, and she would know that soon.

Even though I had been half out of my mind with fever when she visited me, I knew enough of the princess already. Maris was a coddled girl, childlike and with no awareness, no fear or respect for the reality of this world. I couldn't be with someone like that. She would sense that I wasn't truly with her even when we were together. There would always be someone else there, a ghost hovering between us. A girl with stars in her eyes, full of dreams that didn't belong in this world. Maris would come to hate me for that.

"You're right. I do not. But a ruler must do things they don't always like. Choices have to be made."

"If you care about your daughter, don't force this marriage between us."

He shrugged and waved a hand with a scoff. "Don't be sentimental. Maris is an instrument, a weapon to be used and waged. Just as you are. You both have your duties."

He cared little for his own daughter. I couldn't appeal to his love for her. He wasn't that different from my father. That should have made him easy to understand. I should have been able to predict his next move if I simply thought of him in those terms. Gazing at him, I could almost confuse his cold eyes for my father's.

"What say you, Fowler? Do you know your place in the order of things?" He lifted his laced fingers one at a time, bringing them down slowly like dominoes falling. "Do I need to make myself any more clear?" He arched an eyebrow.

Studying him, I angled my head to the side as a calmness settled over me. He meant he expected my fealty—to Lagonia, to him. I don't think there was a distinction. A bad taste coated my mouth. "Yes, I know my place, Your Majesty."

He smiled that oily smile again. "Smart boy. I'll leave you now." Smart indeed. I knew to say what he wanted to hear. "I imagine Maris is skulking around the corner, waiting for me to leave so that she can descend on you again." He patted my knee through the bedcovers. "Get well and we'll start planning these weddings. Maris is eager. She's only been waiting her entire life for this." He waved a hand. "She has a bounty of ideas. Not all realistic, mind you. Her proposed menu alone is going to require adjusting."

She had been waiting her entire life to marry me. While I was on the Outside fighting, trying not to die, watching others die horribly, she was daydreaming about a boy she didn't know and a lavish wedding. It was all the evidence I needed that I couldn't spend my life with her. I couldn't spend my life *here*, under Tebald's thumb. I'd made that decision years ago without even meeting her.

I needed to escape here the same way I had escaped Relhok. Only this place was going to be harder to leave. After my father killed Bethan he thought me broken. No one had thought to watch me. No one thought that one day I might simply walk out of the gates at midlight and never return. Here they would watch my every move.

I had the same choking sensation I felt when I was in Relhok. As though a great weight was bearing down on my chest, pushing and shoving all the air out.

I would find my breath again. I'd say whatever lies I had to say. I'd fake whatever I needed to, but I would leave.

And when I did, I was taking Luna with me. The thought of Luna made something the king said penetrate. "Your Majesty, pardon me. Did you say . . . weddings?" As in more than one? Grimacing, I forced myself back up on the bed.

Halfway to the door, he stopped and turned. "Ah, yes. Luna shall marry into our house as well." He smiled slowly, his eyes gleaming with satisfaction. "Come, Fowler, did you think to hide who she really was from me? Ah, from your expression I suppose you did. I knew her mother, wasted many a season paying court to her. With one look, I knew who she was." Tsking his tongue, he shook his head. "You won't insult me by denying it, will you?"

He knew. I shook my head numbly. As soon as I was on my feet, we'd put this place far behind us. "If you know who she is, why bother with me?"

"I've learned the wisdom of having a secondary strategy in place. You're a nice spare to have around."

I stared, truly without words. My arms started to shake and burn and I could no longer hold myself up.

I collapsed back on the bed, my hands opening and closing into fists at my sides as I stared up at the high beams in the ceiling, listening as the king of Lagonia's faint laughter faded from my chamber.

FIFTEEN

Luna

SLEEP WAS IMPOSSIBLE. The bed was too big. The room too empty. The castle creaked and settled all around me, the eons-old stone sighing its old bones. The wind whipped and howled outside, pushing against the mullioned glass panes like a living thing trying to get inside. For a moment, I thought I heard a dweller's eerie cry far in the distance—a world away from here.

I had never been truly alone. I'd always had Perla and Sivo, if not in the same room with me, then in the room beside me. The cadence of Perla's gentle snores lulled me to sleep through childhood. When I finally left the tower, I'd had Fowler. Even on the

Outside, in the great open space fraught with danger, he'd been there beside me every night.

The murmur of voices at my door brought me into a sitting position on the bed. I flattened my palms on the mattress, ready to push up and bolt if needed.

The door creaked open. Robes rustled and I smelled the faint aroma of incense. The bishop.

I crouched on my knees atop the bed. "What are you doing in here?" So much for the guard protecting me.

His ankle joints popped as he advanced with more speed than I would have thought a man of his size capable.

I scrambled to get off the bed, but he was there, the great mountain of him blocking me. I fell back, desperate to avoid contact, the heels of my hands holding me up on shaking arms. His intent was harm. I smelled it on him, bitter as charred ash on his sweating skin.

"You should never have come here," he hissed, his voice wild in his zealotry. "You'll bring ruin on us."

I cringed at the stink of his onion-laced breath gusting in my face—and there was the stale aroma of that drink that had made me fuzzy-headed. "I don't suppose it makes a difference that I don't want to be here either."

He continued as though I had not spoken. "The king doesn't understand, but I do. You'll bring war to Lagonia."

"Aren't we already at war? With this eclipse? With dwellers?"

"Precisely why we don't need the addition of a war with Rel-hok." He reached out and closed his hands around my neck. "I could open those doors and toss you off the balcony. It's a long drop down. Can't even see the bottom at midlight. No one would ever know what happened to you."

I gasped at the dig of sausage-thick fingers around my throat. "Let me go," I choked out, clawing at his slowly tightening grip. I hadn't been through so much, come so far, to let it end like this.

"I could end you now. Save us all. God would forgive me."

My legs thrashed, nails scoring the backs of his hands as he squeezed, crushing my windpipe.

I couldn't breathe. A roaring filled my ears. It seemed the worst thing. Not dying, but dying like this. I had assumed it would be at the hands of dwellers.

The pressure in my head suddenly lightened and I felt like I was drifting. I didn't feel the sweating, fat hands at my throat anymore.

Then the lightness vanished.

Pain returned as air filled my starved lungs. I clutched at my burning throat. It was a blissful sort of agony, though, because it signaled life. I wasn't dead. Those crushing hands were no longer on my throat.

Dimly, volume returned. I sucked air in over the sounds of scuffling and harsh voices. Bone cracked against something thick and solid. Frand cried out shrilly.

I sat up, listening, one hand still wrapped around my throat, massaging the tender skin.

"Please, please, Your Highness," Frand blubbered, dragging

himself on the floor to get away from the prince. "I beg you! Stop!"

The prince's boots followed after the large body, biting hard into the stone floor. His silken voice slid over me, filling me with a strange sort of relief. "You're fortunate I'm nothing like my father, Bishop Frand, or you would not be leaving this room alive."

"Th-Thank you, Your Highness! You are so generous," the bishop babbled. There was the sound of a sloppy, wet kiss on the prince's boot.

"Get off me before I change my mind!"

Frand whimpered and retreated, bringing his hands up to cover his blubbering face.

Chasan crouched over the pathetic man. "Now heed me. If anything, anything at all, happens to this girl, I will come for you. Your head on a pike in the courtyard. That will be your fate . . . your legacy."

The viciousness of his threat startled me. I would not have thought he cared enough to bother. When his father proclaimed that we should marry, he did not seem any more happy about it than I was.

The bishop gasped. "I can't be the only one here with a thought to harm her. Your Highness, your admirers alone . . . any one of them or a member of their family might think to harm her. Half the noblemen at court have been pelting their daughters at you in a bid for marriage!"

"Then you best hope they don't harm her," he cut in smoothly.

I swallowed, wincing at the pain of the action. The bishop

here was not my only danger? I'd landed myself in a vipers' nest.

"Your Highness," the bishop edged, his voice cautiously deferential, "you know marrying her is a declaration of war on Relhok—"

"Such matters of state do not concern you. Keep to what you do best: delivering lies from your pulpit whilst you lose yourself in gluttony and groping the serving maids. Never cross me again. Someday I'll sit on the throne. Never forget that. Now go, before I decide to toss you into the dungeon."

Frand lumbered to his feet with great panting breaths. "Yes, yes. Of course. Th-Thank you, Your Highness."

His heavy tread shuffled from the room. The door thudded behind him and it was just the two of us.

"H-How—" I stopped, my voice coming out a hoarse whisper. I swallowed, cringing against the raw scrape of my throat. "How did you know that I was in trouble?"

"When I walked past your door, the guard wouldn't meet my gaze. It seemed strange."

I nodded slowly. "Thank you."

He stopped beside my bed. I scooted to the edge, dropping my legs over the side. I couldn't stand without coming chest to chest with him, so I stayed sitting, attempting to hide just how much I was shaking.

When his hands landed on my throat, I jumped. I should have sensed his impending touch, but pain addled my head. I inhaled his warmth, the musk of his skin, his rich, windswept smell. He had been Outside recently. Since I last saw him tonight. I felt a stab of envy that he had the freedom to come and go.

He pulled back slightly, his fingers a brushstroke on my neck.

The air crackled as I felt his stare on my face, so close and probing. I resisted the urge to reach out and feel his face so that I would know him, so that I would have a sense of this face staring at me.

"W-What are you doing?"

"Just checking your neck. Should I call for the physician—"

"No," I blurted. "The fewer who know about this, the better." I didn't want anyone to think I was an easy target. Now that I knew precisely how much in jeopardy I was, I would be more guarded against attacks.

"Good point, but I want to make sure your injuries aren't too grave."

I moistened my lips. "You agree with me? And why is that?" Why should he care what happens to me at all, much less what anyone in Ainswind knew about me?

He sank down beside me. "This shouldn't have happened to you. I don't want anyone to know that I permitted such a thing to ever happen to you."

I snorted. "You didn't *permit* anything."

"It happened," he stated flatly, tension radiating off him. "It never should have. It makes me look weak. You're my betrothed—"

"No," I insisted with a swift shake of my head. "I'm not."

He inhaled slightly but said nothing, still staring, and it filled me with all kinds of unease. Never had lack of vision given me such discomfort.

"What is it about you?" he whispered.

My unease heightened. "What do you mean?"

"You're not like the rest of us. It's almost like . . . you belong out there. To the night."

I inhaled, understanding what he meant because it was how I felt. It's what I was. A creature of darkness, just like them.

"Even now," he continued. "It's like you look right through me."

His fingertips landed on the curve of my cheek and I flinched at the unexpected touch.

"Luna." His voice, so close that it tangled with my erratic breathing, sounded strained, bewildered. "Can you see me?"

A strangled little sound slipped out of me. *He knew.*

"You can't," he declared, his voice so certain. "You can't see."

"Is that so important?" I asked.

"It's just . . . you fooled me."

"Not entirely. You're calling me out now." I shrugged. "I don't lie about it. It's no secret."

"And yet you pass for a fully sighted individual."

"Most of the time." Only Fowler had known. Almost immediately, he had known. Heat crept over my cheeks as I recalled walking in on him naked. My lack of reaction had given me away.

"You're full of surprises." For once Chasan didn't sound hard or suspicious. In fact, he lacked his usual armor. More human than arrogant prince.

And his hand was still on my face.

I cleared my ravaged throat, cringing. "It's late. You should go."

"Of course." He dropped his hand and pushed up from the bed. "You'll be safe now, Luna."

He left me alone, shutting the door behind him. I heard his voice as he talked with the guard, all arrogance and hard stone again. Everyone had their veneers, I realized.

Settling back on the bed, I thought about what he said. I was safe again.

I stroked my bruised throat. In no way did I feel that was true, but was safety possible anywhere in this world? Was Allu just a fantasy that I let Fowler feed my needy heart?

Impossible as the notion seemed, Chasan as an ally didn't feel quite so wrong anymore.

SIXTEEN

Luna

I CONSIDERED MY options throughout the day, turning the facts over in my head. I was stuck here, a virtual prisoner, and the king wanted me to marry into his family. He didn't ask me. He simply informed me—stated it as fact. The same went for Fowler. Tebald expected him to marry Maris.

I needed to find Fowler. I needed to talk to him about sorting this out. I was never alone, though. Breaking away would be a challenge, if not impossible. After the midday meal I was dragged to a rooftop courtyard on the left tower with several other nobles, where they performed an archery demonstration. I couldn't help myself. Listening to songs of arrows, feeling the wind of the Outside on my face, the urge called to me. I took up a bow. I wasn't as good as Fowler, but Sivo had trained me well.

They were shooting at a stuffed dummy hanging from a rope. I listened to the others, to the soft thwacks as arrows hit the target, marking the object.

Stepping up, I notched the arrow and let it fly. My chest lifted high as I hit the target, pleasure suffusing me. My hand dove for two more arrows. In quick succession, I let them each go, and both hit the mark.

Applause broke out. A warm hand closed around my elbow. "Bravo, princess."

I turned to face Chasan. "Surprised?"

"That you are skilled with a bow and arrow? Not at all. You strike me as very capable."

I smiled vaguely and inclined my head in thanks. "What about you? Do you shoot?"

"I can shoot, but I have no desire to do it for the entertainment of others."

I sniffed, wondering if he meant to deliberately insult me since I had just done that very thing. In truth, I'd done it for the thrill, not to impress others. I did it for me, but I doubted that he realized that. He didn't know me. He must have read some of my reaction, for his grip on my arm flexed. "I don't judge you," he added, "if that's what you're thinking."

I shrugged and twisted my arm from his grip. "How you perceive me matters little."

"No? I thought it might, all things considered."

"You mean because your father wishes us to wed," I finished.

"I think it's more than a wish."

I crossed my arms. "You think it an eventuality? Does my opinion not matter? Does not yours? What do you wish for, Prince Chasan?"

He didn't touch me, but I felt him lean in. I felt his warm breath at my forehead, felt the heat radiating off him and knew his taller form was crowding me. "You interest me."

Because I was so different from everyone else? That's what he'd told me last. "Because I'm blind?" I asked, challenge in my voice.

"That's only one part of you. I wish to know you better, Luna. Explore all parts of you." His voice dropped, and heat slapped my face. Why did it sound like he was talking about something physical? "Are you opposed to that notion?" he continued in that purring voice. "Should we not at least grow better acquainted?"

"Yes, I could . . . tolerate that." What else could I say? *No, I'm plotting escape.*

"Try not to sound too enthused." He chuckled. "You're very good. This is yours. Keep it." He thrust the bow and shaft of arrows at me.

"For me?" I smoothed my hand over the polished wood, following the arch in admiration.

"Why not? You're one of the few people who actually knows how to use it." Almost to prove his words, another arrow was released. The shooter aimed too low and it skimmed along the ground, too close to bystanders if the sudden yelps and squawks were any indication.

"Thank you," I said, hugging the bow and shaft of arrows close to my side.

"It's nothing. Hardly a gift. At least not the type of present one gives to his betrothed."

I managed a tense smile, marveling at the ease with which he accepted me as his future wife. Maybe because that's all he ever did—follow his father's commands.

Someone else arrived in our midst, his staccato steps stopping beside the prince. His voice was low but not inaudible to my ears. "The hunt master would like a word with you." The servant's steps receded, leaving us alone again. As alone as we could be on a rooftop full of people.

"You're going out there," I murmured. "To hunt dwellers?"

"It's what I do."

"I don't understand. Why? It seems an unnecessary risk."

"I don't have to travel as far from the castle as I used to, to find them. More of them are coming closer to Ainswind, risking the rock terrain. After all these years, there are fewer of *us* for them to hunt. They're getting bolder." I sensed his shrug. "They need eliminating."

"I did not think your father wanted you to leave the protection of these walls, and yet you go out on these hunts."

"He doesn't like it, but he accepts that I'm good at it. I haven't died doing it yet," he joked.

"That's the qualification for being 'good' at something?" I snorted. "Sensible."

Suddenly my fingers were seized as he lifted my hand. Dry, cool lips brushed the backs of my knuckles. "I'll see you this evening at dinner, Luna. We can continue our conversation then."

An invisible band squeezed around my chest. I didn't want another conversation with him. I didn't want to be here for another day.

I managed to nod my agreement. He grazed his thumb over my knuckles once in a lingering stroke before letting go of my hand. I listened as his tread faded away, and released a relieved breath.

Everyone continued to step up and try their hand at shooting. Over laughter and applause, I slipped away, leaving the courtyard behind. Since my bedchamber door was guarded at night, my best chance to see Fowler was now. I hurried down winding steps, but my departure wasn't missed for long. The servant who had escorted me to the courtyard called out above me. My panicked heart jerked in my chest.

Once I hit the corridor floor, I broke into a run, determined to lose my escort. Clutching my bow in one hand, my other skimming the wall to keep my bearings, I turned down the hall. My fingers brushed a thick wall hanging, and I tucked myself behind the tapestry and held still, holding my breath, listening as my escort rushed past. Certain that she was gone, I slipped out from behind the hanging and started down corridor after corridor, pausing at doors to listen.

I passed my bedchamber and kept going, assuming Fowler would be in the same wing. A prince betrothed to the king of

Lagonia's daughter wouldn't be relegated to anything less than a bedchamber in the royal household.

I had to see Fowler. It was more than assuring myself of his well-being. Selfishly, I needed to see him for me. I needed to hear his voice. I needed to tell him what was happening and hear him tell me that there was a way out of this—that he had no intention of marrying Maris. That we could escape together. Fowler had always been that for me. My comfort when things seemed lost and at their darkest.

Laughter trickled through a door to my left and I stopped, pressing my palms to the thick wood. Leaning in, I flattened my ear to the door and listened. Instantly, I recognized the deep rumble of Fowler's voice.

My heart leaped. He was awake and talking. My hand moved for the latch, eager to burst inside and touch him, to feel the proof of him alive under my fingertips. His betrayal seemed a long time ago. The shock had ebbed, and I'd begun to think about how it must feel for Fowler to born to a man as awful as Cullan. He was a victim of birth. As was I: born amid a moment of chaos, my parents lost to me before I ever knew them. The sins of his father weren't his. Fowler could have told me the truth, but I hadn't told him who I was until someone else had guessed it.

"Oh, Fowler, you need to eat this. Don't be difficult now. I don't care if you claim it tastes like horse dung . . . and how you even know that I don't want to speculate." Maris paused to giggle. "You need your strength if you're to leave this bed."

Fowler's soft chuckle followed this. The sound was deep and velvet and full of amusement. It was strange to hear him laughing at all, much less laughing with Maris. I had heard that laughter only a few times. Rare as the sound was, I had prized it. My heart clenched to hear him laugh so freely with Maris, even though it had no right to hurt or ache. It was his laughter and not mine to own.

"I can already see how our marriage will be," Maris teased in a voice full of fondness. "You stubborn but always making me laugh." A long pause followed these words. I heard nothing but the clink of a spoon in a bowl. "I look forward to our future, Fowler. My only regret is that you took so long to get here."

I sucked in a pained breath. I waited to hear his response, his denial or acceptance of her words. Neither came. But then, perhaps his silence was an answer in itself. His silence was acceptance. Perhaps his brush with death had led to this? Perhaps his gratitude to Lagonia for saving his life had changed his mind?

Maybe he had forgotten all about his quest to reach Allu.

Maybe he had forgotten about me.

I turned my face in the direction of my chamber. To hell with all this supposition. It didn't matter. He wasn't mine. He belonged to Lagonia now. Perhaps I needed to embrace the same fate and belong to Lagonia, too.

At least I would belong somewhere.

There were worse fates. I could spend all day counting them. Prince Chasan . . . Maybe something could grow between us. Listening to Fowler and Maris, it was clear that something had already started to grow between them.

I backed away from the door as if it were something tangible that might leap out and bite me. Fowler's voice started to speak again, and I quickly turned away. I didn't want to hear any more. I didn't need to. I'd heard everything I needed to.

SEVENTEEN

Luna

I WAS HALFWAY asleep when the scream woke me. It was a faint cry, drifting from somewhere deep within the bowels of the castle, but I still heard it. I held myself motionless in the colossal bed, counting softly, hoping to give myself something to fixate on besides the goose bumps feathering my skin and the chill chasing my spine. Closing my eyes, I started to relax until it came again, just a weak thread of sound on the air.

Sitting up, I flung the covers back off the bed. I wasn't sleeping anymore. Snatching up my robe, I shrugged into it and slipped out of my chamber.

Another scream shook the air. I followed the sound, my ears perking and straining.

I skimmed a palm along the wall, feeling my way, occasionally brushing tapestries and portraits and decorative sconces in my quest to track the scream.

A part of me acknowledged that this was probably not the wisest course of action, but then I reminded myself that the screams I'd heard were human. I knew a dweller's cry. Someone was in trouble, hurting. I knew the sound of that quite well.

As I continued down the corridor, a low rumble surged on the air. It faded only to surface again moments later. This second surge was smaller, quieter, but this time I had no trouble identifying it for what it was—applause. Cheers.

Someone was terrified, in pain, and people were cheering? I shook my head. It didn't make sense.

I hesitated before I continued, my pace quickening. Rounding the corner, I almost collided with another individual turning into the same corridor from the opposite direction.

"Oh, forgive me, I didn't see where I was going." Soft hands grasped my arms and the smell of dried lavender tickled my nose. I vaguely recalled the scent from one of the ladies at court. The first day I arrived I remembered smelling her sitting beside Gandal, the physician's son. Her voice dropped to a conspiratorial whisper. "I'm guessing you and I are headed to the same destination, yes?"

"Uh—"

"Of course you are. Who told you about it? Maris? The prince? Never mind. Well, you are in for a rare show indeed. Such a treat, I tell you."

I decided to venture with honesty. "I heard a scream. I was following the sound."

"Oh, very bold, are you?" She giggled. Not the reaction I was expecting, but nothing was as I'd expected since arriving here.

"Truly, I heard screams—"

"Of course you did, you ninny. Don't be afraid. It's not what you think."

I wasn't sure what I thought. "What is it, then?" I asked.

"The king likes to act as though these things are a secret. It's special invitation only, but I know a way in." She shared this with a hint of slyness to her tone. "Come on. Follow me. I'll take you to the best seats in the house."

She linked her arm through mine, and together we quickly walked down vast corridors, our steps ringing off the stone.

"I don't think we have officially been introduced. I'm Riana. My father is the ambassador to your own country. . . . I suppose that makes us countrywomen, although I confess I was two years old the last time I set foot on Relhok soil."

"A pleasure to meet you," I returned.

"Likewise," she murmured. "You are quite the hero, unifying two kingdoms that have been on dubious footing for generations. You have managed to do what Papa never has. I suppose that makes my father quite ineffectual and you a marvel."

I inhaled uneasily. From that statement, it would not seem that she viewed me kindly. I especially did not think she would link arms with me and carry on as though we were the best of friends.

I heard myself asking, "And what is it that I have done?"

"Why, you have united both our countries—well, you will

eventually. That will be the end result with your betrothal to Prince Chasan."

"Th-Thank you," I stammered, dubious of her sincerity despite her cheerfulness, and yet I wanted to know about that scream and what *secret* she spoke of.

"Perhaps Papa can work in the royal counting house. He was assistant to the treasurer in Relhok before he was appointed ambassador. You would think that being good with numbers would be an asset. Hmm, but the funny thing is that there is no money left to be had in Lagonia. Currency these days is anything deemed of value on any particular day. You, for instance, are currency."

"Me?" I stiffened and would have stopped if she had not kept pulling me along.

"Yes. King Tebald is suddenly a far richer man than he was before you arrived. You are currency, leverage, a commodity. It's all semantics. With your marriage to Prince Chasan—nicely done, by the way. He is quite the handsome rogue. Every girl here, me included, has been after him for years. What was I saying? Oh, yes. Lagonia is facing a far brighter future now that you are here, but forgive me. Let's not talk policy. Not when there is fun to be had."

My thoughts churned as she continued to lead me. At one point she stopped before a wall. I turned my head left and right. "What's this?"

"I really shouldn't be showing you this, but since we're sharing so much, this palace is full of hidden passageways. I hear all manner of things I shouldn't." She paused and the back of my neck tickled.

"You eavesdrop?"

"It's about the only thing that keeps me from dying of boredom."

I pressed a hand to the wall, skimming my palm over the ancient stone. "What about ways *out* of the palace?"

"Who would want to leave the castle? It's dangerous out there."

It's dangerous in here, too. "Come, now. I want to know all the ins and outs of my new home." I cringed at this last bit. This place did not feel like home. Nor would it ever.

"Well, this castle has been around forever. Back in the old days, it was important to have a means of escape in the event of an attack. Not that this castle had ever been successfully invaded, to my knowledge at least."

"So there is a secret way out?"

"Yes. Through the kitchens. A rug covers the floor of the larger storage room, but underneath it there's a door."

My heart hammered with excitement. I tried to control my features lest too much emotion give me away. "An escape hatch . . . that does sound intriguing."

Riana sighed. "It's just a smelly tunnel."

A tunnel out of here.

Her hand found some hidden spot and pushed. The wall opened up to a passageway. "Come. Whisper only. Voices carry far in these hidden tunnels." The sound of her words vibrated against her fingertips. "We don't want to be caught. Tebald doesn't think this suitable for a lady's sensibilities."

"What?" I demanded as we made our way through the winding, narrow space. Another round of cheers sounded. This time much closer, louder. The origin was just beyond us. Riana stopped and pushed at the tunnel wall, opening yet another door.

She led the way out into a larger space where the air flowed freely. "Keep your voice down. You must not alert them that we're watching." I nodded, curious. "Get down on your knees," Riana instructed. "Torches line the pit. Not many, mind you. Just enough so that spectators can see clearly. Go on. Down with you. It's just a ledge really, but it's perfect for spying. You mustn't stand or they could look up and spot us."

She pushed down on my shoulder, and I obliged, feeling her body lower beside me as well. The din grew, flooding us as we crawled out onto the balcony. I pulled at my skirts to keep them from getting caught beneath me. I smelled the oil-fed fire from torches stuck in sconces sporadically around the ledge. The flames snapped in the air.

We stretched out, lying flat on our stomachs. Overlapping voices congested the air. *Bring on the next one! More, more!*

"What's happening?" I stretched my neck, angling my head to listen better, to try to process what was happening far below us.

"Look right there. Do you see the man?"

I feigned as though I could see, relying on my ears and that additional sense buried deep inside my gut. "What is he doing?"

It seemed a safe question to glean the necessary information—any information at all, really.

Her voice squeaked with excitement. "Oh, they're opening the gates now."

I did in fact hear the faint grind of metal as the gate lifted and locked into place.

"Now it's about to get fun," she breathed beside me. Just as I was beginning to conclude that her definition of fun and mine did not align, I heard it.

I gasped as a shrill dweller's cry warbled on the air, and I started to scurry backward on my stomach until she clamped a surprisingly firm grip on my arm, keeping me from fleeing the ledge.

"W-What—" Fear choked the words from me. Already this place had lulled me into false complacency.

I had almost committed myself to the belief that I was safe. That no dweller could penetrate these walls. Court life had made me weak even in so short a time. How could I have forgotten? This was the world. It has not changed simply because I'd ducked behind these thick walls.

A second dweller answered the call of the first and my skin jumped, rippling to gooseflesh. I felt them prowling below, their sensors vibrating on the air, acclimating to and learning this new environment just as I was. They moved with slow, dragging steps. Even slower than usual.

Over a dozen voices lifted in a cheer. I listened, trying to sift through their words. No one was scared or alarmed. They were jubilant, excited at the arrival of these two dwellers. I heard someone calling for bets, and a flurry of masculine voices responded with their wagers.

And there was the man. He was there in the pit with them, his feet scampering wildly over the circular space, trying to stay out of their reach. His voice lifted over all the cheers and shouts, screaming, pleading. His fear saturated the air, as thick as the loamy odor of the dwellers.

"What's going to happen?"

"I would think his fate would be obvious."

"They're just going to let him die?" I inched closer to the edge, feeling the flow of air on my face as I peered over, tracking the poor man's frantic movements.

"Yes, and enjoy watching every moment of it. This is what happens to criminals in Lagonia. Sometimes you don't even have to be a criminal. Fall out of favor with the king and face the pits." She explained it so casually, as though she were discussing nothing significant.

"That's barbaric."

Riana laughed softly. "And how is that different from anything else in this world? We live in brutal times. Surely you know that, having come from out there."

And yet somehow I thought things would be different inside here. I had started to think that. Started to hope.

The sound of what was happening engulfed me. Cries and panting breaths. The smack of skin on skin, bone on bone. And smells. Familiar smells and tastes. The acrid coat of fear on my tongue. The bitter metal of hot blood. The man cried out and the crowd went wild. First blood.

Riana's breath fell faster. "Oh, my," she sighed, awe hugging her words. "Would you look at that?" The sound of flesh and sinew tearing from bone brought bile surging to my mouth. "He's still alive."

This girl disgusted me. She spoke of a brutal world and yet she had experienced none of it herself. She merely sat back and observed it with sick delight. They all did. Every man in this room did. The air seethed with bloodlust, and suddenly I didn't know who the animals were—the dwellers or the men watching?

Was the king watching? The prince? My stomach knotted. I couldn't stand it anymore. I started to back away.

Quick as a whip, Riana grabbed my wrist. Her grip was surprisingly strong for a pampered lady. She wasn't like Maris, I realized. She was strong, as raw-boned as Digger and any other predator I'd met on the Outside. "What's amiss, princess? No stomach for it?"

I shook my head. "Let me go."

"Oh, come now. Don't be reticent. You certainly weren't when it came to Prince Chasan. You laid claim to him quick enough."

"I'm not enjoying this," I panted from between clenched teeth. The sound of crunching bone drifted from the pit below. Dark dwellers were tearing him apart between them now.

"What's not to enjoy? The king and prince are enjoying the spectacle."

Her biting fingers were cutting off the blood in my arm.

"Stop," I hissed, thinking of the bishop's words right then . . . of his insistence that other people might want to harm me for taking the prince off the market. Clearly, this unhinged girl was one such person.

"Don't be squeamish. Have a closer look." She pulled me, using her greater weight to haul me right up to the edge.

"What are you doing—" The rest of my words died in a wash of panic as she shoved me with both hands.

I resisted, scrabbling for leverage, but it was too late. The force of her push sent me over the ledge. For one fleeting moment, I managed to grip the edge, my fingers curled tightly, clinging for life. Riana's balled-up fists slammed down on my fingers, and I was falling in a rush of wind.

I slammed down hard, pain vibrating through my body.

I was in the pit.

EIGHTEEN

Luna

THE IMPACT KNOCKED the breath out of me.

I forced my limbs to move. Pain buzzed along my nerves, making me agonizingly aware of the fact that I had just fallen from my perch like a felled bird with a broken wing. I was grounded, unable to fly away from this pit.

Scrambling to my feet, I braced my legs apart, readying myself in a fighting stance. And just like that it was me again, back in the Black Woods outside my tower. My hands opened and closed at my sides. *That* was the only difference, the fact that I did not hold a weapon. I had nowhere to run. My hands felt barren, empty. But I was not a novice at this. I wasn't some broken bird helpless before them. I was me.

The first dweller came at me, his feet dragging over the floor of the pit. The other one still worked, slavering over its victim. The man had ceased to cry out. He was past making a sound.

Dimly, I registered the shrieks and shouts from above—my own name was screamed, but I didn't respond to it. I focused all my attention on the dweller charging me.

I sidestepped the creature, whirling around and kicking it from behind, sending it face-first into the ground. I angled my head to the side, listening to the other one, marking it, verifying that it was still too preoccupied to come for me.

Satisfied, I jumped on top of the one I'd kicked to the ground as it was rising to all fours. Gripping it by the back of the head, I used the force of my body and slammed it into the ground. It wasn't the biggest dweller I had ever encountered, and for that I muttered a prayer of thanks.

Again and again I cracked its face into the stone floor of the pit, my fingers aching and bloodless from the strain of my grip. My arms trembled and burned from exertion, but I kept going. The smell of toxin soaked the air as the dweller's sensors burst against the ground.

I didn't stop. Even when the thing ceased to move I didn't stop. Maybe I was crazed or maybe I was just being careful. Sivo always said you could never be too careful. The careful, the cautious . . . they were the survivors.

"Look out!" This single scream stabbed my ears, rising over all other sounds. It was a male voice, deep and smooth as silk even at such decibels. I knew the voice . . . knew him. "Luna!"

Gasping, I spun around and fell onto my backside. I scrambled to get away, clawing the hard stone beneath me, my nails breaking and cracking under the pressure. The other dweller tore at the hem of my nightgown, grabbing my feet, my ankles, my calves as it worked its way up my body, sharp claws digging into me.

I resisted the urge to strike at it. One hit in the face could result in a bite. Even a drop of toxin could ruin me. Who was to say I would be as lucky or strong as Fowler and survive infection?

My legs writhed, working and kicking to get away. Suddenly there was a loud thump of feet landing in the pit with me.

"Luna!" Chasan's boots thundered toward me just as the dweller inched its solid weight over me. They were always heavier than they looked. Thick and dense with their gummy flesh.

I turned my face sideways, whimpering as its head hovered so close. I smelled the sticky-sweet toxin. Sensors swam in front of my face, disturbing the air. I wedged my hands between us, my hands sinking into its fleshy body as I tried to shove it away. This one was bigger. I couldn't budge it.

Suddenly I was free. The dweller was yanked off me. It released an inhuman grunt. There was a sucking wet sound as a blade penetrated doughy flesh.

The only sound was the gurgling flow of blood easing out of the dweller and onto the stone ground.

Footsteps rushed me. Hands snatched hold of my shoulders and pulled me to my feet. "Luna! Are you harmed? Luna!" Chasan shook me slightly.

I moved my head in some semblance of denial, shaking off my trance.

I smoothed trembling hands down the front of my nightgown, trying to reclaim my composure in the face of so many eyes on me. I felt all their stares, their astonishment. They didn't know what to make of me—a girl who fell into a pit and single-handedly, without a weapon, killed a dweller. I'd shown them the girl from the Black Woods. Now they knew her.

"What are you doing here? How did you—"

"I was pushed," I whispered past numb lips. "She pushed me." Disbelief tinged my voice. I still could not believe that anyone would do what she had done to me. Bad people existed on the Outside. I'd met them, confronted them . . . barely survived them. Bad people out there made more sense than in here, though. Desperate situations created those people, but in here all was well and right. No one should resort to such a thing.

"She pushed you? Who?" Outrage spiked his voice.

He was furious, and I realized that Riana's life would not be worth anything if I revealed what she had done. As terrible as she was, I did not want her death on my head, and I knew the king would react with such a punishment.

I bit my lip and shook my head. "No, nothing," I stammered. "I just fell."

"Fell?" He doubted me.

"That's right," I insisted.

"What are you even doing here?" he asked, apparently deciding not to push the point. "How did you find out about the pits?"

I shook from head to toe. From shock? Perhaps it was simply

a release from all the excitement, the near scrape with being dweller food. "Please. I just want to go back to my chamber now. I am quite weary."

His hands flexed on my arms, fingers splayed wide as though holding me together was holding him together, too. "Of course, of course. I understand. I'll escort you."

"No. You don't have to. Someone else can do that." I tried shrugging out of his grasp. I didn't want him near me. He might have jumped in the pit to help me, but he was a part of this. He was the one who went out and hunted dwellers and brought them back here for these sick demonstrations—for the titillation of haughty and overprivileged men. He designed these sick games where people lost their lives.

"Chasan! Come here!" the king called down from his perch. He did not sound happy. I wasn't sure if it was because I was here, because I had almost died, or because Chasan had risked himself to save me.

Chasan sighed heavily. His hands slipped from me, but he stepped closer, his breath fanning my cheek as he whispered, "We're not finished with this."

I shook my head swiftly, silently disputing that point. Yes, we were. We were finished. I was finished. With this. With him. This place.

A shrill scream shattered the air. If not for the floodgate of sobs that followed, I would have thought it belonged to another dweller.

Chasan cursed savagely.

"What? What is it?"

"Riana," he snapped. "Apparently she was the one who pushed you."

I swung my gaze toward where his father sat with others, listening to the sounds of Riana being dragged forward. Over her loud wails and pleas, another man's voice rose in supplication. "Please, Your Majesty! She's just a girl."

"An assault on the princess of Relhok is an assault on Lagonia," the king boomed over Riana's sobs, his hand slamming down on the arm of his chair. "I should have expected better from your daughter. You are both from Relhok. You failed to breed any loyalty into your daughter for your home country or Lagonia, which has served as a home to you these many years."

I jerked and grabbed Chasan's arm. "What will he do to her?"

A small tremor shook Chasan's body. It was gone as soon as I felt it, and for a moment I wondered if it had happened at all. Ignoring me, he peeled my hand from his arm and turned to address a guard who appeared at my side. "See her to her chamber. And send for a maid to attend to her. The physician, too, if need be—"

"No, wait! I'm not hurt," I interjected. My body ached from my fall, and I had no doubt tomorrow I would feel the effects of it all the more strongly, but I was fine. "You didn't answer me!"

He shoved me at the waiting guards, but I wouldn't relent. I snatched hold of his hand. "What's happening?" I demanded.

"Does it matter?" he snapped. "She tried to kill you. My

father won't forgive that." Even as he said it, frustration shook his voice. He didn't relish this.

"It matters," I whispered, my heart sinking.

"You know what has to happen," he replied just as I heard the hiss of steel on air. I knew that sound.

"No." I mouthed more than spoke the word.

"Get her out of here," Chasan growled at the guard.

"Yes, Your Highness." The guard started pulling me away just as Riana's sobs reached a fever pitch. Her own father was screaming now.

It was getting hard to breathe. A part of me wanted to flee, but another part of me, a larger part, had to stay.

"Now," the king commanded, the only calm and steady voice.

A sword whistled on the air. *Thunk.* I jumped with a gasp. The sound reverberated in the enclosed space. Something struck the ground with a thud and then rolled over the stone floor. It covered several feet in the sudden silence.

"Oh." I choked, bile rising in my throat, turning away as if I could see it all. The head severed from her body. The blood, the gore. The satisfied look on the king's face. None of this could I see, and yet I did in my mind.

The guard took my elbow again to escort me back to my chamber. This time I let him lead me. Shaking like the last brittle leaf clinging to a branch, I let him guide me away from the blood and death. Away from Chasan. Away from the pit. Away was all that mattered.

NINETEEN

Fowler

I LURCHED UPRIGHT in bed, a strangled cry lodged in my throat. I was a chronic light sleeper. My years on the Outside ensured that I never slept too deeply.

Something woke me.

Sweat soaked me and I kicked off my covers. I stretched out my arm, ignoring the dull ache, instinctively reaching for the bow that wasn't beside me anymore. My hand groped air. Finding nothing, my fingers curled into fists.

I swung my legs over the side of the bed, scanning the darkened bedchamber for my weapon, confirming that I was alone. Nothing lurked in the shadows.

And yet something had pulled me from sleep. That wasn't imaginary. My instincts weren't dead. I hadn't forgotten what it was like to be on the Outside. I hadn't dropped my guard. In fact, in here I felt more on edge—an animal caged.

My ears weren't as keen as Luna's, but they were sharp enough. At the thought of Luna, I expelled a breath. It felt like forever since I had last seen her. Maris told me she was busy. I knew she must be. Everyone would want a piece of her. They knew who she was now, and they must be filling her hours with all manner of court life. The king would want her to spend as much time as possible with his son. My hands clenched tighter, the joints cold and aching. They'd never let her go.

I heard it then—the sound that had woken me. A cry cut short almost as suddenly as it started. I knew the sound of a human in distress. A vibration of shock echoed in the sound. I knew about that, too. I'd heard it often enough before I arrived here, but it was different closed up inside these stone walls, where the air was stale and thin.

I moved to the door, determined to investigate. There was no sleep for me now. If someone was being hurt inside this castle, I had to find out what was happening.

The latch turned just as my hand landed on it. I pulled back, bracing myself. Dwellers didn't turn latches, but then that wasn't the only threat.

Lantern light spilled into the room as the door swung open. A flaxen head eased inside. "Fowler," a familiar voice whispered.

"Maris?" I lowered my arm, realizing at that moment that I

had cocked my arm back, ready to strike.

She grinned at me, looking from my knotted fist to my face. "Did I startle you?"

"You could say that."

"Oh." She shrugged, clearly unbothered. The girl didn't understand danger. "I just wanted to see you and say hello. Hello." She greeted me as though she wasn't standing in her nightgown in my chamber in the middle of the night, her hair loose and flowing all around her.

"What are you doing here?" I demanded. "You should be in bed."

She looked me up and down, not missing my rigidity. Those wide eyes of her blinked. "Would you really have struck me?"

I ignored the question. "What are you doing *here* in the middle of the night?" I clarified as though that would help get me an explanation. It wasn't seemly. We'd never been alone. She shouldn't be coming to my chamber without a chaperone.

"Were you already awake or did I wake you?" she asked, breathless, her gaze moving from my face and down, lingering on my bare chest. "I was hoping to wake you . . . surprise you, actually."

I eyed her nightgown with its frills and flounces, wondering precisely what kind of surprise she had planned. Shaking my head, I told myself it didn't matter. She could be naked in front of me and it wouldn't matter. Her virtue was safe from me.

I looked over her shoulder, searching the shadows of the corridor behind her. "Did you hear anything? A sound?"

She dragged her bright blue eyes from my chest back to my face. "I'm sure it was nothing. It's an old castle. The stone makes sounds sometimes. Or perhaps it was the wind."

"It wasn't stone settling or the wind. It sounded far away, but it was in the castle. Here in these walls."

She shook her head slightly, an emotion edging into her eyes that was at odds with her usual exuberance. "It was probably Cook butchering a hog."

I studied her, watching her smooth throat work to swallow. She was lying. "It wasn't a hog."

She shifted on her feet and glanced over her shoulder, looking uneasy. "Sometimes others stay up late carousing in private chambers. We all need our amusements."

I stepped closer, not above using my nearness to manipulate her. She had used every opportunity to touch me. I usually edged away, but this time I gave her what she wanted.

Life at court could be as tricky and dangerous as life on the Outside, and manipulation wasn't an unfamiliar practice. Pandering favor often determined fates. I knew that from being a part of my father's household. It would be no different here. For me, it was probably worse. At any time, for any reason, I could lose favor with the king, if I truly even had it. I might be betrothed to Princess Maris, but that would not keep me from getting my throat cut if Tebald so chose.

I brushed a silky blond lock of hair off her shoulder. She released a tiny gasp, leaning into my touch. "Why are you lying to me, Maris?" I whispered. "Clever girl like you, you know everything that goes on in this castle."

Her lips worked before speech found her. "There are all kinds of things you hear at night in this castle. Best to ignore them."

"Tell me, Maris."

"Don't go snooping around, Fowler." For the first time she didn't look so much like a little girl. She looked nervous. I dropped my hand, suddenly feeling wrong about touching her and using her feelings.

She leaned forward like she wanted to chase that hand. "Go back to bed, Maris," I ordered. "You shouldn't be here."

"And why shouldn't I?" She took a step forward, until our bodies practically touched. "We're to be married. What's wrong with us being together now?"

By that logic, nothing. Nothing was wrong with it.

Except we wouldn't marry.

Very soon, she would wake up and I would be gone. Contrary to what I told Tebald, I wasn't about to live out my father's plans and wed Maris.

She pressed a fingertip above my heart and trailed it down my chest. Emotion burned in her eyes as she gazed at me. I couldn't take what she was offering me. I wouldn't be that big of a bastard. Life was hard, full of disappointment and loss. She hadn't experienced much yet, but she would. I'd rather not be the one to deliver her that education.

I set my hands on her shoulders and moved her back from me, setting her very deliberately outside my bedchamber door.

"Go to your chamber, Maris."

Something sparkled in her eyes that should have warned me. Defiance? Determination. She stood on her tiptoes and circled one hand around my neck. Leaning forward, she clumsily pressed her lips to mine.

I placed my hands on her arms and gently tried to push her away from me. She clung, her hand tightening on my neck and her lips mashing harder to mine with a mewl of determination. My eyes were still open as I struggled to break the kiss in the most sensitive way possible. I didn't need to overly wound her ego. The last thing I wanted to do was to send her crying to her father about me. Tebald already didn't trust me. One look in his eyes and I knew that, but I needed him to think I was agreeable to this marriage. I needed Maris on my side. At least until I was gone . . . and then I wouldn't care.

From the corner of my eye I caught a glimpse of movement. With a little more urgency, I gave a final push and set Maris away from me to look down the corridor. Luna and a guard stood a few yards away.

The guard chuckled, looking us up and down with a lecherous grin. "Getting a head start on the wedding night, eh?"

Maris gasped and released a small breathy giggle. "Mind your tongue, guard," she reprimanded without any real heat.

The guard's smile vanished from his face. "My apologies, Your Highness," he said, his tone at once circumspect.

Luna made a small strangled sound. Myriad emotions crossed her face. "Fowler?"

I stepped forward, extending a hand as though to touch her. "Luna . . ." My voice faded at the sight of her taking a sudden step back. She angled her head, staring at me in that uncanny way of hers. As if she could in fact *see* me.

The betrayal was there, written all over her face. Of course she'd heard that kiss. Luna heard everything. Of course she misread the situation. She thought it was mutual.

"Luna." I tried again for speech and then stopped short, glancing uneasily at Maris and the guard. I couldn't very well reveal that I had been a victim of Maris's advances. If I upset her, she would run to her father, and I didn't need to alert him to the fact that I wasn't receptive to marrying his daughter. He could figure that out the day he woke to find me gone.

Maris returned my stare, pressing her fingertips to her lips, looking up at me beneath her eyelashes with a very coquettish expression.

"It's good to have you up on your feet again, Fowler," Luna said, her voice that of a stranger.

"Isn't it?" Maris chimed in, smoothing a hand against my chest possessively, intimately.

I looked back and forth between the guard and Luna, noting she wasn't dressed properly. Were those tears in the white fabric of her nightgown? I took a step closer. "Luna, is anything amiss? Why are you up from bed?"

"Nothing to fret over. Just a little squabble with a dweller."

"What?" Immediately tense, I looked around as if one of the creatures might suddenly jump out at us.

"Yes. It appears that's what they do for entertainment around here. Throw victims into a pit for dwellers to eat."

My gaze shot to Maris. "Is this true?"

"I-I . . . it has nothing to do with me. Father and the other men enjoy it . . . for sport, you know."

"No. I don't know," I growled, thinking of the risk involved with bringing dwellers into the castle. It was stupid and unnecessary. Luna could have died. And who were the chosen victims anyway? What did they do to deserve such a fate?

Maris must have read some of the emotions on my face. She added a second hand to my chest, her voice softly cajoling, "It doesn't have to remain that way. When you and I are wed, we can change things. Make them better here. However you like."

Nothing appealed to me less than staying here and fighting for change in this place where I didn't want to be. Not to mention Maris was a little naïve if she thought I would ever be given any power. Even if her father was no longer a consideration, Chasan was. He would be king next. He wouldn't roll over for his sister or me. No one would be making changes without Chasan's consent.

Recalling what Luna had said, I demanded, "Wait. You said you had a squabble with a dweller?"

"Um. I happened to fall in."

"You *fell* in?" I looked her up and down, searching for injuries. She turned her face away and I knew there was more to the story than that. "Are you hurt?"

"I'm fine. Just a few bruises. Nothing like the poor man those dwellers butchered, and nothing you should worry about." This last she said with pointed antagonism. Her message was clear. I shouldn't care about her. My jaw locked hard. It was too late for that. She wasn't going to get her way in this. We'd come too far, I was in too deep to give up on her.

Chin lifted at a haughty angle, Luna turned to the guard. "I'm weary. Let us go."

They continued, moving away from me. I watched, helpless to pursue her with Maris watching, her hands still locked on me like she would never let go.

TWENTY

Luna

I WAS ALMOST to my bedchamber door when steps sounded behind us. I turned, my heart racing, treacherous hope stirring inside me that it was Fowler, that he had turned away from his princess and come after me. Pathetic, especially knowing he was clearly invested in a relationship with Princess Maris, but I couldn't force my heart to feel any differently.

"Leave us," Prince Chasan's voice bit out to the guard beside me.

"Yes, Your Highness."

I opened my mouth to protest as the guard left me, but warm fingers circled my wrist and tugged me inside my chamber.

"Prince Chasan," I gasped. "What are you doing? You shouldn't be here. This isn't seemly."

The door clicked shut behind us, sealing us in, and a bolt of alarm slithered down my spine. "What were you doing at the pits?"

"I heard the screams."

"And you followed the sound? How could you have thought that a good idea?"

I inhaled sharply. "You know we're avoiding the more important matter."

"And what is that?" he challenged, still holding my arm. I gave it several yanks and he finally released me.

"Why?" I demanded, rubbing my arm where he had gripped me. "How can you stand there and cheer and place bets as a person is torn to pieces in front of you? And then you just let your father execute that girl—Riana! What's wrong with you? With all of you?" I knew bad people and horribleness existed on the Outside, but in here it should have been different. It was that belief that had started breaking me down and convincing me that I could do this. Stay here. Be a wife to someone I didn't know. Forget Fowler . . . as he had apparently forgotten me.

Chasan didn't reply. I heard nothing beyond the hard rhythm of his breath.

Emotion welled up in my throat as I thought about the man who had died tonight, the sound of his cries, the noise his bones made as the dwellers tore him apart. And the thud of Riana's head. Her father's scream.

"Say nothing." I nodded fiercely. "There is not an excuse, not a defense you can offer." I swallowed past the lump in my throat. "I can't marry such a person."

"No?" he quickly retorted, his voice ruthless as a whip. "And who might you marry, Luna?" His voice twisted into something hard and mean. "Your precious Fowler? I just passed him in the hall with my sister. I'm sure you saw them, too. Quite the cozy pair."

He knew exactly where I was the most tender and bruised and he struck me there with a well-aimed blow. "I needn't marry anyone," I flung out.

"If you think that, then you really are a fool. You think you can go against my father? He will never let you leave this place, and if you don't do what he asks you'll be spending the rest of your days as a guest in our dungeon. Or worse."

His words bubbled like toxin in my veins. I cranked back my arm and struck him in the chest with my balled-up fist. "Is that why you hunt dwellers? Because your father demands it? Is that why you capture them and bring them back here? You do it because he tells you to? What else do you do that he demands? Oh, that's right! You marry lost princesses."

"Luna, stop."

"Tell me, Chasan, who are those people that have to die for your amusements? What have they done to deserve that?"

"They've made an enemy of my father . . . of Lagonia."

I shook my head. "I don't want this. I don't want to be here. I'm not a part of this world where you butcher people. You're a coward." I turned away, but he grabbed me and hauled me back to face him.

He gave me a small shake, snapping my head back to focus on him. "You *are* a part of it. No matter what you want. You're going to be a part of it and you'll say nothing to the contrary unless you want to bring the wrath of my father down on you, and trust me, that's not something you want. Understand?"

My breath fell in hard pants.

"Say you understand me, Luna." There was an edge of panic that I had never heard before in his liquid-smooth voice. "Say it," he insisted, chasing the words with another shake. "I won't have you hurt. I can't."

His words, as much unsaid as said, deflated my anger. "You're afraid of him," I whispered.

"He's a monster," he admitted, dropping his hands from my arms, and for the first time I considered that. I considered him. I thought about what it must be like to be brought up by such a man . . . how trapped you must feel when your own father was a nightmare you had to face each and every day. *Not that different from Fowler.*

We stood in silence for a long moment, only our breaths between us. He closed the space, his bigger body radiating heat and vitality as it crept toward me. "We don't have to live in fear forever. We just need to hold on, Luna." His forehead dropped to mine, fingers flexing on my arms. "We just have to wait it out."

Wait for Tebald to die. That was what he was saying. We had to wait until he was no longer in power and we could take over.

"You have a good heart, Luna," he continued, his voice insinuating into my spinning thoughts. "Better than my own. Better than anyone I've ever met before. You want to do the right thing even if it hurts you. Only I don't want you to be hurt." His lips ghosted over mine. I gasped at the brush of contact.

I didn't have time to pull away from his almost-kiss. It was over as quickly as it had begun, but I still felt a tight clench low in my stomach. Regret whispered through me. I could have kicked myself for the weak thought. Why should I feel loyalty to Fowler when he had already forgotten about me?

"I want to try to be more like you, Luna. Together, with you, I think I can. *We* could be good together. We could be good for Lagonia *and* Relhok."

His words wove through me, a seductive spell sinking deep. Could he mean that? I weighed the possibility. Relhok and Lagonia united, without Cullan or Tebald at the helm. The black eclipse and its dwellers would still exist, but things wouldn't have to be so hopeless.

Marriage to Chasan meant not living for myself, but it also meant making a difference in the lives of others. I could make this world a better place. Wasn't that what Sivo and Perla had groomed me to do? They had believed that was my fate. They taught me to believe it, too.

"I can see you're thinking about it, Luna." His hands fell to his sides with a whisper. I nodded once, relieved at the distance between us so that I could think without his hands touching me. "Good. Consider it. You have time. A little time," he amended.

However much time his father would give us.

He moved away toward the door, his steps soft and steady in the great expanse of my room. "We'll talk again soon."

Then I was alone in the pulsing silence of my bedchamber with only my clamoring thoughts for company.

TWENTY-ONE

Fowler

IT TOOK A little longer than I'd hoped to disengage myself from Maris and send her on her way to her own bedchamber. She was tenacious. I would give her that. She had been waiting all her life for me. Not me specifically, but the prince she had been promised. There was a distinction. She didn't know *me*. She didn't care to know me, and she certainly didn't love me. I was merely the prize that had been dangled before her nose all these years. Now that I was here she did not know the meaning of self-control.

I eased out from my chamber, headfirst, relieved to see that there was no guard at my door and no one in the corridor. I crept along, heading in the direction I had last seen Luna and her escort take. I listened at doors, hoping for any indication of which room might be hers.

A door creaked open somewhere ahead of me and I ducked to the side, flattening against the other side of a beam that jutted out from the wall. Peering around the post, I watched as Chasan stepped out of a room and into the corridor. He turned back to look inside the bedchamber before closing the door. In that moment I glimpsed Luna standing a few feet from the threshold, staring in his general direction as he left her.

What was Chasan doing in her room? A wave of helplessness washed over me at the possibility that I was too late, that she had already changed her mind about me.

I gave myself a hard mental shake. She had just happened upon Maris outside my bedchamber. I had no right to these feelings. Jealousy, annoyance . . . the dark impulse to grab Chasan and stomp all over him wasn't something I could give in to. It wasn't something I wanted to feel.

The prince turned and I quickly pressed myself against the wall, pressing hard into the stone, trying to make myself invisible. Chasan passed by without glancing left, then turned the corner.

With a deep breath I collected myself and stepped away from the wall. I strode to Luna's room, determination fueling me. I couldn't be too late.

I knocked once lightly, so as not to frighten her, and then walked inside.

She whirled around as I shut the door behind me. There was a flash of panic on her face, and I hated that I made her feel that way. For all she knew I was a stranger storming into her room.

She sucked in a deep breath—hopefully not to scream—and the alarm subsided from her features. By scent or sound, she knew it was me.

"What are you doing in here?"

"Does Chasan visit your room in the middle of the night regularly?" I couldn't help myself. The ugly beast that had stirred inside me when I spotted him leaving her room insisted on surfacing.

"I don't know. Does Maris visit yours?"

I sighed. "That wasn't what it looked like." I stared at her, waiting for her to offer me the same reassurance. It never came. She crossed her arms over her chest and cocked one eyebrow.

I rocked back on my heels, fighting down the impulse to demand why Chasan was in her room as though it was my right to know. It was a battle lost. "Why was he here?"

"Are you truly asking me that?" Indignation hung on every word. Her implication was clear: How could I ask that after she'd just found me with Maris?

"Chasan is *not* Maris. He's no harmless suitor. He is as manipulative and cunning as his father." And I'd seen the way he looked at Luna.

"Is that so? And how often have you seen him exactly? Talked to him? You've scarcely risen from your sickbed, where Maris attends you ever so diligently."

"I've seen it in his eyes. I know his sort."

She inhaled swiftly, pulling her shoulders back, and I knew I had said the wrong thing. I hadn't meant to make it sound like I viewed her as *less* in any way because of her blindness, but that was precisely what I had done. "Oh, that's right. I'm merely a blind girl. I can't possibly be a good judge of character."

The word *merely* couldn't be applied Luna. Not in any way. She would always be everything. Of course, if I were to tell her that right now, she wouldn't believe me.

Sighing, I dragged a hand through my hair. "I didn't come here to fight with you."

"You shouldn't have come here at all."

"Oh, I shouldn't, but it's acceptable for Chasan to visit you in the middle of the night?"

"He wanted to make sure I was all right after what happened. He saved my life tonight."

He saved her life? It made me resent him all the more. I should have been there for her. I didn't want to think she might need him. "You don't even know him," I shot back.

"He's my betrothed," she replied evenly, but there was a stiffness to her voice that was impossible to miss.

I froze. Hearing this from her curdled my blood. "Is that true? You'll marry him?" My heart raced at the possibility that she had accepted this as her fate.

"Is that not the expectation?"

Not precisely an answer. "I've never cared much about the expectations of others." Nor had I thought she cared. I'd imagined that she'd be eager to leave this place. But if I were to believe her now, she wouldn't be leaving with me.

She snorted and edged even farther away from me. "I just caught you kissing Maris, and here you stand wanting me to define my relationship with Chasan." She flung out her words like a well-aimed arrow and tsked. "Hardly reasonable."

"*She* kissed *me*." The truth, but it rang weakly even to my ears.

Luna released a huff of hollow laughter and shook her head, clearly not impressed with my excuse. "You don't owe me an explanation. I don't own your lips."

My chest swelled on a tense breath. "You know how I feel about you. I haven't hid my feelings—"

"Fowler, don't."

"We need to talk," I insisted, following her retreating form across the room. She used to listen to me, but now she felt distant.

She continued backing away from me, cocking her head at a wary angle. "If you are found in here—"

"They're keeping us apart." I stayed dogged in my pursuit of her, my steps biting into the plush rug covering the stone floor. "You have to see that. Since we arrived here. They don't want us alone together."

She shrugged, twisting her hands into the voluminous fabric of her nightgown. "It matters not. There's nothing we have to say to each other worth risking their displeasure—"

"Risking *their* displeasure? Do you hear yourself? You sound frightened . . . beaten. Where is the Luna that I know?"

"Maybe you don't know me. Maybe you never did. I certainly don't know you." Her chest lifted high on a quick inhalation. I knew she was thinking about me standing in the corridor with Maris, and regret stabbed me in the chest.

"You're wrong." I stepped forward and touched her face. She flinched but didn't pull back. I clung to that. I could still reach her. "Do you feel my gaze on you? Do you feel my heart, Luna? It's yours. It belongs to you. You *know* me." I added my other hand to her face, holding her as gently as a bird in my hands, careful not to crush her wings.

Moisture gathered in her ink-dark eyes. Her voice came out in a hoarse whisper. "I thought I did. I don't blame you for your birth. I'm not angry about that anymore. It's not your fault who your father is. But that doesn't change the fact that I still don't know you. I don't know what it is that truly drives you, I don't know why you're running from your father, I don't know why you're agreeable to staying here, to marrying Maris—"

"You. *You* drive me. It didn't used to be that way. I can't explain exactly when or how it became that way. But that's the way it is."

She didn't speak for some time, various emotions flickering across her face. She looked down at the ground as though she felt the weight of my stare and needed to escape it. "What?" I asked. "What are you thinking? Tell me, Luna. Talk to me."

She gave a slight shake of her head. "Maris—"

"Means nothing to me," I finished for her. "I know how it

sounded. It's how I need it to look."

"What are you saying? You don't really want to stay here and marry—"

"I'm saying that we're getting out of here. I'm saying that we can still go to Allu. It's not some hopeless, distant dream. We can be together, Luna, but they have to believe we want to be here. They have to believe we're content, and when they don't suspect it, we escape."

The longest pause followed. Bleakness crossed her face. "What of Relhok? My kingdom? If neither one of us marries into the royal family of Lagonia, then we leave Relhok to Cullan. I don't know if I can do that. I know weeks ago I thought I could." She gave a slight shrug. "I thought the dream of Allu was the only thing that mattered, but now . . ."

Frustration bubbled up inside me. How much of herself would she give? How much would she sacrifice? She was still willing to give up everything for a country she didn't even know.

I refused to let her do that.

I pressed on, desperate to reach her. "Why are you so tied to Relhok? You have no memory of it." I shook my head. She bit her lip, clearly conflicted. "Do you so badly want to be a queen that you would marry a stranger?"

"It's not that," she shot back quickly, hot color flooding her face. "I'm not that shallow or power hungry. That's never what I wanted. If you claim to know me, you should know that much!"

"Then what is it? Tell me, Luna. Because I cannot stay here and watch you marry him."

The moisture in her eyes pooled and spilled over, dripping down those pale freckled cheeks. I swiped at the tears with my thumbs. When they didn't stop, I leaned in and pressed my mouth over each cheek, kissing the salty tracks with far more restraint than I felt. The need to grab her and crush her to me, pull her inside myself, was overwhelming. I'd never felt this before.

"My father knows you're alive," I whispered hoarsely, pausing to let that sink in, hoping she fully understood what I was saying. "Have you considered what that means?"

She took a sip of air. Her mouth was so close, damp from tears and that sweet dew that clung to her. "It means the kill order on girls is lifted. That's the only thing that matters."

"You know what I'm saying." My thumbs pressed a fraction deeper, as though I could will her to acknowledge it to me. "There is no way he would let you live now. He'll be sending someone. An assassin, soldiers, an entire army. You're a threat to his crown. He cannot let your claim go uncontested. We cannot stay here. Even if we wanted to, it's not possible."

"You make it sound so easy." She rubbed at the center of her forehead as though she was feeling the beginnings of a headache. I felt a twinge of guilt. She had just survived an encounter with dwellers, and here I was hounding her, demanding she agree to put her life in my hands and escape this place with me. But if she didn't agree, she'd likely die here. Nowhere near Tebald was safe. He was a ruthless tyrant. And my father would eventually come for her. Even dwellers wouldn't stop him.

"We will need a strategy, but we can break out of here."

She fell to silence again. She was thinking, stewing. She took a shuddery breath and finally spoke. "I have to confess something."

Unease gripped my chest. "What?"

"I never intended to stay here." She stopped and took a deep breath. "Well, I never considered it for longer than a moment or two."

My chest loosened. "Oh. Then why are we arguing—"

"I was planning to escape . . . except without you."

Without you.

I stared at her for a moment, still holding her face even as she uttered those words that stabbed my heart. She was going to escape without me. Again. Damn it all. I suppose I should be used to her pushing me away at this point, but it would never feel good. I would never be immune to it.

A bleak kind of fury burned through me. I dropped my hands from her face and all that velvet skin, practically flinging her from me.

"Again?" I accused.

She nodded. "I knew if you stayed and married the princess, Relhok would be assured some kind of ruler that was just and good."

"You think that would be *assured*? Ha! Marrying Maris doesn't change the fact that my father still sits on the throne."

"But not forever," she argued.

I shook my head. "Assuming my bastard father dies tomorrow, Tebald would then reign over both kingdoms. After him, it would be his son. And as far as I can tell, Chasan is every bit as ruthless as his sire."

She paled. Clearly, she hadn't thought this through enough. Doubt crossed her expressive face. "I just thought that with you here your influence would do some good." Her voice faded. Her chin shot up, fire in her cheeks. "You're right. I was wrong."

The tension in my shoulders ebbed. Finally, she was starting to see things my way.

Then, she added, "But Cullan still has to be stopped."

"We can escape together and forget about all of this. We'll build a life in Allu. You and me." It was strange to think that weeks ago I had only ever wanted to be alone, but now I couldn't imagine life without her in it.

She dropped her head, hiding her face so that I couldn't see her clearly.

"Luna," I whispered. She made me crazy and reckless. I reached for her, closed my fingers around her arms, and pulled her to me. As though I could somehow absorb her into myself... remind her what it was like between us. Remind myself. The reality of what it felt like to hold her in my arms had dimmed.

She faced me, her expression set into something grim. "I'll escape with you, but I'm going to Relhok. With or without you."

I kissed her, drinking in her sigh rather than arguing with her anymore. Maybe a part of me hoped to influence her, seduce her, get her to say she would go anywhere with me, but I had forgotten what kissing her was like. The first brush of her lips seduced me.

Pulling back, I held her face, skimming her features, engraving them into my soul. I waited, giving her time to pull away if that was what she really wanted.

She didn't pull back. Her fingers circled my wrists, tugging me back to her, so I kissed her again, drove my fingers into her shorn hair, curving my palms around her skull. Her pulse bled into me through the connection of our mouths, the rhythm passing through my palms.

I had ceased all thinking and let sensation take over. The back of my neck pulled tight, goose bumps breaking out over my skin and chasing all the way down my body. A heavy tightness pooled low in my spine as we backed up together. I didn't look up. All my focus was on her mouth. Her scent. The callused pads on her small palms. I vaguely registered a slight bump as we reached the bed.

Then we were on the bed, and all the desperation, all the near scrapes spiraled into this need for each other. We had overcome every impossibility and were still alive and still together. Maybe it couldn't last, maybe it wouldn't, but for now we had this.

Solitude. Hands. Mouths. Warm lantern light gilded her skin as I peeled the edge of her nightgown down to reveal a smooth shoulder. She sighed at my mouth skimming her skin, and then her hands were in my hair, her nails lightly scraping through strands and reaching my scalp, sending shivers up and down my neck.

I inched back slightly, just to look at her, to see her beneath me. Her features so soft, her pale skin flushed pink over the smatter of freckles. I was breathing hard as she brought her fingers to my lips, touching, tracing the shape. I kissed each one; her palm, her wrist, the back of her knuckles.

"Luna, how do you taste like this?" I breathed against her skin, my tongue licking, savoring her flesh.

She sighed in response, and I brought my mouth to hers again, kissing her harder. Her lips slanted against mine hotly, searing me. She knew how to kiss, how to affect me. Our breaths crashed and collided. Her hands moved faster, skimming my arms, my back, dipping lower.

My heart hammered like a wild bird in my chest. Everything felt new. With Luna it was love. It spiked my need, made everything more desperate, more feverish. She thought she didn't need this. Need me.

Everything flew faster then. Hushed words, groping hands, dragging mouths. I tried to hold back, thinking I was too rough, moving too fast, but she nipped at my lips with a growl and then all was lost. I was lost.

There was nothing but sliding skin and smell and taste. The sound of my name on her lips. Her nails scoring my flesh. Her warm breath in my ear.

I buried my hands in her hair, massaging her scalp, holding her to me and kissing her until my lips grew bruised and swollen. I pulled back, watching her, not missing the dark heat in her eyes. Her fingers dug into my shoulders and my name rasped on her lips in a way that lit a fire in my gut.

I settled my weight into the warm cocoon of her body, swallowing her kiss, her moan. *Her.* I thought I was flying out of my skin. She did that to me . . . made me feel like I was soaring. Like I was free.

TWENTY-TWO

Luna

I LAY ON my back, Fowler's arms loosely wrapped around me. I could smell his skin, clean and musky beside me. I knew he would have to go soon. The castle would wake and a maid would come to my room. It wouldn't do for her to find Fowler here. That would create a whole new set of problems we hoped to avoid. Even knowing this, I snuggled deeper into his arms.

His fingers trailed through my hair, which ended near my ears. It still felt strange that it was so short. Each time Fowler started at the roots and stroked his way down the strands I was reminded that it was gone. Fitting, I supposed. That girl was gone, too.

"It bothers me that you think you don't know me." His voice rumbled beside me. I flinched slightly.

"I was angry when I said that."

"Because if you don't know me then no one does. And that matters now. Someone has to know me or it's as though I'm not even here. I don't exist."

I inhaled and released my breath in a steady stream. It felt good to hear him say that. When I first met him, he didn't care about what happened to anyone . . . even himself. He didn't want to care about me. He definitely didn't want to love me. But he did. I ran a finger down the center of his chest. "I know a way out of the castle."

His fingers ceased moving through my hair. He propped an elbow beside my head and hovered over me. "You what?"

A smile tempted my lips. "There's a hidden door in the kitchens leading out of the castle. At least that's what I was told." I knew I should maybe suspect the source, but she didn't have any reason to lie to me about that. I believed her. Or at least I believed it was worth investigating.

He laughed lightly and pressed his mouth to mine. Coming up for air, he murmured, "It shouldn't surprise me that you know this."

I looped my arms around his neck and said loftily, "Well, I did dive underground and rescue you from a horde of dwellers."

"Yes, you did, and now you found a way out of here. You can do anything, Luna."

"You're correct," I teased. "Don't forget that."

"Don't worry. I wouldn't be able to forget anything about you."

My smile faded. I wasn't the only girl he found unforgettable. There was another one. Another girl he couldn't forget. I moistened my lips, deciding it was time to ask him. After everything we'd been through, after tonight, if I couldn't say what was on my mind then I was a coward.

I finally got the words out. "Tell me about Bethan."

His hand stilled, and I tensed in the stretch of silence, every moment that passed convincing me he wasn't going to say anything. Or he was going to change the subject. Disappointment weighed on me.

"I—I've never talked about it." He gave a brief, humorless laugh. "Not that I've had a slew of friends since I left Relhok. It's only that sometimes . . . the guilt . . . well, it eats at me."

"Guilt? Why do you feel guilty?"

He took his time before answering. His voice rumbled out of the dark. "Bethan died because of me. For weeks she wanted to run away to find the Isle of Allu. She believed in every story she ever heard of it. It was all she could talk about. She wanted to flee. She was so frightened of staying in Relhok City, but I wouldn't listen. I thought we had time . . ."

"Why was she frightened to stay there?" In my mind, the walls surrounding Relhok had to offer some comfort. More protection than anything to be found in the Outside.

"She was afraid of my father. She knew he didn't approve of us. And she was afraid of the lottery. Every fortnight, my father sacrificed a human to the dwellers." His pained sigh wormed its way inside me, making me shudder. "I should have listened. She was right. My father wasn't going to permit me to love anyone that did not benefit him. It was simple enough to rig the lottery so that her name was pulled. I couldn't stop him. I couldn't save her."

His words echoed around us in the vastness of my room. A swell of silence rose between us before I said, "You can't blame yourself for the actions of others. Your father is guilty. Not you."

He sighed again. "I know that. It's taken me a while to accept it, but I do know that. That's not why I feel so guilty."

"It's not?" I pulled back slightly, not understanding.

"No."

"Then why do you feel guilty?"

"She asked me to go and I couldn't. I didn't." He took a breath, his fingers moving through my hair again, sifting through strands and making me melt against him. "But you . . . you could ask me anything and I would do it, Luna. For you, I would do anything. For that, I feel guilty." My heart constricted at his confession. "I feel more for you than I've felt for anyone."

Words abandoned me. All those jealous, selfish thoughts I'd had about this mystery girl made me feel small and shamed. She was dead. I had no right to begrudge her relationship with Fowler. Just as I had no right to feel so elated over Fowler's admission.

Since I couldn't say anything, I did what I could. I kissed him.

TWENTY-THREE

Fowler

Now that I was permitted to leave my bed, I conducted a discreet reconnaissance of the palace over the next couple of days. Maris was my constant shadow, but that didn't stop me from assessing, weighing options, and considering the best way for Luna and me to get to the kitchens undetected.

I was learning the layout of the palace under the guise of strolls with Maris. The number of guards, the number of servants; the patterns and routines of everyone inside these walls were becoming as known to me as the back of my hand. I had to know this place and all its comings and goings—especially as they pertained to the kitchens. We'd have only one chance.

There could be no surprises.

Luna and I hadn't had an opportunity to talk alone since I was in her room two nights before. I fought to keep my distance, not trusting myself to keep my feelings for her buried. Just as Maris was always near me, Chasan hovered close to her side.

And yet everything had changed between us. I didn't need to say a word around her to know this. She knew it, too. She sensed whenever I was nearby. Her features would soften. The glow in her skin hinted at secrets. Her lips would fight smiles when she heard my voice or when I brushed a hand against her arm or hip. Casual touches no one would notice. But she knew, and so did I.

At night, I lay awake, my brain busy dreaming of Luna and contemplating our escape. If we left undetected, whilst everyone slept, we could have several hours' lead.

Even when I should have been sleeping and storing my strength, I could only think. I fought the urge to sneak into her room again. Once was risky enough. I couldn't dare it again. Instead I was left remembering what it was like to hold her, kiss her. She was my first taste of water after a long drought.

A hand waved in front of my eyes. "Hello? Are you in there, Fowler?"

I started and looked down at Maris beside me. Her hand rested snugly on my arm as I escorted her into the great hall. All a necessary subterfuge, I reminded myself. The king looked on with approval when we were together. Had it been me walking solo all over the castle, I was certain I would be viewed with suspicion.

"My apologies. You were saying?" She always *said* a great deal, mostly about our upcoming nuptials and our future together. It was hard to focus when her mouth was going.

"Woolgathering again," she mused. "Is this what I should expect in our future? You daydreaming as I chatter on?" She smiled, but there was something in her eyes, an edge to her smile, that warned me she was annoyed. In that moment she reminded me of her father. She wasn't as dim-witted as I'd first judged her. She sensed I didn't reciprocate her level of interest, and she didn't like it.

I forced a smile and covered her hand with my own, giving it a squeeze of reassurance. "Still feeling lethargic from my injury, I suppose. Nothing a nap wouldn't help rectify."

I stifled a wince at the completely inane words. I needed to keep her content. If she wasn't happy, she could go to her father, and I didn't need the king scrutinizing me, questioning my true commitment to Maris and Lagonia while I was still here.

She nodded in sympathy, but something lurked in her eyes. She wasn't convinced. "Of course. Father and I were discussing when we should take our vows. Contrary to all the jests about a double wedding, I'm feeling rather selfish. I want my wedding day to myself." She pushed out her bottom lip and shrugged with a decided lack of remorse. "I deserve that, don't I?"

"Am I invited?" I joked.

She swatted my arm with a tinkle of laughter. "Of course, silly. I meant *our* wedding. How does next week sound? That should be enough time to plan a proper feast. I already have my gown. I've had it for some time in anticipation of this day."

Of course she did. She'd been waiting for this day her whole life.

She fanned her fingers against my cheek, nails scraping lightly over my jaw. "You don't have to do a thing." She leaned across the space between us and kissed my cheek. "I cannot wait to be your bride," she whispered.

"Next week," I echoed, my mind working, plotting, as I stared down the table where Luna sat beside Chasan.

Maris nodded, her hand drifting.

"It won't be soon enough. Next week sounds fine," I agreed.

Luna and I would be gone by then.

The smell of the onions that had gone into the evening's rich stew lingered in the air as we crept through the kitchen.

Everyone was asleep at this hour. Servants either exhausted from a long day of labor or nobles comfortable in their beds, sated from too much food and drink.

A fire crackled in the hearth. Several kitchen maids slept before its warmth, gentle snores weaving on the air. I led the way, Luna behind me, skimming her hand over the wall and surfaces until we reached the room that smelled of dry goods. I'd observed it briefly when Maris gave me a tour of the castle days ago. Lifting the latch, I eased inside, ushering Luna ahead of me. Carefully, I shut the door behind us.

Letting go of Luna, I examined the storeroom floor.

"Is this the room?" she whispered.

"We're about to find out." I set to work, dragging baskets of goods and boxes of supplies to the far sides of the room. A rough straw rug covered the floor, coated with a thick layer of dust and soot. If there was a hidden door underneath, it didn't look as though it had been used in a long time. I flung the rug to the far end of the room, sending a storm of dirt up into the air. Coughing, I waved aside the particles and stared at an iron grate. I unbolted it and lifted the heavy door, flipping it over and easing it down carefully so that it didn't bang.

Standing, I reached for Luna's hand, folding it in my own, the sensation of her slim, cool fingers spreading warmth through my chest. I stared down at the grate of the storeroom floor, flexing my hand around hers.

"It's here," I said unnecessarily, looking at the jagged hole that opened up out of the stone floor. It was dark down there, a yawning hole that brought to memory the time when dwellers had dragged me underground.

"It's cold in there," Luna whispered beside me, peering down into the hole as though she could see into its depths.

Tendrils of cool air reached up and brushed at my hands. I adjusted the satchel I'd packed full of food and supplies, stroking my thumb along the inside of her wrist with my free hand, as much to comfort me as her. She sent me a brave smile, adjusting the bow slung over her shoulder. A gift from Chasan, she had said when I asked where she got it. I resisted the impulse to demand she leave it behind. As a weapon it was useful. I was armed with the sword and bow they had seen fit to return to me—which meant no one suspected I would do something like this. They thought I was perfectly content to marry their princess and be their puppet.

But the fact remained—it belonged to her. I had no right to tell her what to do with it.

"It will warm up once we're Outside."

She nodded. "Let's get moving."

I released her hand. "I'll go down first. There's a ladder built into the side wall." I climbed down, slipping my hands and feet into the carved handholds. I glanced up as I descended, watching her pale face shrink. I wasn't to the bottom yet when I paused. "Go ahead and start down," I instructed.

She slid her legs over the side. Once she found her first foothold, she began climbing down. The temperature continued to drop as we descended. The hole went deep, as though we were sliding into the very bowels of the earth. I almost expected to hear dwellers, their eerie screams bouncing off the tunnel walls. That ear-shattering scream Luna and I had heard, the one that had distracted all the other dwellers and saved our lives, could probably be heard even this far away. I wonder if Luna still heard that scream in her dreams like I did. Did she wonder what was on the other side of it?

The darkness swallowed us whole, but we kept going. After several minutes, we finally reached the bottom.

She dropped down beside me and chafed her hands up and down her arms as we stood there for a moment, acclimating to the ice-cold space.

Taking her hand, I started down the tunnel. Taking a cue from Luna, I skimmed a palm along the cold rock wall. She shivered at my back and I gave her fingers a squeeze. It was good to touch her again. If it wasn't so cold, if urgency didn't pound like a hammer inside me, I'd pull her into my arms and taste her again. But there wasn't time for that now. Soon. When we were someplace safe, where I could kiss her and convince her to forget about going to Relhok.

We moved quickly. I was counting on no one discovering we'd escaped until morning. The kitchen staff woke before everyone else to start preparations for the morning meal. They would discover the open grate in the storage room and alert the soldiers, but we'd be gone by then. I started a light jog. Luna kept pace, and the run at least helped warm our blood. She stopped shivering.

"Does it feel like we're going downhill?" she panted behind me.

"The tunnel must open up at the bottom of the mountain." We hastened along the rocky ground, every step taking us closer. "We'll have several hours' head start by the time they come after us."

The tunnel finally ended. A wall rose up in front of us. I patted the surface with both hands, spreading my arms wide, discovering a narrow space, large enough for one body to pass through at a time. It had to be the way out.

"This way." I took her hand again and squeezed into the passageway. Luna slid behind me easily. As far as escapes went, this wasn't too difficult, but then there probably wasn't anyone in this castle who wanted to go Outside. Ainswind was fortified against invaders. People wanted in. Dwellers wanted in. No one wanted out except us.

My breath came faster. I disliked the sensation of walls pressing in on me. Clearly, this escape route wouldn't work for everyone. Anyone of a certain girth or height would never manage it.

"Are you all right?" Luna asked, inching along behind, detecting my unease. I grunted in affirmation, noting the sudden increase of airflow ahead. "We're almost there, Fowler." Of course Luna would know that. If I sensed the change in air, so did she.

Suddenly we were free. As though we'd just plunged from a pool of water, we stumbled out into the endless stretch of Outside.

Luna sucked in a deep breath beside me. "We did it." Her voice shook and she released a nervous chuckle.

The glow of moonlight limned her features, reminding me of the first time I saw her—armed with a bow, moments after she saved my life. She looked like some kind of dark wood nymph, and I had wondered if she was even real.

I still held her hand. It was easy enough to pull her into my arms. She fell against me, fitting into me like a long-lost puzzle piece. I dove for her lips, claiming them hard, talking against her mouth. "Not touching you, pretending like I didn't burn for you . . ."

She lifted up on tiptoes and leaned into me, and I let myself have her for one moment.

"I'd thank you to take your hands and lips off my betrothed."

Luna and I sprang apart. For a moment I felt like a boy again when my nurse caught me at mischief. Until I remembered that Luna and I were *right*. Not a mistake. I took her hand again and faced the two men waiting for us, pulling my sword free in one smooth move.

Chasan stood there in his leather doublet with his hands on his hips. Beside him stood that hulk of a soldier, Harmon, who had accompanied him the first day we arrived at Ainswind.

Luna, unsurprisingly, knew it was the prince. "Chasan! How did you know—"

"I've been watching the two of you for days. Amusing, really. You try to act as though you aren't interested in each other. *Try* being the operative word." He shrugged. "I thought it best to assign my man here to watch you both. Glad I did."

I should have known. Chasan couldn't take his eyes off Luna. If anyone would have noticed the long glances and the lingering touches, it would have been him.

Luna's chin lifted. "We're leaving," she declared. "You can't stop us."

Chasan smiled, eyeing her up and down like she was a meal he wanted to devour. "I can. I will."

"I'm sorry, Chasan." Luna squeezed my hand and pressed close beside me. "I can't marry you. And I can't stay here."

Harmon drew his monster of a broadsword. It could cleave a man in half. His face was impassive as stone as he lifted it, ready to engage. Chasan crossed his arms and adopted a self-satisfied grin. It was the smile of a man who knew he'd won. Only I didn't know that. I hadn't accepted that. I never would.

I tightened my grip around Luna's hand and lifted my own sword, nodding at Harmon. "Is he going to kill us? Defeats the point, doesn't it? Of bringing us back to Ainswind with you."

Chasan cocked his head. "I don't really care what becomes of *you*." He locked in on Luna, and damn if something didn't heat in his eyes. "It's her I want."

My lip curled. "Easy to make threats and declarations when you've got him." I nodded at the massive hulk beside him.

Chasan's smile slipped. "Oh, you want to finish this?"

I stared at him for a long moment, the soft sounds of the Outside a heady thing swirling around us. Each insect buzz, bat chirp, and sliding rock sat thick as syrup on the air.

In the far distance, a dweller cried, tinny and reedy on the wind.

"You and me." I held his gaze. "It's what I've longed for." Ever since the moment I saw him interact with Luna, even out of my head with toxin fever, this had been simmering up to a boil.

Chasan settled a hand on his man's arm, prompting him to lower his sword even while never taking his gaze off me. "Winner takes all?"

"Agreed." I nodded at the giant. "And he doesn't try to stop us from leaving."

"That confident you'll defeat me?" Chasan started to shrug out of his leather doublet, revealing a fine linen shirt beneath. He handed the garment to Harmon.

"That confident I won't?" I rebutted.

"No weapons," Chasan replied, rolling his cuffs to his elbows. "Only one of us walks away alive."

Luna's hand clenched around my bicep as I tossed my sword down. "No, Fowler! What are you doing?"

I covered her hand with mine, gave it a light squeeze, and then lifted it off my arm. Lifting my bow, I handed it to her for safekeeping. Her wide dark eyes fixed on me, her mouth parted in a small "o" of wonder as I lowered my head and pressed a hard, quick kiss to her lips. "I know what I'm doing."

"I don't know that you do," she whispered back, her head chasing after my lips as I stepped back out of her range.

Turning, I faced the prince.

It was the only choice.

TWENTY-FOUR

Luna

I STOOD IN the familiar Outside, my heart a wild drum in my aching chest, actually wishing that I was back inside the castle. If it meant Fowler would be safe and not locked in a fight for his life with Prince Chasan, then yes. I wished for that.

The air filled with grunts and the brutal sound of fists slamming into skin and bone. They hit the ground, rolling, tussling. I could not distinguish who was who. There were only pained gasps and ragged breaths.

I'd stood by listening as Fowler had fought before. I knew how ruthless he could be, how unrelenting. It was as though he turned off that part of him that felt pain and fear. But the prince was no weakling either. The two were well matched.

Harmon moved to stand beside me, his hot, rancid breath hitching in excitement as he watched the combat unfold.

Suddenly there was a crunch of bone, and Chasan screamed. I winced. Harmon hissed out a breath beside me and I felt him tense as though he was going to step in.

I slapped a hand on his arm and clung to him as he took a step forward, as though I could somehow stop the giant myself. "Stop!" I ordered. "Stay back."

Harmon shook off my hand, but didn't step forward again.

"The next thing I break won't be a finger," Fowler snarled as he launched himself at Chasan. They hit the ground with a loud crash, limbs flailing wildly as they rolled, grappling to get a grip on the other. Chasan struck Fowler. I smelled the spray of his blood, heard it strike the ground.

"Stop! Stop it!" No one had to die. Neither one of them needed to die. "We'll go back! We'll go back with you!"

Perla's voice ghosted through me. Things, words she used to say to me as a child. *Life is full of choices . . . you just might not like any of them.*

I didn't care then. I believed any risk was worth it just as long as I got to *choose*. The only thing that mattered had been leaving the tower and finding something, anything, else. I'd found that freedom. I'd found Fowler. But Perla was right. Every choice led to this. It didn't matter what you did. It was unavoidable.

"Luna!" Fowler cried out amid grunts as Chasan plowed his fist into him.

"Let them finish," Harmon growled beside me. "It's already done. One of them isn't walking away. My wager is on Prince Chasan." Glee laced his voice.

I shook my head, bitter tears stinging my eyes as Fowler's head whacked the ground from the force of a blow.

"Fowler!" The sound of his name must have snapped something loose inside him. With a howl of rage, Fowler sprang up, launching Chasan off him.

Chasan landed several feet away. Fowler dropped hard on top of him. An *oompf* blew out of Chasan. Soon they were locked again, writhing and landing punches.

I listened, leaning forward, the only thing stopping me from jumping into the fray the enormous hand on my shoulder.

All my focus centered on the two boys beating the life from each other. I followed their savage movements, my head angling, listening, concentrating on their location, until, suddenly, the hand on my shoulder lifted. Harmon was gone, ripped from my side.

A new scream intruded on the din. I turned, trying to track Harmon's staggering form.

"Luna!" Fowler shouted.

Harmon crashed into me, his massive body sending me flying before I hit the ground.

I sucked in a breath, ready to demand to know what was wrong with him, when I got my answer.

"Luna!" Fowler crouched at my side, pulling me up as the sounds of a dweller tearing into Harmon penetrated.

For once, I had missed the usual signals, too fixated on what was happening between Fowler and Chasan—either that or the little time I had spent in Ainswind had dulled me more than I realized. Weakened me so that I had missed a dweller creeping up on us. Just another reason why I needed to escape. The castle was making me soft.

I was fortunate the dweller had chosen Harmon instead of me.

"There's too many!" Chasan shouted over a growing buzz of noise, and I heard them then—not just the single one tearing into Harmon but the others.

Layered over Harmon's screams was an army of twenty or more dwellers working up the incline with steady purpose. Twenty. More, maybe. Blood rushed to my head as they clambered in their heavy shuffle, grinding rocks underfoot as they advanced. To venture this far from the comfort of soft, yielding soil, they must be desperate.

I froze, panicked for one moment as I contemplated how to evade so many of them. Firing to action, I shook off Fowler's hand and readied my bow. I let an arrow fly, striking a dweller with a satisfying *thunk*.

"The tunnel!" Chasan shouted. "It's the quickest way back to the castle."

Fowler grabbed my hand before I could get off another shot. We slid back through the narrow opening. Me first, then Fowler, then Chasan. Gasping panicked breaths, we waited on the other side to see if any would follow.

"The bigger ones won't be able to get through," Chasan whispered amid harsh breaths.

"You better hope so," Fowler muttered, "or you've just given them a direct route inside the castle."

"It was either that or lead them to the front gates of the castle," he snapped. "At least they can't swarm us all at once in here. Space is too narrow."

"It was a good decision." I intervened, attempting to mediate.

"Hear that," Chasan goaded.

"Oh, shut up," I snapped. "If you hadn't insisted on fighting, then the noise would never have attracted them. I blame you for this."

Fowler took my hand and gave it a comforting squeeze. I inhaled a shuddering breath, pushing back the tide of emotion.

Both boys reeked of blood and sweat. At least this had brought their little death match to an end. That was one thing to appreciate.

A scratching sound whispered in front of us. Heavy feet dragged on the ground and my pulse jerked at the base of my throat. I knew before anyone spoke. They were following us.

Rasping breath suddenly cleared the barrier of the wall. Receptors snapped and hissed, poisonous serpents reaching, seeking victims.

With a curse, Fowler snatched the arrow I still clutched in my hand. Shoving me behind him, he lunged forward, using the sharp point to stab it into the head of the first dweller to break through.

"Go!" he shouted, his voice a shattering boom in the tight space. "Get her back inside the castle."

I yanked another arrow from my quiver, intent on helping. "I'm staying!"

Fowler jerked his arrow back out of the dweller's head and stuck it into the next one to emerge. "They're coming in fast!"

He was right. They were like water pouring from a spigot.

"Luna, let's go!" Chasan grabbed my hand and started hauling me away from the dwellers streaming into the tunnel.

"No! Fowler!" I strained to break free of his grip.

"I'll be right behind you!"

"Let him slow them down." Chasan tugged on my hand, pulling us ahead into the tunnel. "He'll be fine."

I moved, half dragged by Chasan, my heart pounding. The growls and rasping breaths of dwellers swelled behind us. After a while I couldn't hear the swift *thunk* and pop of Fowler stabbing them anymore.

"Fowler," I cried.

Chasan yanked on my hand again. "He can take care of himself. We would have heard him scream if they got him."

If they got him . . .

I'd just left him. In all our struggles together, we had never abandoned each other.

I would not abandon him now.

With a grunt, I kicked Chasan in the back of his leg. He yelped, his grip loosening. I spun around, my sweating palm flexing around the arrow still clutched in my hand. The hard fall of my boots echoed all around me as I rushed forward. The ripe, bitter odor of dwellers filled my nose. They were close, filling the space with dampness. Toxin dripped off their faces, the copper sweetness sitting like metal on my tongue.

"Fowler," I hissed, trying to hear or sense him amid the creatures slogging their way toward me. "Fowler," I tried again, lifting my bow and notching the arrow, ready to let it fly.

A hand knocked the bow to the side. "Why did you come back?" Fowler didn't wait for an answer. He spun me around and we started running, trying to stay ahead of the mob. Chasan met us.

"You were supposed to get her out of here," Fowler accused.

"She kicked me," Chasan snarled.

I turned my face toward Fowler as we continued. "I wasn't leaving you. Don't ask me to do that again."

He said nothing, and we fell into silence as we dashed up the tunnel, all pounding hearts and labored breaths, trying to get as much of a lead as we could.

Finally, we reached the end. Fowler seized my waist and lifted me up. I slipped my hands into the carved handholds and started climbing. I worked fast, hand over hand, legs pushing. The boys were behind me, their charged breaths floating up to me, egging me on faster.

Memory told me I was close to the top. I reached out a hand to feel for the open space above me. I met with the hard metal of the grate instead.

My heart constricted.

I looked down in horror. "Someone shut it!"

For a long moment, neither one of them said anything. There was just the roar of blood in my ears and the sounds of the dwellers below, frothing like stew in a pot.

I turned back to the grate and pounded at it. It was a dead end. Nowhere to go above and dwellers below.

We were trapped.

TWENTY-FIVE

Fowler

I PEERED DOWN into the darkness at the swarm of dwellers, hoping they didn't suddenly start climbing. Clinging to the handholds, muscles straining, I looked back up at Luna. Her body shook as she fiercely pounded the grate.

"Keep hitting," Chasan shouted below me.

"I am!" she cried, her voice cracking in a way I had never heard from her.

"Harder!" he added. "Someone has to hear you!"

Luna added her voice, shouting. We all joined in, screaming for help.

Luna's unseeing gaze dropped down, her dark hair wild

about her pale face. Her shoulders heaved with exertion. "How long are we going to be able to hold on like this?"

That's when I noticed she wasn't simply shaking from pounding on the grate. "Don't you dare let go," I warned, a lump lodging in my throat. "You'll hang on for as long as we need."

"Fowler," she choked out over Chasan's shouts. He didn't let up.

"Luna!" I removed one hand from its grip in the handhold and used it to support her, bracing it under her thigh.

"Don't! You'll fall!"

"I'm not going to fall," I ground out from between clenched teeth, "and neither are you!"

Suddenly a grind of metal followed by a loud clank cut over Chasan's shouts. Feeble lantern light glowed down at us from the jagged opening. A kitchen maid's wide eyes peered down at us, her flour-dusted face maybe the sweetest sight I ever beheld.

Luna gasped and started up, pulling herself through the hole with the help of the maid. I was fast behind her, dropping down on the storeroom floor with an exhausted sigh. Chasan pulled himself through, slammed the grate shut, and bolted it. He turned on the maid then, one finger lifted. "No one knows you saw us here. Understood?"

The maid nodded and bobbed a curtsy. "Yes, Your Highness. Not a word." With an uncertain look at each of us, she hastened out of the storeroom, grabbing a sack on the way out.

Chasan dropped back on the ground, tossing an arm over

his forehead. A ragged sigh spilled from his lips. After a long moment, he said, "No one will know about tonight."

For several moments, the three of us didn't move or speak.

I moistened my dry lips. "What do you mean?" I finally asked.

"My father . . . if he were to learn of your escape attempt, he'd see you both as traitors. I want Luna as my wife, not wasting away in a dungeon."

I thought about that for a moment, rolling my head to look at her, still catching her breath beside me. Bright splotches of color splashed her cheeks. I didn't want to see her wasting away in a dungeon either. "He's not going to hear about it from us," I volunteered.

As for Luna marrying Chasan, that wasn't going to happen. I reached for her hand near mine and gave it a squeeze, silently communicating that. Considering our escape attempt had just been foiled, we'd have to come up with a new strategy.

I wasn't giving up.

Fortunately, we didn't pass anyone in the hall as we returned to our rooms. Firelight flickered from the sconces lining the corridor, casting long, crawling shadows as we walked. We deposited Luna at her chamber first.

I longed to stay, talk to her, hold her, but with Chasan hovering and morning looming close when everyone would wake, it was too risky. Instead, I hugged her close before letting her go, inhaling her, pressing my mouth into her hair and whispering,

"I'll come to you. Don't worry. We'll figure another way out of here."

She nodded once, her face downcast, the dark short spikes of her hair angling at a slant that obscured her cheeks. She slipped inside her chamber. The door clicked shut after her, and I felt that small sound resound inside me.

With a single hard glance at Chasan, I continued on toward my chamber. I knew his room was in the opposite direction, but he fell in step beside me. "You're not being fair to her."

I shook my head. "What are you talking about?"

"Let her go."

I snorted. "So you can have her?"

"If you let her go, she could be happy with me."

"You think so?" I released a short, harsh laugh. "You don't know the first thing about her."

"I know Luna." He nodded so knowingly, so smugly, that I wanted to take another swing at his face.

"Apparently not, or you would know she could never be happy here." I motioned around us. "This place isn't for her."

"And out there is? How many times has she nearly died out there with you? In here she would never have to see another dweller again."

"She'd just have to marry you to have all of that."

"And that's what's really bothering you. Luna with *me*."

I stopped and faced him. "Oh, it's bothering her, too. Trust in that." I jerked my chin once. "Knowing it's me she wants, me she thinks about every time you're with her? That's something you could live with?"

Chasan crossed his arms, that smug smile back in place. "I can make her forget you. I can make her happy. Eventually."

Fear stirred in my heart. Fear that he was right. I opened and closed my hands at my sides. "Not happening," I said with far more conviction than I felt.

"You might try not being such a selfish bastard. Start thinking about her. I know you don't give a damn about Lagonia, but you should care about Relhok. Think about your country. According to Breslen, things aren't so great back there." His sigh rattled on the air. "Our fathers won't rule forever. If Luna marries me and you marry my sister, the two kingdoms unite. We present a stronger front."

I wanted to say I didn't give a damn about Relhok, but then I saw Bethan's face. Her parents and little brother. All the people I had known in Relhok who weren't terrible. Those people deserved better. Luna would agree with that, too. She always put others before herself.

Maybe I needed to try to do the same.

The following night the hall was bustling, nobility and gentry alike in full attendance. The hounds trotted amid tables, happily gobbling up the scraps tossed their way, growling and snapping when they got in each other's way. Only here did people turn their noses up at food while the peasants of Ainswind rooted for their next meal in the scraps tossed to them after the king and his court dined.

I moved stiffly, still sore from yesterday's fight with Chasan. The only thing that made me feel better was that he looked much the same as I did.

I dodged a dog the size of a bear as I escorted Maris to the head table upon the dais, my stiffness not solely because of my soreness. It felt unnatural touching Maris and pretending that I didn't want to snatch Luna up into my arms.

I didn't need to look to feel Chasan's gaze on me. The threat was there. He wanted to finish what we started Outside. He could, too. He could end Luna and me with one word to his father. The knowledge held me in careful check. A second escape wouldn't be easy. Chasan would be expecting it, but it would happen. It had to.

Maris preened, resplendent in a blue gown that made me remember my last glimpse of the sky before everything went dark.

Clinging to my arm, she greeted friends who called out to her and stared after her with greedy eyes. I suppose a measure of this was due to the gold crown woven into her hair. The head-piece matched her glittering strands. That crown marked her above everyone else. I vaguely remembered what it felt like to be admired, to feel as though anything could be yours because generally it was. I had felt invincible.

It had been an illusion. Losing Bethan wasn't the first hint, but it was the one that pushed me out, made me rush headlong into a world teeming with monsters, because that was real at least. And I wanted reality over illusions.

My gaze drifted down the table to where Luna sat. She'd become my reality.

Tebald was already sitting at the helm of the head table. He nodded at me in lofty regard. My gaze moved back to Luna sitting beside Chasan. I assessed them briefly, even though it physically pained me. The vision imprinted itself on my mind: Luna dazzling in a red gown, her shoulders and throat bare, her dark hair pulled up, studded with jewels. She looked as she should look— as she was born to look. She looked like a queen: achingly lovely but impossible to touch. Except for Chasan. *He* could touch her and hold her arm as they walked. He could brush his fingers over her hand. It made me gnash my teeth.

I couldn't stare at her overly long without attracting undue attention. Even at my brief glance, a slow creep of pink swept up her décolletage and neck. She felt my stare—felt me. That was enough for now.

I lowered my face as Maris warbled on, complaining that her favorite cheese was not on the table. I feigned interest in the food spread out before me, but it was mostly to hide my smile.

My *pretend* interest in the food was cut short when Tebald rose from the table, clanging a spoon against his goblet to gain everyone's attention.

Maris was the last to stop talking beside me. Resting a hand on top of my arm as though she was afraid I might vanish on her when she looked in another direction, she swung her gaze toward her father with mild interest.

"Friends." The king spread his arms wide, the large sleeves of his robes like great purple wings at either side of him. "We have much to celebrate. We are safe behind our walls. Our fortifications have not suffered a breach in these long years."

A cheer broke out in response to this. Everyone quieted as the king continued, "And we will continue to prosper into the next generation with the marriage of my daughter to Prince Fowler." He paused for an eruption of further applause. I shifted uneasily, forcing a smile. Several goblets banged on tables in salute. "Lagonia shall not only survive but thrive with a second marriage that will more greatly enforce the union of two kingdoms." The king lifted his goblet high, and others shouted out and cheered. Even a hound bayed, joining the din.

Everyone drank deeply. I followed suit, deliberately trying not to look in Luna's direction, to see her reaction to this. Would the words prick at her conscience and make her feel obligated to stay and marry Prince Chasan?

The king's voice continued, rolling over the room like a hot vapor and pulling me from my thoughts. "Lift your cups again and toast *my* nuptials to the queen of Relhok."

Stunned silence met the announcement. I blinked and looked around, gauging expressions, questioning whether I had heard what I heard. Everyone else looked as bewildered as I felt.

Maris was the first to speak. "Father, you mean Chasan's marriage to Luna, don't you?"

Tebald's cheeks rounded above his beard as he smiled. "No." He shook his head. "I did not misspeak, daughter. I meant *my* marriage. I've had a change of heart. It's been some years since your mother died. I'm not yet an old man. I'm certain a young bride will invigorate me. A young rose like Luna is the perfect tonic."

My vision clouded for a moment, rage chugging thick as tar in my veins.

"Father," Chasan growled in a voice I had never heard him use with his father before. "Don't do this." The prince clutched the knife at the side of his plate, his eyes narrowed darkly, and for a moment I thought he might plunge it into his sire. I wouldn't blame him for that. The thought of the old man's hands on Luna filled me with a similar impulse.

My reaction was physical—a sick churning in my stomach. Luna had gone pale, the faint pinkness that had been tingeing her cheeks fading away. I lurched from my chair, the blood rushing in my ears as my chair clattered violently behind me.

People stared at me. The king stared at me, but I did not care. I was past caring, past playing the biddable, submissive prince of Relhok.

Chasan rose, too, tossing his napkin down. "She's not marrying you."

The king turned his gaze to Chasan. "Have a care, son."

I cleared my throat, warning myself to stay calm. "I don't think this is a good idea."

The king turned that cruel smile of his on me. "Prince Fowler, I fear you're forgetting the conversation we had." He sat back down. "I warned you, did I not? And you claimed you understood your place."

I nodded once, inhaling thinly through my nose, fighting to control my temper. "I know my place."

Chasan stabbed a finger toward the floor. "You're not putting your rotting paws on her, old man. Not ever. She'll never marry you."

A hushed awe fell over the hall. Maris gaped and then quickly looked down, ducking her eyes.

King Tebald lifted his drumming fingers from the arms of his chair and stroked his graying beard. "You risk much standing here saying such words to me, my son. You know men have died for less."

And yet Chasan didn't back down. "I do."

Maris reached for her brother's arms and tugged, trying to bring him back into his chair. "Chasan, no . . ."

He pulled away.

The king leaned forward. "You know and yet you speak these things to me. You're either very brave or very stupid. Either way, taking a bride and begetting an heir who is more respectful to his sire strikes me as a fine idea indeed."

I fought back the urge to launch across the space separating me from the king and wrap my hands around the old man's neck. I stared at the king, my jaw clenched hard, fighting for restraint.

Maris whispered her brother's name in a beseeching tone. He paid her no mind, simply shook her off.

My gaze found Luna, still bloodlessly pale. That expressive mouth of hers trembled as though burdened with too much pressure. I looked from her back to the king, then to her again. Her features were tight and pinched with desperation for me to hold silent. I shook my head and opened my mouth.

"Perhaps you would like to retire for the evening, Chasan.

You seem quite flushed and agitated. Not yourself at all. Usually you are much more composed." The king arched a bushy eyebrow at his son, offering him a way out; a last reprieve.

I seethed, my hands knotting into fists at my sides. Somehow I managed to hold my tongue during the exchange. I had to keep it together. I could not lose the king's trust. Not if I wanted to get Luna out of here before she was forced to marry the old man.

The king snapped his fingers and guards appeared. "See that Chasan makes it to his chamber. We would not want him to collapse en route." He smiled again, but his eyes stayed cold and lifeless. Tebald managed to convey absolute menace even when only kind words dropped from his lips.

The guards moved to either side of Chasan. He gave his father one last long look, and then departed the great hall.

It was as though, as *always*, Luna could see me. Sensing her stare, I turned to look at her, hoping to convey to her that she had nothing to worry about. We were still going to escape this place. Sooner rather than later. She wasn't going to marry Tebald, just like she wasn't going to marry Chasan.

She gave a hard shake of her head at me, her eyebrows dipping low over her eyes, commanding me to do nothing.

I nodded once, more for myself than for her since she couldn't see me.

I would hold silent and pretend as though Luna marrying an old man who reminded me so much of my father did not send my body into revolt.

The dinner continued, this time with the king salivating over Luna. When he hand-fed her a bit of meat with his pudgy, beringed fingers, I couldn't stomach it any longer. I rose from my chair.

Maris touched my arm. "Where are you going?"

"I fear that I might not be quite recovered from the fall I took earlier," I said, referencing the excuse I had given for my appearance. I didn't know what excuse Chasan had given for his appearance, but no one had pressed me on the fact that I looked like I'd tangled with a tree wolf. Standing, I turned my attention to the king, who was now looking at me intently. "Forgive me, Your Majesty."

"Retiring already, Prince Fowler?"

"Yes, I'm not feeling quite myself."

"By all means, rest. We wouldn't have you sicken on us again. My daughter has her heart set on a wedding next week."

I inclined my head. "Of course, Your Majesty. I would not want to disappoint her."

"As well you should not." The king wore a smile, but the threat was implicit.

It was a threat I would think about on my walk back to my chamber, my hands opening and clenching at my sides as it festered inside me.

He thought he had me—*and* Luna. Two whipped puppies under his control.

He would be wrong, and I would show him just how wrong he was.

TWENTY-SIX

Luna

I LISTENED AS Fowler left, his tread fading to a dull beat over the stone floor of the great hall. I fought the wild need to call him back. It was better if he wasn't here right now. I knew that. I felt his anger and knew he was close to snapping.

Still knowing that, it took everything in me not to call Fowler back. If he had not left when he did, he could have lost the fragile trust he had established with Tebald.

I was not marrying Tebald, but I couldn't declare that. I had to keep that truth bottled up inside. I needed to keep my composure and suffer this meal, suffer Tebald and his roaming fingers.

My heart thumped furiously in my chest. My head buzzed,

the king's announcement running over and over in my mind. He intended to marry me.

After Fowler's departure, conversation revived in the hall. I turned my head left and right, taking it all in. My eyes burned but no tears fell. I squared my shoulders, pulling them back, reminding myself that I was strong. I had survived so much. I would survive this, too.

I lasted through dessert. Tebald attempted to feed me a candied date and I couldn't tolerate it any longer. I pushed up from my chair. "I'm sorry, Your Majesty. All the excitement has tired me. It's not every day a king proposes, after all. I'm quite . . . overwhelmed." Somehow I didn't choke on the lie.

"Of course, my dear." He reached out and grabbed me with one of his hard, square hands. He tugged me down, his grip pinching my skin. I winced, my shoulder joint straining.

His lips brushed my cheek, his beard, as coarse as the bristles of a paintbrush and with the faint odor of rancid meat, prickling my skin. "I may not have won your mother all those years ago, but I shall have you."

Revulsion bubbled through me. His hand squeezed tighter and I whimpered. His breath came hard against my face, putrid and hot on my skin. He was excited at my pain.

I had to get away. "I look forward to that." In that moment, I would have said anything.

I twisted my arm until I managed to free myself. Rubbing where he had gripped me, I gathered up a fistful of my skirts and hurried along the back of the dais.

I charged ahead, mindful of the steps leading down from the

platform. By now I knew the route to my chamber by heart. No one stopped me. They let me go, and that, perhaps, filled me with the bleakest fear of all.

They thought I could do nothing. They thought I had nowhere to go. Deep down, I was starting to fear they were right. Maybe I was never leaving here.

The night was silent. My maid had come and gone after brushing my hair and helping ready me for bed as though it wasn't something I'd done for myself countless times. As though this were any ordinary night and not the first night of my death. Marrying Tebald would be a living death. The thought of marrying Chasan had been bad enough. But Tebald? I shuddered.

I crossed my hands over my stomach, willing sleep to come. Somehow I didn't think I would ever sleep well or fully in this place. Especially after tonight. The memory of Tebald's touch, his words . . . how could I stay here when this place made me feel like my own skin didn't fit my body? I preferred the Outside with all its dangers to this.

My bedchamber door creaked open and I lurched upright, heart pounding. My mind leaped to where I'd left my bow and how quickly I could get to it. After this evening's shock, I fully expected my late-night visitor to be Tebald.

"Luna." At Fowler's hushed voice I sagged with relief.

"Fowler," I cried, and then caught myself, dropping my voice. "You shouldn't be here," I hissed.

He crossed the room and closed his hands over my arms. "Get changed. Where are your shoes? Your boots? You can't go

Outside in slippers. You'll tear them to shreds in minutes."

He let go of me and hurried across the room. Cold swept over me. His boots thudded distinctly. He'd changed already, too. I could smell the leather of his doublet.

I heard him at the bureau, the door slamming against the wall. He rifled through the garments in my wardrobe.

The cold didn't fade. I chafed my hands up and down my arms, hugging myself tight as I scooted to the edge of the bed. "Fowler, do you have a new plan? We can't go through the storeroom again, can we?" I stood and edged forward. "We can't just charge out into the night—"

Fowler spun around and advanced on me, his voice darkly intent. "We can't just stay here and wait for the king to drop any more surprises on us. For all we know he plans to marry you tomorrow. Or maybe he won't even wait for a wedding at all. He might be on his way to claim you this very evening. Have you considered that?"

Bile rose up from the back of my throat. Of course I had. I remembered that hand on me, tight and hurting. I thought of what he'd said about my mother, about me.

I shoved that memory away, shaking my head. I couldn't think about that. "You're overwrought."

He laughed harshly. "Luna, this whole place is a paper tower ready to crumble at the first wind. We can't stay." He pulled me toward the wardrobe. "Now are you going to change? Or do I need to help you?"

I knew he didn't mean it. Despite the gravity of his words,

he wouldn't force me to do anything. He needed my compliance. We couldn't just stroll out the front gate.

I stepped forward and smoothed a palm down Fowler's cheek. "So fierce. This isn't like you." He'd never been rash. Fowler was smart and calculating. He hadn't survived on the Outside these last years because of luck.

His chest lifted on a ragged breath. "Tebald wants you for himself. He won't stop until he gets you."

I nodded and spoke in a placating manner. "But don't you think we stand a better chance of surviving if we stop and come up with a plan? Maybe Chasan would help. He wasn't happy either—"

Fowler laughed roughly, the sound scratchy. "Yes, he'll help himself."

Before I could anticipate his next move, he swept me into his arms and buried his nose in my hair, his mouth directly against my ear.

Turning his face into my neck, he inhaled me before pressing his mouth to the sensitive skin there. "Luna," he breathed. "Just the idea of you with Chasan has been bad enough. To think of you with the king . . ."

I brought both hands into his hair, delving my fingers through the thick mass. "Then don't think about it."

His mouth at my neck sent my thoughts ricocheting. My heart beat like a wild thing as his lips and teeth grazed my skin, making me gasp. My knees threatened to buckle and his arm came up around my waist, hauling me closer and keeping me from falling. He was good at holding me together. Except when he was sending me flying apart. One touch, one kiss from him did that.

The creak of hinges wove its way through the fog of my thoughts.

We weren't alone anymore.

TWENTY-SEVEN

Fowler

TOO LATE, I heard the click of the door and realized neither of us had thought to bolt it. A gasp sounded. It was ugly and obscene, as though ripped deep from someone's soul. The peace of our sanctuary, the intimacy between us, shattered.

We had been discovered. Even so, I felt like I was giving up a part of myself to disengage from Luna and face the door.

Maris stood there, eyeing us both up and down with her wounded, childlike gaze. "Fowler? What are you doing?" Her perfect features froze in horror as she stood on the threshold. She asked the question, but she knew.

Luna's lips worked for speech and she took a step forward. I shook my head, beyond pretending, well past further subterfuge. I was done. I seized Luna's hand and pulled her to my side. "I'm sorry, Maris. There was never going to be a you and me. Luna and I are leaving."

Luna made a small sound of distress, turning her face toward me. "Fowler . . ."

"You and Luna?" Maris's eyes darted back and forth between us, her voice shrill. "When?" she sputtered, her gaze dropping to where I held Luna's hand. "How?"

Suddenly robed figures appeared behind the princess. A bejeweled hand fell on her shoulder, moving her to the side for the arrival of others. Tebald took his daughter's place, a great figure in his fine robes of purple, his face a mask of controlled ire.

He strolled into the bedchamber, casual, elegant even. He gestured idly, flicking a hand at Luna and me. "It's always been the two of you. Since before you even arrived? Isn't that correct?"

I narrowed my gaze on the older man. His small eyes stared back at me, cold and emotionless. I tugged Luna behind me. She resisted, placing herself firmly at my side, her shoulder brushing my arm. Her chin went up at that obstinate angle I knew so well. "I will not marry you. I will not marry your son."

The king smiled slowly; a thin slit of yellowed teeth flashed amid his beard. "Thank you for that bit of truth. Finally." His gaze shot to me. "Your honesty is appreciated. We can at last end the pretense with each other."

"It's time for us to leave," I said.

"Father!" Maris stomped her foot on the ground and crossed

her arms over her chest, glaring at me and Luna and then looking back at Tebald as though he could do something, change this
from happening. Or stop it altogether.

The king did not glance at his pouting daughter. He stared
directly at me.

"We appreciate your hospitality and you allowing your physician to care for Fowler," Luna rushed to add. As though good
manners would make any difference. I had already accepted what
she had failed to yet comprehend.

The king rocked back on his heels and looked up at the rafters, studying the high wood beams as if they held the utmost
fascination for him. "Yes. Saving Fowler. That was perhaps an
exercise in uselessness." He brought his gaze back down, resting
it on us again. "Pointless considering he shall probably die within
the fortnight. The conditions of the dungeons are far from favor-
able. No one lasts very long there. And if my dungeon doesn't
end you, fights in the pit eventually will." Tebald lifted a hand
and snapped his fingers.

A breath shuddered through me alongside grim acceptance.

"No!" Luna grabbed my arm as if she could keep me beside
her.

Guards stepped around Tebald, advancing on me. I covered Luna's hand in my own and faced her. "Shh." I rubbed her
smooth, cool fingers, imbuing as much comfort as I could into
the motion. "It's going to be fine. You'll see. Don't fight them."

"How can you say—"

"Listen to me, Luna. Everything will be fine." They were

words. I had to say them—hoped they were true. I pressed my lips against her cheek for one quick kiss, sliding my mouth close to her ear to whisper, "Don't let them break you. Be strong; be the bold girl I know. You will come out of this. You know how to survive." There was the escape hatch and Chasan. She was right. Chasan hated his father enough that he would try to help her.

I curled my grip around her fingers, attempting to peel them loose from my arm. She tightened her hold, hanging on with a death grip.

"What about you?" she whispered, turning her face until our noses practically touched, our lips brushing with each word spoken.

I bit back the response that *I* didn't matter, that I was already lost. It would give her no comfort. It might very well feed into panic, and I needed her to feel calm. She couldn't think or defend herself if she was panicked, and above all I needed her alert and ready to protect herself. "As long as you are well, as long as you are alive . . . thriving . . . then I am well. I will be with you always."

Guards took hold of my arms. My calm acceptance fled. I resisted. Straining toward her, I grabbed her face. Ducking, I stole one last kiss from her lips, hard and swift. Something to take and keep with me.

Tears skipped unchecked down her cheeks as she clung to my wrists, trying to keep my hands on her face. Trying to keep me. "No, no."

"This is nauseating," Maris's voice called out, dripping venom.

"Stop! Stop it! Don't take him!" Luna's hands slipped from my wrists as they pulled me away.

A single guard stepped in front of her, holding her back from coming after me.

They dragged me across the chamber. The king stood on the threshold, smiling. The guards paused with me before him. "I do hope you last a long time in my dungeon, Prince Fowler. I should enjoy very much watching you battle in the pit."

I forced a smile, matching his chilling grin with one of my own. He frowned slightly at the sight of it, and that gave me immense satisfaction. Let him worry. Let him see the real me. No more pretending and acting like someone other than myself. "Don't worry," I promised. "I'll be around for a long time." I nodded once with promise, fully meaning it. "We'll be meeting again."

His smile returned then, hair-shrouded lips peeling back over yellowed teeth. "I admire your temerity, boy." He chuckled. "It reminds me of myself."

"You and I are nothing alike. I never forced a girl to do anything she didn't want to."

His smile vanished. "You think you are so much better than I am."

"I don't think it. I know I am." One of the guards landed a blow directly to my stomach. I bent at the waist from the force. Luna cried out.

"Let's see how you fare in another week, boy. Something tells me you won't be nearly so cocky."

I forced a grin. "I just might surprise you."

"Doubtful." He sneered and flicked his hand toward the door in dismissal. "Take him to the dungeon."

They yanked me out of the chamber and pulled me down the corridor so fast my feet could hardly gain purchase.

Footsteps rushed behind us. Maris caught up with us, holding up her lush blue skirts, her face flushed a splotchy red as she planted herself in front of us. The guards stopped lest they run her over.

"Fowler," she snarled, her words flying like daggers. "You should have loved me. You should have married me."

Maybe I should have felt some sympathy for her, but one look at her bitter expression and she reminded me of her father. She was spoiled and shallow. She wished me in the dungeon. As if to confirm this, she added, "Make friends with the rats; maybe they'll keep you warm."

She fell back, and I was glad for that. I didn't want to see her face anymore or hear her words. I wanted to take the memory of Luna with me. Her voice. Her kiss. *Her* love.

I meant what I'd said to Tebald. This wasn't over. I was going to be around for a long time. I would be seeing the king again, and the next time there would be no armed guards between us.

TWENTY-EIGHT

Luna

As Fowler was dragged away, I crushed all evidence of my tears. I couldn't look weak. It would be up to me to escape—up to me to get Fowler out of the dungeon. For a moment the realization rattled me, but then I remembered all I'd done up until now. It couldn't be any harder than infiltrating a dwellers' nest, and I had done that before.

Squaring my shoulders, I faced the king. "Spare his life. I beg you." The words choked me, begging *him* for anything, but I managed to get them out.

Fabric rustled. "Leave us," Tebald announced to his men.

I bit my lip, squashing the impulse to call them back as they marched out of my chamber, leaving us alone.

Tebald's slippered feet padded over stone, advancing on me with measured steps. He brushed the side of my face with pudgy fingertips. I jerked from the touch but held my ground. "You plead so prettily, Princess Luna. I quite like this look on you. It's softer. You're usually so standoffish. I'm accustomed to women who are more accommodating. You'll have to remember that. I have expectations."

Because they had no choice. He was the king.

He continued, "Your mother was the last person to ever deny me. She was close to accepting my suit until she met your father."

I suppressed a shiver. I may not have known my mother, but Perla and Sivo had told me so much of her that the idea of this man *almost* with her made me slightly queasy. I pressed a hand to my stomach, fighting off the nausea.

Tebald continued in scathing tones, "Once your father began courting her, she never looked at me again." His voice turned bemused here. "It's gratifying to have you here . . . subject to me. It's funny how life comes full circle."

"What will it take?" I lifted my chin a notch, determined to try to appeal to him. "What do you want?"

He tsked. "You know the answer to that, my clever girl."

"We can unite our kingdoms without me having to marry you. We can forge an alliance—"

He laughed harshly. "Such a child. Do you know how many alliances have been forged between Lagonia and Relhok over the generations? They never last. Uniting our two houses through marriage is the only way." His voice sobered and became something dark and severe. "You know what I want."

My eyes started to burn and it hurt to breathe. I sucked in a deep breath that felt like razors going down my throat. I fought to keep up my chin. "I do."

"You can consent," he said, his voice all lightness, fingers back to grazing my cheek. "Go along gracefully like a good girl, and Fowler lives. Fight me, and I win. It just won't be pleasant for you."

He would have his way in this. There was no stopping him. Not if I wanted to save Fowler. I shuddered at the idea of Fowler in that pit.

No matter what I decided, no matter what I did, Tebald won. But whether Fowler suffered and died . . . that decision was entirely mine.

That left me only one choice.

TWENTY-NINE

Fowler

IT TURNED OUT Maris was right about the rats, except they didn't keep me warm. They scampered in dark corners, edging close with their hungry squeaks and twitching whiskers until I lashed out with my boot and sent them fleeing.

I was given a cell to myself, excluding the rats, of course, but that didn't stop other prisoners from calling out to me through the bars, jeering taunts about my fine garments and clean boots and how quickly I was going to die down here. I laughed once, hard and mirthless, my head lolling against the slimy stone wall. I should have died a long time ago. Still, I was here. I glanced around my cell, trying to convince myself that

I was going to get out of here.

Time was lost inside these walls.

I stared into the dark, my mind wandering, groping through the blackness, bumping into the hope that I would get out of here. Survive yet again. Take Luna and run. Be free. I could have been down here an hour or a day. It was impossible to tell if midlight came or passed. The eclipse could have even ended. I wouldn't know.

Footsteps thudded outside my cell. I looked up, one leg stretched out, one bent to my chest. Chasan's face arrived, illuminated by the light from a torch he was carrying.

I chuckled roughly. "Ah, come to delight in my accommodations? Should have expected as much."

Chasan propped a shoulder against the bars, his head angling to the side. There was a stillness about him that hinted toward violence held barely in check. "I'm not much in the mood to delight in anything."

"Ah, that's right. Your father betrayed you? Didn't he?" I flexed my fingers around my knee. "Can't say I don't know how that feels. Pull up a cell. We can commiserate."

"He's going to make you wish for death, you know." His voice rang flatly, as if he were remarking on the weather. "He'll keep you alive for weeks, months, maybe longer. Starve you. Torture you. Make you play for him in his pits. If you sicken, he'll nurse you along just enough to keep you alive."

I nodded once, envisioning the scene well. I knew men like Tebald. My own father was of the same ilk. It was Chasan I wasn't certain about. Who he was . . . *what* he was. What he wanted here. With me. I couldn't say. I didn't have a read on him.

Chasan leaned in, closing his fingers around the bar. "You say the word, and I'll end it for you."

I stared at his shadowed features. "Are you offering to kill me? How generous of you."

"It'd be a favor."

I chuckled. "That right? Because we've been such good *friends*."

"Just say the word at any time. I'll see it's done. I don't enjoy torturing people. This world is ugly enough."

Silence fell between us, crackling with tension. This world was ugly, but it wasn't hopeless. I wasn't giving up yet. People clung to the belief that the eclipse would end because according to legend it had happened before. It had ended before. Mankind had survived it and would again. Why couldn't those survivors be Luna and me?

"You really want to do me a favor?" I asked. "You could let me out of this cell. Let me take Luna and go."

It was his turn to laugh. I watched him through the bars as he shook his head. "I can't do that."

"Right." I clenched my teeth. "Your favors only extend so far. What about Luna? How are you going to help her?" I knew he wanted to. I just had to persuade him that he could.

Chasan looked away, staring at some point in the darkness. "I can't go against my father."

"Your feelings for her were real," I continued. "They *are* real.

You can't fool me. You liked her. You still do. You thought the two of you could have been good together. Maybe even happy? You believed that." I shrugged. "Who knows? Maybe that could have happened someday . . . but your father killed that possibility. Didn't he?"

Maybe, years from now, she would forget me. Or at least look back on me, on *us*, as something that existed in a dream. A whim of youth when we came together and helped keep each other going. As bitter as that was to swallow, it was better than envisioning her with Tebald. I could see her with Chasan, standing in sunlight, surrounded by children.

I could face the pit. I could die with that image burning in my mind and be content.

Chasan shook his head. "I don't know—"

"You'll let your father have her? He'll break her." My voice grew thick as I envisioned this. "Bit by bit, he will destroy all that she is until there's nothing left of her." Chasan sighed, and I took that sound as encouragement to keep talking. I let go of my knee and leaned forward. "If you don't want to free me, then just let her go. She can survive on her own out there." I gestured. "You just have to make it so that she can slip out of the castle."

Chasan's gaze shot back to mine. "It's not that simple."

"It is. It is that simple. Give her a chance. You know you want to."

Chasan let go of the bars and stepped back as if needing distance from me and all that I was asking him to do. "Offer still stands. Let me know if you want me to spare you." Turning, he walked away stiffly, disappearing into the darkness, leaving me to my cold cell.

I sat there alone, stewing in my thoughts, wondering at what point any of this could have been avoided. It all seemed so inevitable. I had come full circle.

Years ago, I had sat in a cell, helpless as my father took Bethan's life. It felt like I was living through the same nightmare again. Only this time it wasn't Bethan. It was Luna.

The pain, the fear . . . it was different. Worse.

A pair of guards came by. Unlocking my cell door, they entered the dank space and tossed in a bucket of soupy slop. It tipped over, the swill spilling onto the floor.

"Eat up, prince. You'll need your strength when it comes time for your turn in the pit." The guard laughed and kicked me savagely, for the sheer pleasure of it. Grabbing the bucket, I flung it at him, spraying soup through the air. The bucket knocked him in the face, sending him crashing to the ground with a cry.

I sprang to my feet and launched myself at the other guard, beyond rage. I couldn't help Luna. Maybe I couldn't even help myself. Perhaps this was really it—the end—with me rotting in this dungeon, emerging only when it was time to fight dwellers for the amusement of Tebald and his nobles.

But I could do this. In this moment, I could inflict pain.

I pummeled at him, swinging my fists, bone striking bone, skin breaking, warm blood flowing. Mine. His. It didn't matter. It was release.

I hit and hit, roaring until two guards pulled me off. They

turned on me then, beating me with hot, spit-flying curses. Boots. Fists. I took it all, curling into a ball on the moldy stone floor. I took every blow they dealt, absorbing the pain, welcoming it because it paled beside the agony of losing Luna, leaving her with Tebald. I grunted, jerking from the volley of fists and boots until my world faded to nothing.

THIRTY

Luna

I WAS LEFT alone in my chamber. It seemed forever that I paced, my pulse racing at my throat as I thought about Fowler stuck in that dungeon and my impending wedding to Tebald.

A maid came, as always, to help ready me for bed. I sent her away and went through the motions myself. I didn't want the company. Lying in the center of the massive bed, I surrendered to the tears I'd held back in front of Tebald. Once they ran out, the numbness crept in.

I wiped my cheeks dry, sniffing loudly in the cavernous silence of my chamber. Tears were weakness. I was alive. And because of my agreement with Tebald, Fowler would live, too.

I inhaled a shuddery breath. I could do this. I could live this life. It wasn't the one I'd planned for myself, but it could be worse. People were dying without hope, without friends or loved ones, without having ever known love. I could have been one of them, and yet I wasn't. I'd always have that.

Any time things became too unbearable I only had to think of Fowler alive and well somewhere out there. Maybe in Allu. A wobbly smile shook my lips. That would be enough to get me through.

I stilled at the sound of soft voices murmuring outside my door. I knew Tebald had stationed two guards at my door, but they had been silent for the last several hours since he'd left me.

My heart seized in my chest as the door creaked open, and I remembered Fowler's ominous words to me, how Tebald could claim me now even without the formality of the wedding.

I swallowed back a whimper and clutched the bedcovers at my throat. Propping myself up on my elbows, I turned my face in the direction of the door and the individual standing there. I felt his gaze on me across the length of the room.

I stretched my senses, trying to detect his identity, his intent. I knew it wasn't Fowler. Even if he wasn't in the dungeon, even if I hadn't lost him, I would know him. I would recognize his presence.

The door clicked shut and steps sounded toward me, each one making my heart plunge deeper into my twisting stomach. I sat up, covers pooling around my waist. It was definitely a he, and *he* was coming for me. The bed dipped slightly with the weight of one knee.

I scurried backward, my pulse a wild beat at my neck,

threatening to burst from my skin as I pressed myself into the ornate headboard. I opened my mouth to scream. A hand slammed over my mouth, forcing my head back, silencing me. I kicked and punched but it was useless.

His weight pinned me, filling me with impotent rage. I freed one arm and sent my fist rocking into his jaw.

A familiar voice cursed and the hand over my mouth loosened.

"Chasan? What are you doing here?"

"Apparently getting my jaw broken."

I shoved at him, scrambling out from under him. "It's what you deserve."

"Even if I'm here to help you?"

I stilled, my heart stalling for a moment. "You'll help me? What about Fowler?"

He sighed, shifting his weight. "I suppose I can't help you without helping him, too. You've made that fairly clear."

"You'll help us," I repeated as if I needed that agreement from him written in blood.

"That's right. Get yourself dressed and we'll go get him. Unless you want to stick around and marry my father."

"No," I gasped, springing from the bed. I started toward the armoire, but stopped, turned back around, and launched myself at Chasan. I hugged him tightly. "Thank you. I knew you were different."

"Yeah. My father has been complaining about that all my life," he grumbled, his breath lost in my hair.

I pulled back and touched his face, brushing my fingers along his cheek. "That's a good thing. Never be like him, Chasan. Someday you'll rule this country. Lagonia needs you."

"Yes. I only wish you needed me, too." His breath fanned my face warmly and he covered my hand where it pressed against his cheek. "But you don't. You, Luna, queen of Relhok, don't need me, or anyone for that matter."

"That's true, but I *want* Fowler." I turned my hand over and squeezed his hand lightly, feeling a strange camaraderie swell between us.

"I know." He sighed. "I know." He rose from the bed and gave me a gentle push toward the armoire. "So let's go get him."

THIRTY-ONE

Fowler

THE SOUND OF my cell door clanging open woke me from troubled sleep. My entire body ached from the beating the guards had given me, in addition to the injuries from my fight with Chasan. I wasn't in the best condition. I inhaled, wiping the blood from my nose and lip with the back of my hand as I struggled to rise.

I blinked past the fog obscuring my vision to the slight figure hovering in the threshold of my cell.

"Fowler?" a soft voice asked, so at odds with everything inside this sordid, wretched place. The gentle sound of my name stood out starkly against the hardness of everything around me.

"Luna?" I blinked again, shaking to clear my head. "Am I imagining you?"

She stepped deeper into the cell, emerging from the shadows and revealing her familiar pale features, the delicate lines and hollows cast in sharp relief. A smile played at the corners of her lips. My heart constricted. I shook my head, the too-long strands of my hair falling in my face. I shoved them back. "What are you doing here?"

"We've come to get you out of here."

"We?"

She motioned behind her.

I looked up to find Prince Chasan standing there. He entered my cell, hands on his hips. "No time for reunions. You can kiss later. I've got a few girls distracting the guards, but that will only grant us so much time. They'll return to their posts eventually. Right now it's time to leave."

We followed the prince through the sleeping castle, below the dungeon and down into the bowels of the castle, until I was certain we could go no farther without reaching the very core of the earth; a bleak thought, as I imagined the center of the earth was overrun with dwellers.

"I thought there wasn't any other way in and out of the castle," I said as we turned a corner into a narrow corridor that forced us to walk single file.

"You mean other than the not-so-secret tunnel in the kitchens? Everyone knows about that, you know. My father let everyone know about it. He calls it his decoy tunnel so that if there was ever a mass exodus from the castle, that one would be overrun. This one is truly secret. Only the royal family knows of its existence." The prince grimaced. "The castle has never been breached by dwellers, but as a precaution, at the beginning of the eclipse, Father had a team of engineers build this tunnel that leads out of the castle. Then he killed each and every one of them so they could never speak of it."

Luna gasped.

Chasan continued, "He claimed you could never be too safe. Never know when we might need to run. In that event, he didn't want to compete with a stampede of people trying to get out."

"How awful," Luna muttered.

I gave her hand a squeeze, ignoring the ache and sting in my bruised knuckles.

"We're almost there now." Chasan's pace picked up slightly. "I've left two horses with supplies waiting on the other side. Weapons, too. Fowler, your bow, of course. I know your penchant for it. Assuming they haven't made too much noise and lured dwellers, the horses will still be there."

We reached an iron door set in the damp stone wall. The prince unbolted it. He pushed open the thick metal door, its well-oiled hinges silent. Chasan stuck his head out to peer into the darkness before passing through. Unlike the last tunnel, this one did not go on and on. I followed. It was only a few feet until I emerged Outside. I paused, looking around in the pulsing darkness as Luna stepped out beside me.

The horses were twin shapes etched against the chronic night. They nickered softly in greeting. I hurried forward, helping Luna up onto her mount. Turning around, I faced the prince. He stood framed on the threshold of the secret door.

Clearing my throat, I extended my hand for him to take. "Thank you. I was wrong about you." It was hard to admit, but it was the truth. It wouldn't have been the worst thing in the world for Luna to have ended up with him.

"Ride hard. Get as far down the mountain as you can. He'll come for you the moment he realizes you're gone."

"What about you?"

Chasan grinned, his teeth a flash of light in the darkness. Always a cocky bastard. "I'm his son. What can he do to me?"

I thought he could do a great deal. I wouldn't put anything past the man. "Don't underestimate him," I warned because I felt as though I had to. After the favor he did us, I couldn't just toss him to the wolves.

The prince's gaze flicked up to Luna sitting atop her horse. "Believe me. I won't make that mistake again." I knew he was thinking about how he'd thought he would be the one to marry Luna.

"You can come with us," Luna offered.

I surprised myself by agreeing. "Yes. Come with us." I still didn't like him. He didn't disguise his interest in Luna and I would always have to keep one eye on him.

He smirked at me as though doubting the sincerity of my offer. "My place is here. Lagonia needs me, especially considering who my father is. Someday he'll be gone. Someday this eclipse will end, as before. I'll be here to pick up the pieces and rebuild when that happens."

Nodding, I swung up onto my horse, holding the reins loosely in my hands. I had never held out much hope for the end of the eclipse. This world was darkness. I wasn't waiting for light to return to start living. I wanted Luna by my side in this life, come good or bad. "Good luck. And thank you."

"Now go. Don't get recaptured and let my efforts go to waste." Chasan swung his gaze to Luna, and I knew he was speaking mostly to her as he added, "Take care of yourself." There was a wealth of meaning in those words. She meant something to him. Even now, saying farewell and leaving him behind, this prickled at me.

Chasan sent me a hard glance and slapped my horse on the rump. I lurched forward. He called out as we started moving away, "Try not to die."

My horse slid into a trot. Luna followed. I glanced behind me, watching as she turned in her saddle to wave back at the prince. She called a farewell, but he was already slipping through the door back into the castle, as though he could no longer stand the sight of us.

The heavy metal door thudded shut behind him, sealing himself in and us out.

Once again we were together on the Outside.

THIRTY-TWO

Luna

It took a day to get down the mountain. We rode hard, Fowler pushing the horses down precarious slopes that had us arching sharply in our saddles. I didn't complain, biting back any fears or concerns, knowing we had to cover as much ground as possible as fast as possible. Mammoth bats flew overhead, their great leathery wings slapping the air as they hunted for prey in the great maw of night.

We stopped only briefly, when necessary, to rest and water the horses. On the second day we were still moving over rocky terrain. Fortunately, we hadn't come across any dwellers. It stood to reason our luck couldn't hold forever. Not in this world.

Still, at that first, inevitable sound of a dweller, I froze. Its tinny and shrill call bounced off the rocks of the canyon we were passing through. The eerie sound reverberated across the air, carried far by bat-stirred winds. Even though a part of me had missed the Outside, I hadn't missed that.

"The ground is getting softer," Fowler murmured beside me.

I nodded in acknowledgment and swallowed, all my senses squeezing and stretching as far as they could go. I listened. I knew firsthand how one dweller could turn to two to twenty in a blink.

"Luna?" Fowler queried, and I knew he was asking if I detected anything else with my more sensitive hearing.

After a moment, I shook my head. The dweller must have moved on, for we didn't hear it again.

We kept moving.

We didn't speak much in those first couple of days, too intent in our flight from Ainswind, too trapped in our own thoughts.

"You have to eat, Luna," Fowler said as he pushed a piece of dried meat into my hand.

Nodding, I brought it up to my teeth and tore off a chunk. It tasted like leather but I forced myself to chew.

"Do you think Chasan is all right?"

"I think he'll always land on his feet." He sounded testy.

"Are you angry?"

"I think we're out here and Prince Chasan is snug inside his castle. He's fine."

We fell to silence again. I felt chastened. "Do you think he's coming?"

"Tebald?" I felt the motion of his shrug. "It's risky. He doesn't like risks."

"He'll come," I stated hollowly even though I had posed the question. I wanted him to persuade me otherwise, but I knew. I had thought of little else except Tebald's voice in my ear, his determination to have me that went deeper than his desire to unite our countries. "With an army, if need be," I added.

"We can travel faster than any army. It's just the two of us. He will make the mistake of bringing too many men with him. Too many men will attract dwellers. They'll be swarmed. They'll have to fight."

I nodded again, heartened by these words.

Fowler rose from where he was sitting and settled down beside me, his arm aligned with mine. "You're worrying too much. It's not good for you." He bumped me slightly. We'd been alone for the last couple of days, but we'd hardly touched.

"Easier said than done, isn't it?"

He lifted his arm and draped it over me, a comforting weight. "Nothing is easy," he murmured, and I sighed as his fingers brushed the hair back from my temple. "Except this. Us. That's easy."

I smiled a little. "Except when it wasn't. I remember when we first met and you would hardly talk to me."

"That's because I liked you, and I didn't want to."

"You were so . . . hard. And unfeeling."

"I thought I had to be. I thought not caring was the way to protect myself from this world. From losing and hurting again. I actually told myself we could just be travel companions. That I could spend months with you and not love you."

I turned my face, dropping my forehead against the side of his face. "I'm sorry."

"What are you sorry about?" Bewilderment rang in his voice.

"If Sivo hadn't forced me on you, then you would have kept going. You'd be halfway to Allu by now. I was exactly what you didn't want. Entanglement. Someone to drag you down—"

He kissed me, crushing my words. His hands held my face, pulling me toward him so that I crawled in his lap and straddled him. This kiss was ruthless, desperate. A release from the fear of almost losing each other. From days of running without time for breath.

"Don't you ever say that," he growled against my lips.

His hands burned a trail everywhere, roaming my back, callused fingertips stroking my nape and burrowing into my hair. I trembled as he tugged my head back, his lips gliding over my throat before coming back to my mouth. "You're the best thing to ever happen to me and I wouldn't want to be anywhere except here with you."

My fingers delved inside his doublet, smoothing over taut shoulders. I clutched him through the layers of his shirt, hungry for the sensation of him. He winced and I remembered his injuries. Gasping, I pulled back. "Oh, I'm sorry!"

He seized my hands and positioned them back on him. "I want your touch."

I nodded, a happy breath shuddering out from me because it was what I wanted, too. More than anything. Gently, I slid my hands over the curve of his shoulders. "I'll be more careful."

Fowler leaned back slightly to shrug out of his doublet. "Don't worry about me." His arms came back to wrap around me, and we were kissing again. Hard, deep, soul-bending kisses. Fowler's bigger body curled over mine, taking us down. Dried bits of grass crackled under the blanket cushioning us as we kissed until I could hardly catch my breath. "You're all I need."

I framed his face in my hands and reveled in the texture of his skin, the silk of his hair, the delicious weight of him over me. I traced his features, soaking him up, absorbing all of him. "I love you, Fowler," I whispered, following his instructions and living in the now. Not worrying. Not thinking. Only feeling.

I listened to the strong and even cadence of Fowler's heart beneath my ear. His chest rose and fell in slow draws. If he wasn't asleep, he was very relaxed. I smiled softly. He needed rest.

My ears pricked and I lifted my head from the pillow of Fowler's chest. A bark sounded in the distance. I lifted my head. "Did you hear that?"

"What?" Fowler asked, his voice alert and wide awake.

I rose to my feet. "It sounded like a . . . bark."

"Your wolf?"

"No." I wished it was Digger, but that wasn't his bark. Digger rarely even barked. He was all stealth. "A dog, I think." I angled my head to the side, listening harder.

Fowler moved to stand by my side, pulling his shirt over his head. I faced the direction of the sound. "There. I heard it again."

"That's south. Not the direction of Ainswind."

I turned to face him. "That's good, right?"

"I don't know." He hesitated a moment, listening by my side. A dog barked again. "I heard it," he confirmed. It was a distinctive bark, low and hoarse. This time closer.

Fowler jumped into action, sliding back into his doublet, gathering up our things as one bark turned into two, then three. I joined him in packing up our belongings, our breaths fast and choppy with anxiety.

The barks overlapped now. There was more than one dog out there, and they were on the trail of something. Something like us.

Fowler turned in the direction of the barks again and froze.

"What is it? What's happening?" I demanded, dread building as I tracked Fowler where he stood so still.

"My father used trained dogs. Whenever a group left Relhok City, the hounds would accompany them. He never traveled without them. They can track. They can detect dwellers long before us. They can also fight, attack on command, if necessary."

"Your father?" I shook my head, bewildered. "He came himself?"

"Yes. My father. Cullan." He paused. "He's come for us,

Luna. He's come for you."

I shook my head. "No. That can't be—"

Fowler grabbed my hand and tossed me atop my horse. "It's him," he declared as he mounted his own horse.

We rode hard side by side, no longer concerned with the amount of sound we made. Alerting the dwellers to our presence was the least of our worries. We moved at breakneck speed, running away from a greater threat than those monsters.

I followed Fowler, keeping pace. If there was even a chance he was correct, then we needed to move. The barking grew closer, right on our heels, but we kept pushing. An arrow hissed on the air and my horse cried out, tumbling out from under me and sending me flying. I landed hard, all the air escaping me in a pained whoosh. I lay on the ground for a stunned moment.

"Luna!" Fowler's shout rose over the thunder of hooves.

I blinked, chasing away the shock of my fall. Hands grabbed me, hauling me to my feet. I whipped my head around, trying to process the flurry of voices, horses, men, and scurrying dogs. It was an overwhelming din. Even the air tasted musky and sweat-laced. Bitter with fear. My fear.

"Luna! Luna! Are you hurt? Let her go! Let her go, you bastards!"

I shook my head, searching for my voice, trying to filter through the chaos of sensations bombarding me.

"Fowler." A gruff, scratchy voice rose over all other sounds. "You look well, if not a little rough at the edges. Don't tell me that King Tebald was not hospitable to you."

My skin shivered with an innate, gut-deep knowledge. My voice welled up, a thick, jumbled lump of words in my throat. This was Cullan. The man who had murdered my parents. Untold, innumerable lives had died at his command. I'd waited my entire life to confront him. True, I'd hoped to have more leverage when that day arrived, but here I was.

My chance was now.

THIRTY-THREE

Fowler

I FACED MY father. I wasn't certain the last time I had seen him. Days weren't something one counted in this life. There were no seasons to mark the passing of time. No birthdays to celebrate—but it felt as if I'd lived a lifetime since the last time I stood before him.

He traveled with over a score of soldiers, all armed to the teeth. A dozen dogs circled the group impatiently, excited over their recent chase. I should have known if anything would rouse my father from the protection of Relhok City, news of Luna would do it.

He looked the same. The years had been good to him. Only

faint lines fanned out from his face. His well-trimmed beard was lightly peppered with gray. He still wore his hair long, pulled back in a single plait. I had hoped that age and disease might take hold of him and spare the world, but that clearly wasn't the case. I reached inside myself, searching for the familiar hate, but there was only dispassion—emptiness when I stared at this man who had failed me in every way.

"So this is the princess." Cullan's white teeth flashed in a smile as he dismounted to stand before Luna, where she dangled between two soldiers. "She is the spitting image of her mother, but I'm sure Tebald told you that already. He was rather obsessed with the woman. Pathetic man. Weak, losing his head over any female." He tapped his temple. "That's the difference between us. I use my head. That old fool thinks with other parts." Cullan laughed and the rest of his men joined in.

I struggled against the hands that held me back. In the distance a dweller cried out—not surprisingly, given the noise we were making—but the sound hardly alarmed me. Right now I faced a far greater menace.

"Don't touch her," I warned, glaring at my father, staring at green eyes so similar to my own and yet not. These eyes were dead inside. Impossible to breach. They felt nothing for no one.

Cullan laughed. "Speaking of weak men, you, my son, always did pick the worst girls to attach yourself to." He shook his head with a tsking sound.

His words made me think of Bethan and what he did to her. And that had not been personal to him. That had been about me. Luna was personal to him. She was a threat to everything he held important.

My father continued, "I blame your mother and that nurse of yours. They made you soft." His voice turned hard and accusing. "Such a disappointment. I should have taken you in hand from the start and made a man of you."

The dweller that had cried out moments ago called out again. It was close. I scanned the horizon, spotting it, visible now. Its pale body shuffled toward our group. It was only one. It didn't concern anyone. My father's men would dispatch it quickly.

Cullan followed my gaze to the lone dweller. A slow smile eased over his features. "Ah. What do we have here? A friend come to join us?"

An icy finger of dread scraped down my spine as my father turned to face the creature. Cullan studied it as it shuffled closer and then looked back to me. He turned his gaze to Luna, arching an eyebrow in consideration.

She hung between two burly soldiers, shaking, her face pale. I wondered what was going through her mind. She'd heard about this man all her life. Cullan had taken everything from her. Her parents. Her home. Her very identity was something she'd had to hide for fear of him.

A soldier started toward the dweller, sword drawn.

"Wait," my father called, holding up a hand to halt him. "Why don't we give it what it wants?"

The statement, the casual expression on my father's face, was so reminiscent of when he had taken Bethan that a black wave of rage swept over me. I swung and struck the guard on my left, catching him by surprise. He fell to the ground.

I turned on the other one, attacking him viciously with an elbow to his nose and a fist to his throat. He went down with a groan. I lunged toward Luna, but didn't make it two feet before other soldiers were on me, pinning me to the ground.

My father's voice fell hard with command, fast as an arrow. "The girl," he snapped. "Take her. Give her to the dweller."

I watched as they dragged Luna toward the approaching dweller. She struggled, digging in her heels, landing a few blows, but it was useless. They overpowered her.

I screamed, spitting up dirt and saliva. I screamed until I was hoarse, my throat shredded.

I screamed even when I was struck repeatedly in the head and shoulders and cursed to stop. The dweller's movements became anxious, rapid and jerky as it smelled the humans approaching.

My father's voice sounded in my ear, breaking through my screams. "What do you think is going to happen? It's always interesting to guess, isn't it? Will it stop and eat her right here, right now? Or will it take her below and save her for later?"

I bowed my head, salty tears scalding my throat and rolling down my face. A sob choked me, shaking my shoulders as I gazed up at the man who'd given me life. "Father," I choked out, addressing him as I had done when I was a child. "Please . . . don't."

"Oh." Cullan squatted before me. "You really care for her?"

I had survived this before, but this time I wouldn't. I couldn't.

He might as well feed me to that dweller, too.

"Such weakness. How are you my blood?" My father fisted his hand in my hair, yanking hard on the strands, forcing my head back up. "Watch this. You don't want to miss it."

The soldiers stopped a yard in front of the creature and tossed Luna to the ground at its feet. In seconds it was on her, its taloned hands wrapping around her.

Her scream shattered the air, shattering me.

Broken, I sobbed, calling her name as the creature turned and headed in the opposite direction, dragging her with it. I watched as together they faded into the darkness. I watched until I could see nothing anymore.

THIRTY-FOUR

Luna

I WAS BELOWGROUND again, trembling in the wet cold. Except this time I wasn't here to rescue anyone. I was the victim and no one would be rescuing me.

Fear coated my mouth in a wash of copper, and bleakness rolled over me. My muddy hair dangled in my eyes and I swiped at the bothersome strands with my free hand. My other arm was held in a death grip.

It was only Fowler up there, and he couldn't do anything for me. The sound of his screams and cries echoed inside my skull and the bleakness faded to a hollowness inside my chest. I had never heard him like that. The sound of him hurting . . . hurting for me . . .

I had to get back to him. No one was coming for me, so I had to get myself out of here.

Whimpering, I jerked against the grip on my arm. My boots slipped and skidded as the dweller dragged me, its talons digging through the fabric of my sleeve and scoring my arm. Everything was dripping earth and slimy ground and crumbling walls. The metallic stench of blood and death filled my nose. The dweller dragged me down earthen tunnels, its moist breath rasping beside me. The receptors at the center of its face writhed on the air like hissing serpents. Inhaling, I smelled the tinny sweetness of toxin.

I stopped fighting, fearful of getting poison on my skin.

The air suddenly opened up and I knew we were in a wide space. Dozens of dwellers roamed the area and I shrank inside myself. The dweller started leading me over a honeycomb network of holes. I could hear other humans in pain, trapped here as I was. Their cries vibrated through me, rooting deep into my bones.

A screech shattered the air. I jumped, my heart clenching painfully in my chest before galloping ahead.

I'd heard that cry before. I heard it when I was belowground with Fowler. It belonged to something huge, sitting just beyond the stretch of honeycomb. The scream faded, and then there was its sloughing breath, similar to the other dwellers except louder, deeper. It rumbled on the air like building thunder.

The dwellers froze in response. The people down here weren't as easy to silence. They started crying out in earnest, sobbing and shouting as though they had a hope for rescue.

All at once it released a long, shrill, earsplitting call. The dweller holding me started moving again, dragging me forward.

In the distance, in other tunnels, I heard more dwellers moving toward the nest where I was, answering the call.

My hand drifted to my thigh where my dagger was strapped. My mouth dried as I contemplated when to use it. Dwellers crowded around me, continuing to pour into the nest like water from an endless spigot.

My dweller pushed me, leading me toward the big creature on the other side of the nest, guiding me past holes like the one that had trapped Fowler. I wasn't the only one being delivered up to this monster. Another person, a man, wept and struggled as another dweller pulled him forward too. He reached the monster before I did.

"No, no! Help me, no, please!" he cried. His voice cut off suddenly on a wet, gurgling shout.

Bones cracked and blood flowed like hot copper on the air. I flinched, bile rising in my throat. I fumbled to free my blade. Its hilt filled my palm, solid and comforting. I held tightly to it as I was launched through the air.

I fell at the feet of the beast, pain jarring my knees. The ground was sticky with warm blood and bits of fleshy material I dared not contemplate.

The monster's great jaws worked, crunching and grinding the last of the man sacrificed before me.

I shoved myself to my feet, squaring up in front of the massive dweller as it finished eating its victim. The beast's size alone told me it was no ordinary dweller, but there was also the way the other dwellers followed its command. It ruled them. It was so big I doubted it possessed much mobility. They served it . . . this thing was their queen.

I felt its arms stir on the air as it reached for me. I dove to the right. Stretching out my hand, I skimmed a palm against its dense, pasty body, circling it. I had to risk touching it, getting close. It was the only way.

Moving as quickly as I could, I jumped on its back and crawled up its great girth, stabbing with my dagger into the dense meat of its body as I went, using my blade for leverage.

Once I neared its head and its squat neck, I reached around with my arm and started sawing through the doughy skin. Panting, I kept going, digging deep with my blade, ignoring its writhing movements and the hot, slippery flow of blood over my fingers. Its agonized scream stabbed my ears. I choked in relief as that scream reduced to a wet gurgle. It finally stopped moving.

Gasping, I slid down the length of its body and landed shakily on my feet. The air continued to wheeze out of me. Saliva flooded my mouth.

I wiped bloody hands against my trousers and listened to the faint breathing of the other dwellers. They all stood immobilized, frozen, their attention fixed on me. Waiting for my next move.

THIRTY-FIVE

Fowler

SHE WAS REALLY gone.

Nothing mattered anymore. Pain mingled with numbness. Pain at losing Luna, but numbness over my fate. The future didn't matter. Whether there was a tomorrow didn't signify.

I didn't even care when more horse hooves thundered over the air. Tebald and his men arrived, and I sat there, staring into the swirling dark as the two armies of soldiers drew swords on each other. They could fight their stupid battle, play out their senseless war with each other. The reason they were fighting didn't matter anymore.

It would better serve the world if they killed each other off. I accepted that fact grimly. I would do nothing. I would stand amid it all, staring without seeing, without caring, because Luna was dying somewhere without me. Dimly, I registered my father and King Tebald hurling challenges and insults back and forth at each other. I stared ahead, my eyes burning as I focused on the spot where I had last glimpsed Luna.

Gradually another sound penetrated through the bantering threats and insults. I frowned, peering into the darkness where I had last seen Luna.

A cacophony of cries rent the air with the suddenness of wings flapping in the sky. Dwellers' cries. An entire herd of them, more than I had even witnessed outside the village of Ortley, where Luna and I had gone for the kelp. I snorted, enjoying the irony that my father would die at the hands of dwellers when he himself had sent so many people to face their insatiable hunger.

The soldiers panicked, crying out and breaking formation as dwellers materialized out of the dark. The creatures' sawing breaths formed a humming fog on the air. For some reason they stood in a perfect, uniform line, gazing at the army of scattering men, waiting, it seemed, for some*thing*.

The dogs whimpered and broke, running away, wise enough to know their odds of survival were poor. Tebald's and my father's commanding officers shouted, trying to whip the men into some order. The soldiers attempted to form their own lines, lifting up their shields and swords in readiness. Several started shooting arrows into the tide of dwellers as if that would make a difference with an army of creatures this size.

I watched, laughter bubbling up from my chest, indifferent to any threat to myself. I looked back and forth between the two kings who had wrought so much damage. My father must have sensed my stare or heard my laughter. His wild-eyed gaze found mine.

"The day won't be a total tragedy," I called to him. "Not if both of you die." I could almost imagine Luna smiling over this. My satisfaction ebbed as pain constricted my chest. *Luna.*

My father and Tebald shared terrified expressions as the reality of this moment sank in. Then they looked at me with hatred in their eyes, as though I were somehow responsible for this. I wished I had been.

I faced the line of dwellers again, finished running, ready to accept my fate.

The line of them broke, parting at the center, revealing a yawning hole in the darkness. Something stirred, moving out of the dark chasm like a ripple in water. A figure came forward, step by slow step.

Luna advanced, stepping forward. She was covered in blood but looked unharmed. She stood abreast with the line of dwellers. None moved toward her. It was almost as though she were one of them, accepted, embraced.

Suddenly she flung her arms high above her head.

I blinked, trying to understand what I was seeing. With that single motion, the dwellers on either side of her unleashed themselves, charging forward with more speed than I had ever seen from them. The earth shook beneath the storm of their stampeding weight.

Stunned, I watched in awe. They more than accepted her.

They obeyed her. She was in control of them. She was queen.

Luna moved with them, walking almost elegantly through their haphazard charge. She made her way to me, finding me as chaos broke out all around us.

I pulled her into my arms, holding tightly amid screams and whistling arrows and clanging of swords. "You're doing this?" I whispered against her cheek.

She nodded, burrowing her face into my neck, her lips forming a wordless whisper. *Yes.*

I smoothed a hand over the back of her head and made a comforting hushing sound over the volley of noise around us. "You saved us. You've saved us all." She may, in fact, have just saved the world.

As men dropped all around us, I spotted my father through the sea of dwellers. I glimpsed his stricken expression, the flash of his teeth in an agonized scream the instant before he went under a mob of feeding dwellers.

My arms wrapped harder around Luna. We clung to each other through it all, until the last body fell and the last cry sounded.

Then everything was still.

She lifted her for head from my neck and turned her face out, assessing the carnage in the sudden ring of silence. Dwellers stood as one and looked to her, waiting patiently, toxic feelers at their face whispering on the stagnant air.

"Go," she whispered to them, and then louder, gaining courage. "Leave us."

They obeyed, slipping back into the night like fading ghosts.

Silence draped over us. I stroked her face, staring down at her in the darkness, feeling shaken and overcome and in awe of this girl . . . this queen who I held in my arms. The queen I loved.

"It's over," she said.

"No, Luna." Trembling, I pressed my lips to hers in a long, lingering kiss. This wasn't the end. "It's just the beginning. Finally. We can really begin."

EPILOGUE

Luna

I STOOD AT the balcony of my bedchamber, listening to the sounds of the unrelenting night. The dwellers were quiet this evening. They were quiet most of the time now, even when darkness blanketed the world. They were quiet because *I* willed it.

Ever since I'd destroyed the dweller queen, I'd felt a connection to the creatures. A connection, I learned, that was reciprocal. They waited for my bidding, following my commands. *I* was their queen. Their alpha. They wouldn't harm me or anyone else I didn't wish them to harm. As long as they were in proximity, I could influence them.

After the dwellers destroyed Cullan and Tebald, Fowler and I returned to Lagonia for a short time to apprise Chasan of everything that had transpired. By the time we left him, he was fully dedicated to his role as the new king of Lagonia. As we traveled, I'd felt the presence of dwellers more keenly than ever. Out of sight, but always there. At my back, in front of us, beneath, in the ground, like blood flowing under my skin.

"Come. It's time. Everyone is waiting."

Turning, I faced Perla with a smile. I approached her, but before stepping into the ermine-lined cloak she held out for me, I embraced her, inhaling her familiar scent. I had missed her so much—a fact I did not fully realize until she and Sivo were returned to me.

"Ah, sweet girl." She patted the back of my head, where she had coiled my hair into an elaborate arrangement of tiny plaits. "This day has long been coming."

Fowler and I returned for Perla and Sivo after leaving Lagonia. Together the four of us made the trek to Relhok. In the last few months, I had learned what it was like to rule a kingdom. I was *still* learning. With Fowler at my side, Relhok had embraced our return. Cullan was gone, and he'd taken his reign of fear with him.

I put an end to the human sacrifices and worked toward fortifying and spreading the perimeter of our walls. Even if I controlled the dwellers, we needed to be cautious and defended against all threats. It was still a perilous world. We sent out hunting parties, building up our reserve of game and resources. With Sivo's supervision, we worked toward cultivating farmland. The population grew as we brought in more people from the Outside. Survivors like us.

Perla pulled back with a wet sniff, draping my father's heavy cloak more fully around my shoulders. "There now. You look like a queen."

"Almost." I smiled.

"Well, let's see to making it official, shall we?" She took my elbow. "A crown awaits you."

We exited the chamber. Fowler pushed off the wall where he was waiting.

"Your escort looks very handsome," Perla said approvingly.

Fowler took my chilled hands in his and pressed a kiss to them. When he lifted his face, I brushed his cheek with one hand. "Yes. Yes, he does." I didn't need to be sighted to know this was true.

He tucked my hand into the crook of his elbow. Perla fell into step behind us as we began walking.

"Ready for your big day?" he asked over the swish of my skirts.

I tsked. "My coronation?" I shook my head. "It's a formality. This is my kingdom. I've always known it. I've always felt it in here." I pressed a hand over my heart, feeling its strong and steady thud.

He trailed his thumb down my cheek. "Of course you have. They've been waiting for you. Like I have. And like me, they love you."

"There's another day soon approaching that I'm anticipating much more," I confided with a smile, leaning slightly into the length of his side.

Fowler turned to face me. "Is that so?"

With an exasperated grunt, Perla passed us. "Don't tarry. You've an entire city waiting."

In the distance, I could hear the dull roar of a crowd outside the castle, waiting for their queen. Waiting for me.

Fowler lowered his head and kissed me, slow and lingering. "Would that day happen to be our wedding day, Your Majesty?"

"It would." I smiled against his lips, relishing his mouth on mine, his gaze warm and tender on my face.

This must be what sunlight felt like.

The light had not yet returned to the world, but someday it would. Until then, this was the closest I could get, and it was enough.

As far as I was concerned, the darkness had passed. And I lived in light.

LOVE SOPHIE JORDAN?

Read on for an excerpt of her deliciously romantic

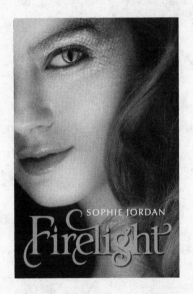

1

Gazing out at the quiet lake, I know the risk is worth it. The water is still and smooth. Polished glass. Not a ripple of wind disturbs the dark surface. Low-rising mist drifts off liquid mountains floating against a purple-bruised sky. An eager breath shudders past my lips. Soon the sun will break.

Azure arrives, winded. She doesn't bother with the kick-stand. Her bike clatters next to mine on the ground. "Didn't you hear me calling? You know I can't pedal as fast as you."

"I didn't want to miss this."

Finally, the sun peeks over the mountains in a thin line of red-gold that edges the dark lake.

Azure sighs beside me, and I know she's doing the same

thing I am—imagining how the early morning light will taste on her skin.

"Jacinda," she says, "we shouldn't do this." But her voice lacks conviction.

I dig my hands into my pockets and rock on the balls of my feet. "You want to be here as badly as I do. Look at that sun."

Before Azure can mutter another complaint, I'm shucking off my clothes. Stashing them behind a bush, I stand at the water's edge, trembling, but not from the cold bite of early morning. Excitement shivers through me.

Azure's clothes hit the ground. "Cassian's not going to like this," she says.

I scowl. As if I care what he thinks. He's not my boyfriend. Even if he did surprise attack me in Evasive Flight Maneuvers yesterday and try to hold my hand. "Don't ruin this. I don't want to think about him right now."

This little rebellion is partly about getting away from him. *Cassian.* Always hovering. Always there. Watching me with his dark eyes. Waiting. Tamra can have him. I spend a lot of my time wishing he wanted her—that the pride would choose her instead of me. Anyone but me. A sigh shudders from my lips. I just hate that they're not giving me a choice.

But it's a long way off before anything has to be settled. I won't think about it now.

"Let's go." I relax my thoughts and absorb everything humming around me. The branches with their gray-green leaves. The birds stirring against the dawn. Clammy mist hugs my calves. I flex my toes on the coarse rasp of ground, mentally counting the number of pebbles beneath the bottoms of my feet. And the familiar pull begins in my chest. My human exterior melts away, fades, replaced with my thicker draki skin.

My face tightens, cheeks sharpening, subtly shifting, stretching. My breath changes as my nose shifts, ridges pushing out from the bridge. My limbs loosen and lengthen. The drag of my bones feels good. I lift my face to the sky. The clouds become more than smudges of gray. I see them as though I'm already gliding through them. Feel cool condensation kiss my body.

It doesn't take long. It's perhaps one of my quickest manifests. With my thoughts unfettered and clear, with no one else around except Azure, it's easier. No Cassian with his brooding looks. No Mom with fear in her eyes. None of the others, watching, judging, sizing me up.

Always sizing me up.

My wings grow, slightly longer than the length of my back. The gossamer width of them pushes free. They unfurl with a soft whisper on the air—a sigh. As if they, too, seek relief. Freedom.

A familiar vibration swells up through my chest. Almost like a purr. Turning, I look at Azure, and see she is ready, beautiful beside me. Iridescent blue. In the growing light, I note the hues of pink and purple buried in the deep blue of her draki skin. Such a small thing I never noticed before.

Only now I see it, in the break of dawn, when we are meant to soar. When the pride forbids it. At night you miss so much.

Looking down, I admire the red-gold luster of my sleek arms. Thoughts drift. I recall a chunk of amber in my family's cache of precious stones and gems. My skin looks like that now. Baltic amber trapped in sunlight. It's deceptive. My skin appears delicate, but it's as tough as armor. It's been a long time since I've seen myself this way. Too long since I've tasted sun on my skin.

Azure purrs softly beside me. We lock eyes—eyes with enlarged irises and dark vertical slits for pupils—and I know she's over her complaints. She stares at me with irises of glowing blue, as happy as I am to be here. Even if we broke every rule in the pride to sneak off protected grounds. We're here. We're free.

On the balls of my feet, I spring into the air. My wings snap, wiry membranes stretching as they lift me up.

With a twirl, I soar.

Azure is there, laughing beside me, the sound low and guttural.

Wind rushes over us and sweet sunlight kisses our flesh. Once we're high enough, she drops, descends through the air in a blurring tailspin, careening toward the lake.

My lip curls. "Show-off!" I call, the rumble of draki speech vibrating deep in my throat as she dives into the lake and remains underwater for several minutes.

As a water draki, whenever she enters water, gills appear on the side of her body, enabling her to survive submerged . . . well, forever, if she chooses. One of the many useful talents our dragon ancestors assumed in order to survive. Not all of us can do this, of course. *I* can't.

I do other things.

Hovering over the lake, I wait for Azure to emerge. Finally, she breaks the surface in a glistening spray of water, her blue body radiant in the air, wings showering droplets.

"Nice," I say.

"Let's see you!"

I shake my head and set out again, diving through the tangle of mountains, ignoring Azure's "c'mon, it's so cool!"

My talent is *not* cool. I would give anything to change it. To be a water draki. Or a phaser. Or a visiocrypter. Or an onyx. Or . . . Really, the list goes on.

Instead, I am this.

I breathe fire. The only fire-breather in the pride in more than four hundred years. It's made me more popular than I want to be. Ever since I manifested at age eleven, I've ceased to be Jacinda. Instead, I'm *fire-breather*. A fact that has the pride deciding my life as if it's theirs to control. They're worse than my mother.

Suddenly I hear something beyond the whistling wind and humming mists of the snow-capped mountains at every side. A faint, distant sound.

My ears perk. I stop, hovering in the dense air.

Azure cocks her head; her dragon eyes blink, staring hard. "What is it? A plane?"

The noise grows, coming fast, a steady beat now. "We should get low."

Nodding, Azure dives. I follow, glancing behind us, seeing only the jagged cropping of mountains. But hearing more. Feeling more.

It keeps coming.

The sound chases us.

"Should we go back to the bikes?" Azure looks back at me, her blue-streaked black hair rippling like a flag in the wind.

I hesitate. I don't want this to end. Who knows when we can sneak out again? The pride watches me so closely, Cassian is always—

"Jacinda!" Azure points one iridescent blue finger through the air.

I turn and look. My heart seizes.

A chopper rounds a low mountain, so small in the distance, but growing larger as it approaches, cutting through the mist.

"Go!" I shout. "Drop!"

I dive, clawing wind, my wings folded flat against my body, legs poised arrow straight, perfectly angled for speed.

But not fast enough.

The chopper blades beat the air in a pounding frenzy. *Hunters*. Wind tears at my eyes as I fly faster than I've ever flown before.

Azure falls behind. I scream for her, glancing back, reading the dark desperation in her liquid gaze. "Az, keep up!"

Water draki aren't built for speed. We both know that. Her voice twists into a sob and I hear just how well she knows it in the broken sound. "I'm trying! Don't leave me! Jacinda! Don't leave me!"

Behind us, the chopper still comes. Bitter fear coats my mouth as two more join it, killing any hope that it was a random helicopter out for aerial photos. It's a squadron, and they are definitely hunting us.

Is this how it happened with Dad? Were his last moments like this? Tossing my head, I shove the thought away. I'm *not* going to die today—my body broken and sold off into bits and pieces.

I nod to the nearing treetops. "There!"

Draki never fly low to the ground, but we don't have a choice.

Azure follows me, weaving in my wake. She pulls close to my side, narrowly missing the flashing trees in her wild fear. I stop and drift in place, chest heaving with savage breath. The choppers whir overhead, their pounding beat deafening, stirring the trees into a frothing green foam.

"We should demanifest," Az says, panting.

As if we could. We're too frightened. Draki can never hold human form in a state of fear. It's a survival mechanism. At our core we're draki; that's where we derive our strength.

I peer up through the latticework of shaking branches shielding us, the scent of pine and forest ripe in my nostrils.

"I can get myself under control," Az insists in our guttural tongue.

I shake my head. "Even if that's true, it's too risky. We have to wait them out. If they see two girls out here . . . after they just spotted two female draki, they might get suspicious." A cold fist squeezes around my heart. I can't let that happen. Not just for me, but for everyone. For draki everywhere. The secret of our ability to appear as humans is our greatest defense.

"If we're not home in the next hour, we're busted!"

I bite my lip to stop from telling her we have more to worry about than the pride discovering we snuck out. I don't want to scare her even more than she already is.

"We have to hide for a little—"

Another sound penetrates the beating blades of a chopper. A low drone on the air. The tiny hairs at my nape tingle. Something else is out there. Below. On the ground. Growing closer.

I look skyward, my long talonlike fingers flexing open and shut, wings vibrating in barely controlled movement. Instinct urges flight, but I know they're up there. Waiting. Circling buzzards. I spy their dark shapes through the treetops. My chest tightens. They aren't going away.

I motion Az to follow me into the thick branches of a towering pine. Folding our wings close to our bodies, we shove amid the itchy needles, fighting the scraping twigs. Holding our breath, we wait.

Then the land comes alive, swarming with an entourage of vehicles: trucks, SUVs, dirt bikes.

"No," I rasp, eyeing the vehicles, the men, armed to the teeth. In a truck bed, two men crouch at the ready, a great net launcher before them. Seasoned hunters. They know what they're doing. They know what they're hunting.

Az trembles so badly the thick branch we're crouched on starts to shake, leaves rustling. I clutch her hand. The dirt bikes lead the way, moving at a dizzying speed. A driver of one SUV motions out the window. "Look to the trees," he shouts, his voice deep, terrifying.

Az fidgets. I clutch her hand harder. A bike is directly below us now. The driver wears a black T-shirt that hugs his young muscled body. My skin tightens almost painfully.

"I can't stay here," Az chokes out beside me. "I've got to go!"

"Az," I growl, my low rumbling tones fervent, desperate. "That's what they want. They're trying to flush us out. Don't panic."

Her words spit past gritted teeth. "I. Can't."

And I know with a sick tightening of my gut that she's not going to last.

Scanning the activity below and the choppers cutting across the sky above, I make up my mind right then.

"All right." I swallow. "Here's the plan. We separate—"

"No—"

"I'll break cover first. Then, once they've gone after me, you head for water. Go under and stay there. However long it takes."

Her dark eyes gleam wetly, the vertical lines of her pupils throbbing.

"Got it?" I demand.

She nods jerkily, the ridges on her nose contracting with a deep breath. "W-what are you going to do?"

I force a smile, the curve of my lips painful on my face. "Fly, of course."

2

When I was twelve, I raced Cassian and won.

It was during group flight. At night, of course. Our only authorized time to fly. Cassian had been arrogant, showing off, and I couldn't help it. We used to be friends, when we were kids. Before either one of us manifested. I couldn't stand seeing what he'd turned into, watching him act like he was God's gift to our pride.

Before I knew it, we were racing across the night sky, Dad's shouts of encouragement ringing in my ears. Cassian was fourteen, an onyx draki. All sleek black muscle and cutting sinew. My father had been an onyx, too. Not only are they the strongest and biggest among the draki, but they are usually the fastest.

Except that night. That night I beat Cassian, the prince of our pride, our future alpha—trained since birth to be the best.

I shouldn't have won, but I did. In the moon's shadow, I revealed myself to be even more than the pride's precious fire-breather. More than the little girl Cassian gave rides to in his go-cart. Cassian changed after that. Suddenly, he wasn't focused on being best, but winning the best. I became the prize.

For years I regretted winning that race, resented the additional attention it brought me, wished I couldn't fly so fast. Only now, as my bare feet scrape over rough bark, preparing to take flight, I'm grateful I can. Grateful I fly as fast as wind.

Az shakes behind me, her teeth clacking. A whimper escapes her lips. I know what I have to do.

And I just . . . go. Dropping from the tree, I surge through the air, wings pulled taut above my back, two great sails of fiery gold.

Shouts fill my ears. Engines rev, accelerating. Loud, indistinct voices overlap. Hard male voices. I whip through trees, the hunters in hot pursuit, crashing through the forest in their earth-eating vehicles. A smile bends my mouth as they fall behind and I pull ahead. I hear myself laugh.

Then fire erupts in my wing. I jerk, tilt, careen wildly.

I'm hit.

Fighting hard to keep myself up with one wing, I manage

only a few strokes before I slip through air. The world whirls around me in a dizzy blaze of lush greens and browns. My shoulder swipes a tree, and I hit the ground in a winded, gasping, broken pile, the scent of my blood coppery rich in my nose.

My fingers dig into moist earth, the rich, pungent smell nourishing my skin. Shaking my head side to side, dirt fills my hands, sliding beneath my talons. Shoulder throbbing, I crawl, clawing one hand over the other.

A sound burns the back of my throat, part grunt, part growl. *Not me. Not me,* I think.

I curl my knees beneath me and test my wing, stretching it carefully above my back, biting my lip to stifle a cry at the agony jolting through the wiry membranes, penetrating deep into my back between my shoulder blades. Pine needles scrape my palms as I push and try to stand.

I hear them coming, their shouts. Motors rise and fall as they ascend and descend hills. An image of the truck with its net flashes through my mind.

Just like Dad. It's happening to me now.

From *New York Times* bestselling author Sophie Jordan

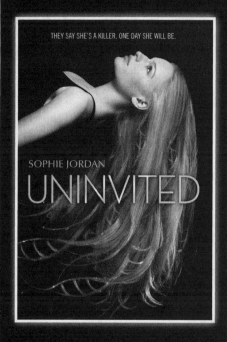
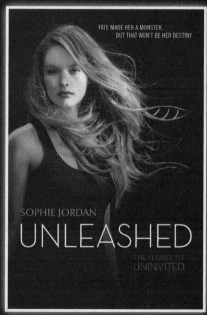